MORTAL HEIR

THE THIEF'S TALISMAN: BOOK ONE

EMMA L. ADAMS

1

With feet lighter than a human's could ever be, I crept down the corridor, following the enticing scent. Like a kid raiding their parents' liquor cabinet in the middle of the night. Except I'd never had a childhood like that, and if I got caught, I'd face a more severe punishment than being grounded.

But I never got caught. Good thieves don't.

If I had the ability, I'd have used a glamour to make myself invisible. But my weak faerie blood wasn't strong enough even to make my pointed ears look like human ones, so I had to rely on keeping as quiet as possible. My feet barely made a sound, trained to avoid creaky floorboards and noisy steps, to tread gracefully and not leave an impact. This was a human establishment, so they'd never know I was here. I'd slip in and out like a ghost. A handkerchief wrapped around my head covered my bone-white hair. I had a number of handkerchiefs, but I saved the rose gold one for special occasions. It was my birthday in less than an hour, and that counted as a special occasion in my book.

I paused as I found what I was looking for—a chocolate cake, fresh, icing dripping onto the work surface. I stuck my finger in the icing and licked it, tasting the sweetness on my tongue. Apparently such things used to be commonplace before the rationing kicked in after the war with Faerie. Now luxuries were only for the elite. I'd spent weeks packaging them for rich humans when I'd worked here. Before the 'incident'.

Finders, keepers. I closed the box carefully to make sure the icing didn't leak out. Slipping the box inside my coat—a thick fur-lined winter one I'd swiped from a clearance sale in the local market—I retraced my steps to the window.

Climbing out was my favourite part. It was also the riskiest. My feet fit carefully onto the windowsill, and I hung on with one hand, the other keeping the box from falling out of my coat. I shimmied across the sill to the drainpipe, and began the three-floor climb one handed. Maybe a particularly athletic human could do this, but not as easily as breathing like it was for me. Faeries were typically built like dancers, or athletes, and could move infinitely more gracefully. Even in a thick coat concealing a birthday cake. If not for my cumbersome load, I'd have thrown in some acrobatics. As it was, when my feet touched the ground, I turned to face the shop and gave it a rude gesture. I'd lost my job here after a particularly vindictive human colleague had decided to put pieces of iron in my pockets as a prank, and then laughed when the shards burned my hands to blisters. I'd had no magic to curse the bastard, so I'd punched him in the nose and got myself fired. Stealing a cake was a petty form of revenge, but a delicious one.

The cold breeze did its best to tear my handkerchief loose so I held it down with my free hand, lowering my gaze to hide my too-bright blue eyes, which marked me as part of a Court I'd never set foot in. I picked up speed, heading for my least favourite part of the walk home. The contraband in my pocket sat heavily and the first drops of rain had begun to fall.

Noises followed me as I walked alongside the hedge bordering half-blood territory, shrieks and growls and whispers from the beasts in the forests that had once been small patches of woodland and had now grown to cover a huge section of the city. It was pretty much a replica of the Summer and Winter Courts, minus half the magic and with a few added rules like *don't kill anyone, half-bloods and humans included.* Such rules didn't apply in Faerie—one of many reasons I thought staying here was the better option for everyone. I didn't quite get how the faeries had ended up invading this realm in the first place, but they were here to stay, and so were we.

As I prepared to pass by the gate, a horse rode out into the road, bearing a tall elven knight. At first, I thought it was one of those half-blood guards who liked to play dress-up as nobles. Then I saw the insignia on the banner.

This was a legit, *pure-blooded* faerie from the Winter Court itself.

I kept very still. I wouldn't get into trouble for stealing, but pure faeries are well-known for being cruel and capricious, and they show us no more respect than they do regular humans. I held my breath as the horse halted, and a second rider came out through the gate. Then another. What was the Winter Court's messenger patrol doing here of all places? There might be more travel between here and Faerie than there used to be, but it was an unusual occasion that required true Sidhe to show up. Something big was happening. Unfortunately, it was between me and my way home.

The knights turned as one, and vanished in a dazzling flash of white-blue light.

The surge of Winter magic lifted the hairs on my arms. I

didn't really feel the cold—the coat was to hide my spoils—but a full-on shiver broke out all over my skin. I'd just watched them walk *into* the Unseelie lands that overlapped with this part of the mortal realm. I hadn't seen so much as a glimpse of the world behind the white flash, but some traitorous part of me couldn't help imagining all the same. It wasn't much help, though—only pure-blooded Sidhe had the ability to cross between realms, not that they'd really used it in the past. Aside from when they decided to come here and steal a human away for fun.

I waited sixty seconds for more knights to appear. Then I started walking again. I'd left Dad for long enough already, and if he'd seen that flash of light, he might have thought it was *her.* Or that I'd left for the Court. That was his new obsession these days, and the reason I didn't like sneaking out at night as much. He thought I was like the other half-bloods, and wanted to go back to Faerie.

"Absolutely no chance of that," I'd informed him the last time he'd asked. "I'd be lucky to last five minutes there, considering the pure faeries don't think much of mortals."

He flinched. "Don't say that. You're not one of them."

"Don't worry about me," I'd told him. "They don't have any claim on me."

Famous last words, Raine. On that cold night, I had zero desire to follow the knights, but I didn't know any half-faerie who hadn't fantasised about being picked up by the Court. It was our version of a faerie tale, if you ignored the Sidhe's murderous tendencies and their hatred of anyone who wasn't a heartless immortal. Really, I was lucky to escape them, and so was Dad. If I ever met the faerie who kidnapped him, I'd punch her in the nose. Which would be kind of awkward, considering she was my mother.

Family drama. Half-faeries have that in spades. Those of

us who are lucky enough to still *have* a family, that is. Often, when the faeries steal someone, they have no intention of giving them back in one piece. But for whatever reason, my mother had decided to leave my father right where she'd taken him, minus a few memories, and with an added bonus. Me.

The tension in my chest loosened as I reached the front door to our flat, on the ground floor of a run-down house converted into apartments. Not much of a home, but enough for the two of us. I sang under my breath as I unlocked the door.

"Happy birthday to me, happy birthday to me..."

"Happy birthday, Raine."

I jumped. Denzel, half-satyr and the closest to a friend I had, stood beside me. He must have silently followed me to the door. Fur covered his legs up to his waist, and instead of feet, he stood lightly on twin hooves.

"Don't sneak up on me, Denzel."

"I came to wish you many happy returns."

"You're spending too much time around humans. Birthdays are nothing to celebrate."

"I beg to differ." He reached past me and pushed the door open.

"What are you doing? Dad's asleep."

"I won't wake him."

Rolling my eyes, I let him into the flat. Denzel was okay. All right, he was shifty as hell and made me look like a saint by comparison, but he protected his friends, and I fell into that category.

"What do you want?"

His face fell. "Am I that obvious?"

"Yes."

His mouth twisted. "All right. So I'm in a bit of trouble..."

"Why am I not surprised."

"With the mages," he went on. "Apparently selling amulets is a serious crime. Even if they're genuine elf-forged ones."

"If they're genuine, I'm a leprechaun."

I pulled the cake box out of my coat and set it on the coffee table, then retrieved a bottle of wine from the sideboard. "Want some?"

"Where'd you get *that?*"

"Hen do." I flashed him a smile. "Nobody noticed when one of the bottles wandered off of its own accord."

"You're a terrible person."

"They're rich humans. They won't miss it."

"I'd prefer elf wine, but you take what you can get."

"Damn straight." I poured two glasses, keeping one eye on Denzel in case he slipped anything into his pockets. The light-fingered little shit was a thorn in my side, but he wouldn't call on me in the middle of the night without good reason.

"So." He trod from one hoof to the other. "I might be in a bit of difficulty. See, I… sort of took out a loan from the Crusher."

I choked on the wine. "You what?"

The Crusher was a half-troll with just enough human blood to know how to string a sentence together, and just enough troll blood to be able to flatten a person with one step. Nobody in their right mind crossed him. Though Denzel wasn't what you'd call *all there.* I fought the urge to groan. I'd sworn not to get dragged into any of his dodgy dealings again.

"That's why I need something to sell."

"You know most of the stuff I steal is worthless, right?"

Honestly, I have no idea where my magpie-like habits come from. It's not helpful. Fake gold doesn't pay bills. But I know what does.

I sighed and handed him a coin. Not a human one, but a faerie antique I'd swiped from a visiting contingent from Summer's Court who'd nearly trampled me with their horses.

"Hey—*hey*. Is that…?"

"It's worth more than my life. Don't lose it."

"You're a lifesaver."

"You're a liability."

"Love you too." He blew me a kiss and drank the wine in one go. "I should probably leave. The Crusher wants to see me in the morning."

"Good luck. Try not to get trodden on."

He clip-clopped out the flat.

Shaking my head, I put the wine away. Hopefully Denzel would manage to keep his head. Literally. *The Crusher*, of all people. And I thought *I* had a penchant for getting into trouble. It was a miracle I'd made it to my twenty-fourth birthday. Tomorrow would be… trying. Dad always acted weird on my birthday. I figured it was to do with losing his memory of the day I was born. When mortals fell into the hands of a faerie, they often lost their memories and most of their sanity, forever dreaming of a world they'd never see again. I didn't remember any of the years I spent in Faerie at all. Maybe they wiped my mind, too, or maybe the memories faded with age.

It'll be okay. You have the cake, anyway. I yawned, tugging off my boots.

There was a knock at the door.

I frowned. Denzel didn't usually knock. He just walked in.

Knock. Knock.

"All right." I was kind of pissed off by now. If Dad woke up, I'd have to deal with the fallout. Who'd come here in the middle of the night, anyway?

Did someone see me stealing the cake? No—impossible. I'd been careful not to be spotted.

The image of those Winter knights flashed through my head again and a chill raced down my back. Drama was going down in half-blood land...

"Who is it?" I hissed through the door. "It's nearly one in the bloody morning."

"Raine," whispered a male voice. "It's me."

It'd been a while since I'd fallen off a roof, but the impact of hearing his voice was pretty close to the sensation. My stomach dropped, my heart sinking as though I'd missed a step on a high staircase. I hadn't heard that voice in a long time.

"Go away."

"That's not nice, Raine."

I forced a laugh. "You can't claim the moral high ground, Robin."

I was too angry to be curious as to why my ex—the man who'd started and ended my performance career—was doing here in the first place. I'd never given him my address. Mostly because he hadn't spoken a word to me since the day he ended our four-year relationship and trounced my career in one fell swoop.

Despite myself, I inched the door open a fraction to make sure it was really him and not an illusion. But anyone with faerie blood can see through glamour, and he wasn't wearing any. He looked exactly the same as he had three years ago— beautiful in the way only faeries could be. Pointed ears, pale skin, cornflour coloured hair, elegant features forming an expression that almost resembled remorse. If I didn't know better.

"I'm sorry," he said now.

"You lost your chance to say sorry. Words are cheap."

"You're speaking like a human. You aren't."

"I might as well be," I shot at him. The closest I'd come to having my own magic was being part of his act, and that was long gone. Nothing was worth being reminded of something I could never have again.

Something I didn't *want* again.

"Look, can I come in?"

"No. You're a few years too late for an apology. It's done. *We're* done."

"That's not why I came."

"Really." I crossed my arms. "Well? What's so important that you had to come all the way here?"

"There was… a message from the Unseelie Court."

Unseelie. Winter. Those knights.

I edged the door open a little. "Okay. What does *that* have to do with anything?"

"They're here for us. We can claim our heritage and find out who our fae parent was. Yours… well. You'd be better off finding out yourself."

"Wait, *what?*" I'd never met my faerie parent. No half-blood had. They didn't want us. "That's a lie. Not a funny one, either."

"It's true." He moved closer into the doorway. "The Sidhe came here. They saw how many of us are left, and… that woman with the faerie magic, Ivy Lane, she asked them to claim us and allow us access to the faerie realm."

I laughed humourlessly. Sure, I'd heard the rumours about Ivy and her visit to the Courts, but she had faerie magic. I didn't. I'd never survive in Faerie. "You can't force a faerie parent to claim a child."

"No," he said. "That's why it's taken so long. It took me a while to find mine out."

"Do you want a medal?" I scooted back, having had about enough of him attempting to sneak into my flat. "Knowing who they are doesn't change anything."

"Raine," he said softly. "It does. Your parent is Sidhe. A Sidhe Lady of the Unseelie Court."

I didn't respond. I wasn't sure I could, even if the right words showed up. No wonder he'd spoken to me again.

I was half-Sidhe. Royalty.

2

"**I** don't believe you," I finally said. "You know I can't even cast a glamour, let alone use the kind of magic the Sidhe do."

Damn. I hadn't meant to open my heart to him again, even if he already knew about my lack of magical prowess. He had that way about him—a manner which invited you to let him in, to tell him everything. A promise he'd never use those words against you. *Yeah, and look how that turned out.*

"It's true. It took some time for the Sidhe to work out your parentage, but it's unmistakable. Your mother is Lady Nessa Whitefall of the Unseelie Court."

The more he spoke, the more absurd he sounded. "You'll have to do better than that."

"I can bring proof. I have a letter with the royal seal."

"Since when were you acting as their messenger boy?"

He ignored my barbed comment, pulling a piece of paper out of his pocket. Paper thick enough to be called parchment, covered in text I couldn't read. Faerie text. The stamp—a wolf's head—did match what I'd seen of the Unseelie Court.

And the name—Raine Warren/Whitefall. My name. Listed as heir.

Okay. It *looked* official. But that didn't mean they hadn't made a mistake. A monumental one.

"If it's true, I appreciate you telling me, but I'm no Sidhe. I'm happy where I am."

"Really." He eyed the dingy walls of my flat.

I moved to cover the view—it was none of his damn business. "Yes. If it's so hard for you to believe, I'm not going to bother explaining. You go to Faerie, you get eaten alive. I'll stick with my human side."

"There's no human side to us, Raine," he said. "We're all faerie or none. And you have a legacy."

"Legacy? I mean absolutely nothing to them. Anyone who thinks otherwise is deluding themselves. Don't you have a family to meet?"

He blinked. "Yes. I do."

"And?" I couldn't help my curiosity. I wanted to know his parentage.

No, I don't. Not just because we were finished, but because it wasn't a competition. I wanted no part in this game at all. The Sidhe had probably sent him to me on purpose. Why they'd bother playing a prank on me, of all people, who knew. Maybe because they were now free to openly walk into the mortal realm, they'd decided to find a new audience for their cruel games. It was harder for them to steal mortals away with all doors to Faerie under close watch now, so screwing with us lowly half-faeries must be their substitute.

"The house of Lady Hornbeam. Of Summer."

"Obviously." He had brown eyes, not green, but I knew his magic. Intimately.

I know, Summer and Winter faeries aren't supposed to be involved with one another. In the eyes of the Courts, it's almost as bad as murder. Things like that didn't matter here in the mortal realm. At least, they didn't before the Sidhe shoved their way into our lives.

"I thought—"

"Thought what? I'd take your hand and walk with you into Faerie as though I don't have family here? Unless the Sidhe show up in person, I'll be staying put, thanks."

"You…" He looked past me again at the flat.

"Yes, Dad's here. Go away and leave us in peace."

His mouth twisted. "Are you sure you don't want to come? Because this might be your only chance."

"Honestly, Robin, I ran out of fucks to give a long time ago."

I closed the door in his face, and took in a couple of calming breaths.

Okay. I might have handled that better. I couldn't think of a reason he'd lie to me about my heritage of all things— which I'd always assumed I'd never know. How they'd found out was a mystery, too, because the Sidhe never kept track of mortals they'd stolen. Right?

"Who was it?" Dad asked sleepily.

"Nobody," I said firmly. "Go back to sleep. It's not morning yet."

Though it would be in a few hours. Some birthday this was turning out to be.

The door opened a fraction, and Robin whispered, "Sorry."

I turned back to him, glaring. "You might want to time your bad news better."

"It's not bad news." His forehead pinched as he looked past me at the neglected state of the flat. He'd never known about Dad—and he'd not been as bad back then, anyway. "I'm sorry for the timing. The Winter contingent just left, and it felt important that I tell you right away. I'll come back tomorrow."

"Try it and you'll leave here in a body bag."

He winced. Good. Let him try putting me under a spell again. Why they'd sent him to deliver a message when we belonged to opposite Courts was odd, too, but I was through playing games. I'd take it up with the Sidhe messengers themselves if he kept bugging me.

"Bye, Robin." I closed the door, properly this time.

Dad didn't speak again, and I checked his door was closed before returning to my own room. Like most half-faeries, Robin worshiped the Courts despite never having set foot there, but he'd built a life here in the mortal realm like the rest of us. He'd been an orphan before he'd started the performance company to entertain mortals. I'd quickly risen in the ranks as the main attraction. Half-faeries make humans look uncoordinated and clumsy, but to stand out amongst us, you have to be extraordinary. He made me feel that way, once.

I earned every smile, every sidelong look, revelled in the attention as I soared high, and held the crowds under a spell. Even now, I wasn't sure how much of that was me and how much was him. I couldn't explain the sensation when his magic and mine—the little there was—clicked, like I could do anything as long as we were connected. Except it wasn't real. Since he'd gone, the stage lights had lifted. I remembered every moment he'd looked past me as though I was only there when convenient, and turned them into armour.

Half-faeries are pretty resilient. It's the mortal blood inside us. When you have little time to live, you rebuild fast. It'd take a while for the latest bombshell to sink in, though. I couldn't be descended from the Sidhe. Absolutely not. Maybe if Robin realised I wouldn't rise to his bait, he'd find someone else's life to ruin.

I shoved all thoughts of Robin, the Sidhe and hidden legacies firmly from my mind when I got up that morning. No thievery today—I had enough food in the house for the next few weeks. I mostly stole from the mages' stores, since they got first pick of every supply truck that came from outside town. Supposedly, it was only fair because they did more than any other supernaturals to defend everyone. Maybe I couldn't deny that, but I was glad I'd picked my obnoxious former employer's place to steal the cake from.

I put on my best jeans and shirt and covered my white hair with my rose-gold handkerchief again, grimacing at my reflection. Aside from the hair, eyes and pointed ears, the most distinctive sign of my nature was the marking on my face, a half-moon shape where my jaw met my neck. Like the Winter Court's way of reminding me of its never-ending hold over my entire existence. Not being able to use glamour was the worst part, because it ensured that I couldn't blend in amongst humans, let alone my own kind. I tugged up my collar to hide the mark, and tried to wrench my thoughts back into birthday mode.

Dad was already awake, reading a month-old newspaper in the battered armchair.

"Hey Dad," I said brightly. "Guess what day it is?"

He looked up. He wasn't all that old, but Faerie had aged him, turned his hair to wispy grey and his face to wrinkles.

"It's your birthday."

"Yep. I'm officially Old."

"You're eighteen."

My heart sank. "Nope. Twenty-four. Mentally, though, yeah, I'm a teenager. Being mature is overrated." I skipped over to the kitchen and opened the cupboard, throwing bacon into a pan.

In daylight, the risks I'd taken last night seemed foolish, but no more so than any I'd taken before. After Robin's revelation, the memory of those faerie knights felt like a dream.

Just like that, they'd vanished into Faerie in a flash of white-blue light—

I told you not to think about that, Raine.

When that didn't work, I thought, *that's what happened when your mother left you and Dad behind.*

Dad stared at the wall, a habit of his. There were times where he looked at things I couldn't see, spoke to people I'd never met, and the most painful part was knowing he *wanted* it. No mortal could resist the siren song of the Sidhe.

Maybe only a Sidhe could have damaged him the way my mother had.

My throat tightened. So much for not thinking about it. But it only affected my whole life. My entire past. Even the bit I couldn't remember. The whole world was changed thanks to the faeries, although I didn't think my mother had been amongst the Sidhe who'd attacked our realm twenty-two years ago. Either way, a lot of half-bloods had been left stranded here. Would any be left after they'd been collected and taken to the Courts? What would become of those of us who remained behind? And seriously, if I went after Robin into Winter, how in hell was I supposed to get home?

As I was loading our plates, there was a knock on the door.

Dammit, Robin.

Gritting my teeth, I snatched up the nearest weapon—a knife with wooden handle that protected my hands from the iron of the blade. Apparently he couldn't take a hint.

"Miss Warren?" said a voice.

Two human men greeted me at the door, and I swiftly hid the knife behind my back. I hoped they hadn't seen it.

"Yes?" I said warily. Human authority figures rarely came with good news.

One of the men said, "It's come to our attention that your father, Mr Harold Warren, has been seen causing damage to the property of your neighbour Mr Branson. His ornamental gnomes were found in your garden."

My heart sank. "Yeah. He gets confused sometimes. It's all right. I watch him most of the time. I'm his carer."

"They were decapitated."

"Oh."

I stepped forwards into the light, so they'd have no doubt at all that I wasn't fully human. At times like these, my too-blue eyes came in handy. Both of them took a step back, exchanging glances. It was a glance I'd seen too many times to count, a look that communicated that I was one of *them.* The usual human rules didn't apply—not if we didn't want them to. And obviously they had no way of knowing whether I was the type of half-faerie who cooperated, or the type who'd blast them in the face with Winter magic and cause icicles to grow on their noses.

The first guy continued with his spiel. Something about *the council will have to take action,* and a bill with far too many zeroes on it. Who the hell spent so much on lawn ornaments?

"And if your father can't speak to us himself…"

More words followed, even more unwelcome. If the authorities came poking into my life, they'd find out about the thievery pretty quickly. They'd take Dad away, lock him up, and I'd be completely alone. Maybe even lock *me* up. Denzel's antics hadn't helped matters at all.

"I'll pay," I said quickly. "Just—I'll pay. I swear it won't happen again." Because I'd take care of the ornaments first. Bloody humans and their constant fascination with all things faerie.

The humans left, and I stared after them, my heart sinking. There went this month's rent money. And next month's, too. If I didn't think of something good to steal, and fast, we'd be out on the streets by the month's end.

Before I could close the door, there was a flash of light, and a small figure materialised from thin air. The little winged man spun around and bowed at me. A sprite, eight inches tall, made of a wispy substance that wasn't quite solid, wasn't quite air. He wore a tuxedo of all things, and carried a stack of papers.

"The Unseelie Court formally extends an invitation to Raine Whitefall to come to the Winter territories of Faerie to accept her inheritance."

"Not interested," I told the sprite. "I've made my decision, and I decline the offer. I'm staying here in the mortal realm."

The sprite's brow furrowed, then he inserted a finger into his overlong ear as though he thought he'd misheard me.

"No, you heard me right. I'm not Sidhe. I don't have magic. I don't qualify for this, even if I wanted to come to Winter. Which I don't."

"You belong to the Whitefall bloodline, and you will inherit riches beyond imagining. A palace of ice, and—"

"Stop," I said, before temptation could sink its claws in me. I was all Dad had left, and they'd taken his life away from him. They'd do the same for me. No question. Whoever my mother was, she wasn't worth it.

You will inherit riches beyond imagining. The Sidhe lived for hundreds of years. How big a fortune could you amass in that time? Never mind rent money—if I claimed it, we'd be able to move out of this shithole. Pity it belonged to the one place I'd sworn never to set foot in, not even if my life depended on it. And the faeries never gave anything away for free. No—I'd be better off selling fake amulets on the black market.

"I'm *not* interested," I said. "Tell the Winter Court that. There's nothing binding me to them. It's my decision."

The sprite bowed again. "As you wish, Lady Whitefall."

He vanished in a swirl of blue glitter, which fell to the

ground like fresh snow. The pieces of glitter hit the same spot on the ground in a flash of light, turning into a small piece of paper. What'd he left me, a business card?

Words were written on the paper: *It's in your interest to come to the Unseelie Court, Raine. I trust you'll make your decision shortly.*

"Nice try." I ripped it in two, then tore each piece into two more and threw the pieces outside. Then I went back into the flat.

A rustling noise came from behind me. I turned to see the paper lying on the mat in the hallway. In one piece. It was bespelled. Obviously. Thanks for that one, Faerie.

The bacon was cold. I didn't care, and apparently Dad didn't either. My good mood—or what was left of it—had thoroughly evaporated. Why would the Winter Court think I'd be thrilled about their invitation to leave my home? Maybe because, to most of us, Faerie *was* home. The others didn't have ailing parents to take care of, or no magic to defend themselves with. If my mother wanted to meet me so badly, she could come here herself. This façade was all about the Sidhe showing this Ivy Lane and the mage council that they kept their word and helped us poor, helpless half-bloods find where we belonged. Never mind that we'd never fit into either realm. We were built to die, to wither away as our blood signalled our demise. Pure faeries lived forever, ever-burning candles, not snuffed out in the slightest breeze like we were. They might be pretending to be polite to us now, but they could as easily turn against us. No inheritance was worth the risk, even if it'd save us from being turfed out of the flat. Faerie was the last resort possible. I wasn't out of tricks yet.

"Who was at the door?" Dad asked me.

"The neighbour," I said. "Did you really destroy Mr Branson's lawn ornaments?"

"They looked evil. They were watching the house."

I sighed. "You're lucky the humans think I'll curse them with faerie magic if they dare put up more of a fight against us." It was no use telling him about the lack of money. Dad couldn't work, and it'd only distress him. "Please don't mess with the neighbours' ornaments. The human authorities don't like it."

"Humans," he muttered. "They're a joke, aren't they?"

"Yeah, sure. I'm half of one, remember?" I didn't know if he remembered he was fully human. Not with his mind permanently altered by Faerie. Sometimes he seemed to think he was Sidhe. I'd had to throw away all the mirrors in the flat after he broke them in a rage, tormented by the reminders of his own mortality.

"You're not like them." He stroked my hair, his eyes crinkling with tears. "I—I'm so sorry, Raine. I tried to stop them."

My throat tightened. He said things like this sometimes. I'd figured he meant, *I tried to stop your mother from kicking us out of Faerie.* It'd also been my birthday when we'd been abandoned here in the mortal realm, apparently. So it might not have been the day I'd been born. On days like this, I felt a thousand years old.

I shrugged. "It's okay. Ignore them. Today's *our* day. Wanna light the candles now?" If nothing else, at least we'd have had our moment if someone else decided to show up and trash the place. At this rate, we wouldn't even be able to afford to eat next month.

"I'd like that."

I lifted the cake onto the coffee table and went to retrieve the matches—to prevent accidents, I kept them hidden in my room. A shuffling noise came from the flat door, and I paused. *Okay, if Robin's left something alive outside my flat, I'll shove it up his nose.*

The door flew wide, nearly coming off its hinges, as a

giant and furred shape barrelled through. A hellhound. My knife was too far to reach, but its attention was on Dad.

"Dad, run!" I yelled.

I ran, clearing the table in one jump, and then the beast was on me.

3

I dodged the creature's lethal bite, kicking it hard in the side. Its teeth snapped at the doorway, gouging holes in the plaster. The tight space of the hallway made it difficult for it to charge, but it could still fit through the entryway into the flat. Its teeth dripped acid-like drool onto the mat—and at me. I ducked, pulling my handkerchief over my head just in time to avoid the splatter of drool. Walking back a couple of steps towards the coffee table, I reached to grab the nearest weapon—which happened to be the cake knife.

My hand closed around the knife handle as the beast jumped, forcing me to throw myself flat. The coffee table shattered under its weight, sending glass, wine and cake flying everywhere. Dad yelled from behind the bedroom door, which he'd closed. I heard him dragging furniture against the door from behind.

As the beast shook broken glass from its bulky body, I stabbed it in the eye with the cake knife.

The beast's legs buckled as the blade sank into its eye, splattering the floor—and me—with blood and grisly jellylike stuff. More drool dripped onto the floor, burning holes in the rug as the hellhound's head slumped at my feet.

Pulling my handkerchief off my head, I inspected the damage. The hellhound's drool had eaten holes in that, too. Great.

"You okay, Dad?"

He whimpered from behind the door. "Raine? What's that?"

"A hellhound." I wiped the bloody knife on the ruined handkerchief. "Who sent that in here?"

Obviously, I didn't expect an answer. Now faeries were attacking me at home? I'd thought hellhounds had gone extinct. They belonged to Winter—I thought—but had been known to easily fall under the control of anyone who wanted a quick and deadly way of disposing of their enemies.

I think someone tried to assassinate me.

My mind seemed slow to keep up with the obvious. Mostly, I was stumped on how I was supposed to get this great hulking monster out of the flat to a place it wouldn't draw attention. I kept hold of the knife and backed out of the flat door.

That bloody letter remained outside in the hallway. Even the beast barrelling through the door had left it untouched. I crouched down to examine it again. The ink was still wet. No —the message had changed to a fresh one.

I did warn you, Raine. Others seek your inheritance, too, and they will not hesitate to take your life before you can ever set foot in Faerie.

Well, that wasn't ominous at all.

If I hated anything, it was being coerced or threatened. I glared at the letter, leaving it where it was. As though an attack on my home would ever make me think it was safe to leave. The Sidhe could suck it. As for the fey beast, I wasn't going to let it rot here in the flat. Which meant carrying it outside, without getting any drool on me.

I went into my room and put my thick coat on again, grabbing a fresh handkerchief. Then I returned to the living room to find Robin staring into the flat.

"Get out," I snapped.

"Raine." His voice cracked. I stared at him, momentarily distracted by his dishevelled appearance. His arm was wrapped in a bloody bandage, and a nasty-looking scratch marred one side of his perfect face, inches away from his left eye.

"What happened to you?"

"Winter beasts." He looked at the hellhound. "They came for you, too."

I strode over to him. "Let me guess. I have to go into Faerie otherwise they'll keep trying to kill me. Real original."

His jaw worked. "I—Raine. There are things you… things you should hear from them. Not from me."

"If it's so important, my so-called family can come here and tell me themselves. I'm not leaving Dad here alone with hellhounds invading my flat."

"It's you they're after," he said. "I'd be happy to help move your father to a safe house. But Raine, it's urgent. They need you in Faerie. If not—the people who want you dead won't stop until they've taken down everyone you know."

My mouth dropped open. "What the hell's so important about me? I'm a half-blood without magic. That's not worth murdering people over."

He looked over his shoulder. "May I come in? I don't want to risk anyone overhearing."

"You're not allowed in here."

"I can help you get that creature out. You can't leave it here. It'll attract other Winter monsters, and so will its blood."

"Even five year olds know that. Don't patronise me."

"Sorry."

Apologies meant little coming from him, considering what he'd put me through already. "If you're going to stick around, make yourself useful and help me get this thing out of here."

Unfortunately, he was dead right—its corpse would draw every creature attracted to faerie blood, and magic, in the area. Not to mention put a beacon on my head for a week, unless I got the blood out of the carpet. The house had no iron wards on it, because the effect of the iron would spread to me, as well as any fae creature that tried to get into the flat.

I tugged on a pair of leather gloves and grabbed the hellhound around the middle, pulling it along the carpet. Robin made a feeble attempt to help. I might move quickly but I'm not that strong, and Robin's injured arm was clearly bothering him. Between the two of us, we didn't make much headway, and it took several minutes of cursing and tripping over hellhound feet for me to notice we were being watched.

A half-blood male stood outside the building, eying the hellhound through the open front door. He had shoulder-length dark hair, and pale skin marked with a curved scar on his right cheekbone. His pointed ears were the only other visible signs of his faerie heritage.

"Need a hand?"

"If you're offering one." I glared at Robin. "Stop walking sideways. It's not helping."

"Allow me." The man stepped inside the hallway, taking the hellhound's front from me. The drool didn't seem to bother him—and then I looked closer and saw he wore some kind of armour, black and form-fitting and downright fancy compared to the second-hand crap I usually saw on half-bloods playing at being real Sidhe. Who was he?

"Thanks," I said, when we were outside. I brushed sweaty hair from my eyes with the back of my glove, and I was sure his gaze jumped to the mark on my neck. I didn't know him. I was fairly sure I'd remember a half-blood who dressed like a noble. Maybe he was here to collect me. "You don't look like you're from around here."

"No, I can't say I've been to this particular area of the city before. It's… different."

"You mean it's a hellhole. I know it is. Doesn't mean I wanted a hellhound chewing my carpet up." I hauled up the hellhound's flank again. "There's a place nearby we can take him. Down the street, turn left. Let the mercenaries take care of him."

"The human ones?" The stranger arched an eyebrow. "Are you sure?"

"Of course I'm sure. Robin, can you go and close the door? If you go back inside, I'll know about it."

Robin gave the stranger a suspicious look, but did as I said. Good. I bloody hoped no other hellhounds had been sent to the flat, but Robin could handle them.

"The name's Cedar, by the way," said the stranger.

"Raine. I'd offer to shake your hand like the humans do, but I have hellhound drool all over my gloves."

He laughed, the typical melodic laugh of a half-faerie. "It's delightful to meet you, Raine."

Sure it is. He must be here for some purpose, but I was too preoccupied trying not to drop the hellhound to get a closer look and figure out which Court he belonged to. I'd thought he'd leave the beast at the road's end, but instead, he helped me carry it all the way into the alcove between two abandoned houses. The mercenaries frequented this area a lot, because it practically wore a sign saying "easy-to-kill faerie beasts here". Hellhounds, however, did not fall into the category of "easy kills", especially as they hadn't been seen in this realm in over a year. That I knew of, anyway.

"I don't suppose you saw where it came from?" I asked Cedar. "You were outside my flat, right?"

"Unfortunately, I didn't. I heard screaming and ran this way. If I'd reached you sooner, I'd have been able to help."

I let go of the hellhound's legs, grimacing at the trail of blue-tinged blood all over my coat. That'd be fun to dry-clean.

"Well, you didn't quite arrive in time to save me from the evil monster, but I'll take what I can get at this point."

Cedar smiled. "You don't look like someone who needs saving. And not just because it looks like you killed that thing with a blunt knife."

"Believe it or not, that's the nicest thing anyone's said to me all day. And yeah, it was my birthday cake knife."

"Happy birthday, then, Raine." He turned his smile up to full effect, which on a half-faerie, is like being punched in the face by the sun. He had the sort of striking looks that would cause heads to turn even amongst half-bloods, which would have suggested Sidhe heritage if not for his light hazel coloured eyes which showed no marker of his Court. I'd guess he came from Summer, but I wouldn't know for sure unless he used magic. All my suspicions went up to max. Usually half-bloods flaunted which Court they belonged to—or, like me, had no way of hiding it. I hadn't spent my life around criminals to be fooled by a pretty face.

"Cheers," I said. "All right. Mind telling me why you were near my flat? Running an errand for the Courts?"

"The Courts? Not at all. I was visiting half-blood territory and decided to take a shortcut home."

Home. Did he mean here—or Faerie? He wore a smile which might have been an open book… or a mask.

I dropped my hands to my sides. "What do you want from me?"

"Nothing more than to see you home safely, Raine."

I rolled my eyes. "All right, have it your way." I started walking, one eye on him. After a heartbeat, he followed, easily, arms at his sides as to show he was unarmed. Considering the armoured coat he wore, he didn't fool me for a second. Half-bloods might look out for one another, but his timing was a little *too* perfect. I definitely hadn't seen him before, much less in a mostly human part of town.

Bu even without magic, I could still sense others', though muted. No evil intent came from him, and the lack of a distinct marker of his Court suggested his own magic wasn't powerful, either. That, or he was taking care to keep it on mute.

Luckily, it appeared the hellhound had come alone. Robin crouched beside the door, tipping something from a small container onto the bloodstains on the doorstep.

"I'll see you around, Raine," said Cedar, and gave me one last smile before walking away.

"Sure you will," I muttered. Sad to say, nobody offered anything for nothing in my experience, and now I watched him walk away, he looked even more suspicious. He walked swiftly, checking over his shoulder every couple of steps, and was lightly glamoured to disguise his pointed ears from any human onlookers. My Sight let me see through glamour and his wasn't particularly sophisticated, but there was something... odd about it. I still couldn't sense whether he was from Summer or Winter.

Given his clothes and manners, I'd bet my right hand he was from the Courts. But he hadn't asked me to come with him. *Hmm.*

"Who was that?" Robin asked. "Did you know the guy?"

"No, I didn't. What are you putting on the carpet? Iron filings?"

"They'll deter anything from coming to your door."

"And give me blisters if I step outside barefoot."

"Did you plan to do that?"

"You never know." I clamped my mouth shut, determined not to let him reel me into conversation again—because that way led to the dreaded Sidhe. Instead, I returned to the flat, checked Dad was still in the bedroom, and grabbed a dustpan and brush from the kitchen to clean up the broken glass.

Robin joined me a minute later. "This looks bad."

"Any clue who might have sent it? Not everyone has hellhounds at their disposal."

"No." He paused. "Ideally we need a witch spell to clean the floor. Or we can just pull the carpet up."

"You're the one with magic."

"And you're the thief. I saw some spells in there…"

He'd been peeking at my hoard after all. "They're not for you. And they can't clean up hellhound drool, for crying out loud. I'll shift this lot."

I tipped the last of the glass into a plastic bin bag. A shard pierced my palm and I hissed in pain. Great. More faerie blood on the carpet, this time mine. My blood wasn't worth anything, but it'd still draw attention.

Maybe it is worth something. Someone wanted to kill me for it.

With Dad hiding in the room behind me, I didn't dare question Robin any further about the Court's message. I used the knife to cut out the damaged section of carpet—not hard, because the hellhound's drool had eaten through it anyway— and sealed it in bin bags under Robin's hovering. Then I stripped anything the blood had splattered on and shoved that in another bag, with the exception of my coat. That, I kept on until the bags were outside. I'd dump them some- where later. The iron would deter anything else from coming inside, anyway. I dug in the cupboard for a spare rug and threw it over the missing carpet. Done. Relatively. Pity I hadn't been able to salvage the cake, though.

Robin stood on the side taking orders, which I figured was because he had more to say to me. Once we were done cleaning, I hauled the last bag of ruined carpet out into the corridor and beckoned him to come with me.

"All right," I growled at him. "Now I expect a detailed explanation from you as to why a hellhound came into my house in the first place. I thought they belonged to Winter."

"They belonged to one part of Winter," he said. "But they mostly work for whoever gives them orders."

"How do you know it isn't the Winter Court who want to kill me?"

"Because they would never turn on one of their own."

"And I'm one of them." It still felt *wrong*. I was my father's daughter. Not this faceless Sidhe Lady's mortal offspring. What did she even want with me? As a mortal, it wasn't like being her heir actually meant anything. The Sidhe lived forever, after all. So they ran off and had affairs with mortals and left half-blood children all over the place.

"Of course you're one of them," he said. "Though—there's something you should know first. I'd rather explain it to you when we're in Faerie."

"Tell me here."

His gaze flickered to the door to Dad's room. A surge of anger gripped me. My hand brushed against the iron part of the knife and pain lanced up my palm. Ow.

"Tell me," I said. "I'm not in a good mood today, Robin."

"It's your—your mother," said Robin. "She's dead."

The world rocked and swayed then went deadly still. For the second time in less than twelve hours, I stumbled, my heart plummeting like I'd been shoved off a cliff into free-fall. All words fled my tongue, leaving a gaping silence behind.

I should feel something—grief, sadness, something other than shock. But I didn't. All I knew of my mother was that she'd captured my father, bewitched him and then used her magic to permanently damage his mind. I'd never forgive her for that, even in death.

But the Sidhe didn't die. They were immortal.

"Now do you see why the Sidhe would prefer it if you came in person? There's the matter of the inheritance to sort out, and—"

"Inheritance?" I didn't give a crap about faerie trinkets, but money… money would be good to have. Really good. Maybe I'd get compensation for someone setting hellhounds on me after all.

"It's the reason you're being attacked. You're set to inherit something very valuable—I don't know what it is, because I'm not in the same family as you are. But I heard them whispering about it. If you don't claim it, someone else will. If you stay here, others will attack you because they believe you possess it."

"Possess *what?*"

But I knew what. Nothing would make every faerie lose their collective minds and murder one another—nothing short of a genuine faerie talisman.

"I—I can't say, because I don't know. It's your family's treasure, not mine. But there are rumours. Whatever it is, it's valuable enough to kill for. Several people have already died."

Once again, he'd rendered me speechless. *Why me?* The question was childish, but of all people, couldn't they have picked someone with more magical gift than a pencil?

Maybe this talisman would be the source of magic in my family. *Wait. That makes sense.* Maybe… if I had the talisman, I'd get magic.

The idea seemed about as appealing as dancing for Robin right now. I mean, people had died. A fae monster had almost torn my throat out in my own living room. And far worse would await me in the Winter Court.

I looked at the closed bedroom door. Dad didn't seem aware of what was happening, which was probably for the best. If he figured out Lady Whitefall was dead, the Sidhe alone knew what he'd do. He'd worshipped her, in the way a mortal worshipped a living goddess. A form of enslavement, no matter how you looked at it. Finding out she'd died might be the final crack that caused him to shatter. I wouldn't be responsible for that. Never.

But that explained why the sprite had said I'd inherit *riches beyond imagining.* If there was nobody else to claim those riches, then maybe I could use them to dig us out of our current financial hole. It wasn't like I was wandering into Faerie unprepared. I'd be going with a group, and I'd be back here before Dad even realised I'd gone. It'd be selfish of me to leave him, but even more selfish to stay and put his life in danger. *I'm doing this for your sake, Dad. I won't let them keep me captive like they did to you.* Over my dead body.

The letter said to come to Faerie. It didn't say anything about *staying* in Faerie. I'd just take my inheritance, get an explanation of my mother's fate from someone whose word I actually trusted, and come home. Done. Finished. Minimal disruption.

"Okay," I said. "Here's what's going to happen. I'm taking *one* trip into Faerie, to collect my inheritance. Then I'm coming home."

"You—"

"Don't," I snapped. "We both know I don't belong in Faerie, and with my mother dead, there's nothing keeping me there. My life is here. I'm not rearranging my entire future because the Winter Court suddenly decided to remember I exist."

His mouth thinned. "It's not a wise choice. The Court would protect you from those who seek to do you harm."

"You mean whoever sent the hellhound? Child's play. If I get this valuable inheritance, so much the better."

"This isn't a game."

"You think I'm laughing? You just fucked me over. Big time. Not that I should be surprised, but this is as reasonable as I'm willing to be. You might be happy to leave everyone you know in this realm hanging. I'm not."

Which was the heart of our issues. He'd happily left me behind, content to carry on as though our relationship had never existed, as though I'd never been his inspiration, his greatest performer. Those words, as it turned out, meant as little as his promises.

I'd trust nobody. The Sidhe, least of all.

"I'm sorry, Raine. I really am."

Maybe he did mean it. But he'd still, indirectly or not, ruined my life again. "Fine. I'll see you tomorrow, then."

In the weeks following the break-up, I'd dreamed of saying those words. In no way had a dead hellhound and a summons from Faerie been involved, though. At least he left without a fuss. I sighed, rolled up my bloodstained coat, and shoved it in the washing machine, hoping hellhound drool wouldn't be the final straw that caused the rickety old thing to break.

Dad's door inched open. "What was that?"

"A fae monster," I told him. "It's dead now. We're safe."

I didn't bring up tomorrow. Not yet. I'd tell him when things had calmed down. When I'd found the words. And how in hell was I supposed to explain this to Denzel?

Ugh. Forget it. I'd be back within less than a day, and Faerie would never bother me again.

I didn't really believe it, but the thought made me feel a little better about everything. Battling the dryer and cleaning the flat took care of most of the rest of the day. I didn't sleep much that night, though, knowing Robin would show up early in the morning to drag me into Faerie. Every noise made me jump, thinking another hellhound had come to attack us. I gave up on sleep at five a.m. and put a call through to the mercenaries to send someone to watch our flat. One mention of the hellhound and I had no fewer than six volunteers, all keen to claim a kill. I hoped they'd be disappointed, but at least Dad would be under guard in case anyone came after me.

"What're you on the phone for?" Dad asked sleepily, coming into the living room as I hung up. He eyed my ragged boots, even more ragged jacket and torn up jeans—maybe I was being petty, but if Faerie expected me to show up in my best dress, they could keep it. "You're going out?"

"Yeah." I put my phone in my pocket—it wouldn't work in Faerie, but would help convince him I wasn't going far.

There was a knock on the door.

"Dad," I said. "I'm off to run a few errands. There's a chance I might not be able to come back tonight. Will you be okay? You remember how to use the microwave, right?"

"Of course I remember how to use the bloody microwave." He looked at me with eyes more lucid than they usually were. "It's them, isn't it? They've called you."

I paused. "Yes."

He held my gaze for a long moment. "Be careful, Raine. They're not like us."

"Tell me something I don't know." I leaned forward and hugged him. "I'll be fine, Dad. I'll be back before you know it."

That, I can promise. I'd keep my word, and if anyone stood in my way, I'd cut them down.

I stepped back, the glint of the iron knife on the table catching my eye. If I took the knife with me, it'd signal I had no intention of playing nice with my newfound family, whoever they were. Iron was a direct threat to every faerie I came across. It'd blow any chance I had of making friends.

It might also save my life.

I tucked the knife into my belt and walked out the door.

4

Robin tried to start a conversation a couple of times on the way to half-blood territory, but gave up after I responded tersely. My mind was elsewhere, torn into two pieces. I'd never felt the separation between my two halves as keenly as I did now, and I didn't usually think of myself as half a faerie or half a human. Just me.

Here, though, it was impossible to forget. The territory was a haven of magic in the middle of a human city, a blazing beacon. Literally, because two half-bloods were in the middle of a magical duel right by the entrance. Bright blue and green light clashed with the effect of fireworks colliding in mid-air as a female faerie with thorny hair did battle with a long-fingered winged faerie with blue sparks dancing from his hands. Summer and Winter, getting along like a house on fire. As usual.

The Summer faerie unleashed a blast of green energy from her palms, sending her opponent flying into the nearest hedge. Thorns had sprung up where the Summer magic hit the ground, already withering under the Winter magic from half-blood territory that signalled the end of autumn.

"Hey," said a Summer half-blood wearing armour and carrying a bone-white sword. "Stop that. Get inside or get out."

The Winter half-blood detached himself from the hedge, glaring all the while at the Summer half-blood. I stepped around the thorns to avoid treading on them in my ragged old boots. Behind them was the gate, grown in a pattern of intertwining branches between the hedges. The armoured half-blood was clearly a guard, but his armour looked to be of a cheap human-made material rather than whatever the Courts used. Certainly not like the stranger I'd encountered yesterday. I wondered if Cedar would be here. It'd be nice to know someone aside from Robin, who I likely wouldn't see again if he moved to Summer permanently. The thought was something of a relief. After today, if I played my cards right, the Sidhe would be out of my hair forever.

Frost-covered grass crunched beneath my feet as I walked with Robin to join the others in the field's centre. Winter's special effects were beginning to creep into the territory as the days shortened and the nights lengthened. I'd never felt a particular attachment to the season, but how could I, without magic? Frost coated all the bare-branched trees, and a chill breeze blew through the air. I scanned the crowd for a familiar face, but found a bunch of strangers—a mixture of Seelie and Unseelie. On a superficial level, there weren't too many differences between the two, though the most powerful Sidhe often had bright green or blue eyes, matching their Court allegiance. Otherwise, they were human-appearing, ranging from children to adults. Most were young, though a side effect of faerie magic meant ageing was slowed even with our shorter lifespans. And some had wings or tails, features of partial shapeshifters who hadn't figured out how to control their magic. There were even some pure fey like hobgoblins and brownies amongst the group who must have ended up in this realm when the invasion had shaken every-thing up. They tended to have weaker magic and must surely know they wouldn't last long in Faerie, but the lure was too strong to resist. Faerie wasn't a place for the weak, and Winter least of all.

"It's her," a winged female half-blood whispered to another at her side. "The Whitefall heir."

Whispers spread through the crowd, making me wish I could glamour myself and turn invisible—not that it'd make a difference in a field of Sighted individuals. Apparently everyone had been given a detailed description of my appearance so they could embarrass me. I settled for wearing a stony expression and keeping my eyes ahead. Robin moved closer to me in sympathy, but I ignored him. It was his fault I'd landed in this mess in the first place.

"Hey," said the winged female faerie, fluttering over to me. "Haven't I seen you before? Did you used to perform for the mortals?"

Damn. I hadn't known some of them would remember my past. I'd thought of that as belonging to the human world—after all, humans were my audience, mortals entranced by my performance in the way only people who haven't experi-enced the real Faerie can be. But half-bloods had frequently attended too, drinking in the magic pouring from the stage as we wove our spell.

"Years ago," I said, trying to keep my tone even. Aside from the wings, she was human in appearance, with delicate, elfin features and a mischievous grin that might have caught my eye if she hadn't been poking into my history.

"Thought so. You were the best act."

I put on a fake smile and said, "I don't do that anymore, sorry," and used the restlessly moving crowd to extricate myself from the conversation by hiding behind an eight-foot-tall half-troll.

Even there, I wasn't safe. Two short half-goblins pointed at me, jabbering at one another in their own tongue. Some species of faerie had their own language, including the Sidhe themselves. I didn't know if they spoke modern English, but there was a rumour that their magic enabled them to be understood no matter what language they spoke, and that they knew every human language. Most of the stories about the Sidhe sounded like exaggerated tales, but I wouldn't rule anything out as far as the faerie realms were concerned.

As the group spread, it divided seemingly of its own accord—by species and by rank. Some half-Sidhe ensconced themselves in a group away from the others, and from the jabbering of the half-hobgoblins, they weren't happy about being pushed aside. *This is what happens when you suddenly impose Faerie's hierarchy on a bunch of people who once lived in relative peace.* What would happen to the friendships between people of different Courts? There'd be no visits between Summer and Winter. Good job Robin and I hadn't lasted, really.

Another half-faerie sauntered over, a girl of maybe sixteen or so with Asian heritage on her human side. She smiled at me with pointed teeth. Her eyes glowed neon blue, too bright to be contacts. "I've wanted this my whole life," she said. "We're finally going home."

"Uh-huh." I couldn't even feign enthusiasm. "Home. Right."

"You're Raine Whitefall." She tilted her head on one side. "Your mother's dead, right?"

Even *that* had got out? "Yes," I said stiffly. I didn't care if the Sidhe didn't want everyone finding out—if not for them, I wouldn't be here. "I'm going to collect my inheritance."

"You're that confident you'll win the trial?"

I blinked. "Trial?"

She laughed. "You didn't think you'd just get to stride into your family's palace and take your heirloom?"

Well, yeah. "I was under the impression I would."

"You have to earn it," she said. "Or one of your siblings will get it instead."

I had *siblings?*

"What?" I didn't need to feign ignorance. "I don't see any other Whitefalls."

"Oh, they don't live here. But they're somewhere in this realm. We're not the only ones crossing over today."

"How do you know my family?"

"Everyone knows," she said. "You're famous. Not just because of the dancing thing, though that's pretty cool, too. Didn't you get to perform for the Chief?"

"Yes," I said. "Once. How many… how many siblings?"

"Three."

Dad hadn't had other kids. So they must be half-siblings. The Sidhe woman, my mother, she'd had more than one mortal. It shouldn't have surprised me, but… were the others living in the same kind of circumstances as me? Did they have mortal parents to protect? Like Dad? Would they understand my situation?

"Quiet!" hissed a voice. A half-hobgoblin climbed onto a tree stump to address us. "Attention!" he rasped, not much louder. Everyone kept talking.

A bright white light exploded in the middle of the field. All the nearby half-bloods moved back with cries of alarm as the air split in two, and several horsemen stepped out of the air.

My jaw hit the floor as magic washed over me in a way it never had before. It was like inhaling fresh air after being locked in a stuffy room. Cool air, beckoning, dizzying, alluring.

As the doorway widened, and Faerie opened in earnest, I

was forced to confront the truth… part of me wanted this. Part of me sang with joy when the dizzying iciness of Winter's magic washed over me, invigorating, awakening all my senses. All of us moved towards the gap as though under a spell. Which we were—the powerful enticing aura of the realm that called to our blood and magic.

The path on the other side wound through trees coated in snow. I ought to be cold, but it felt *right*. Some of the others were shivering, though, especially the Seelie fae. There was a noise like a collective intake of breath as the horsemen turned to face us. Each was clad in armour of either silver, black, or grey. They carried swords, too, prominently displayed, and most had banners bearing symbols I assumed belonged to the major Winter families. The half-hobgoblin spoke into the silence: "Please welcome the messengers of the Unseelie Court."

So these guys were only the messengers. But they must be Sidhe, to cross realms in the first place. Maybe lower ranking ones. I hadn't realised even the Sidhe had a hierarchy. All I knew was that bloodlines affected which territory we'd be assigned to, and everyone belonged to a family, which were generally quite extensive—they lived forever, after all. But other than that, I didn't know what to expect. If my mother was dead, surely I'd have other relatives. Maybe more half-bloods. Several of the half-Sidhe-looking faeries might be related, though it was hard to tell with faeries.

However enticing Faerie might be, this wasn't the moment to indulge my long-buried curiosity about my own history. Time to collect an inheritance, and bugger off home before this place ensnared me in its grip.

"All Unseelie fae are to follow me. The Seelie fae will be collected in five minutes." The Sidhe in front beckoned, and we followed, like children dancing after the pied piper. Minus the music. Aside from the howl of the wind in the trees, Winter territory was pretty quiet, actually. The trees were all bleached white, stripped of bark, and twisted in gnarled shapes like the screaming faces of torture victims.

Three winding paths later and I concluded that I'd never be able to find my way back on my own without getting lost in the forest. Winter had a not-unfounded reputation for being the home of most of the nasty fey—redcaps, ogres, trolls, lorelei. We were never far from some horrible noise or other—screeching, ripping and tearing noises, bringing the scent of blood from some unfortunate creature in the woods. Not so different from half-blood territory… though the group's enthusiasm had died down some, and most people walked in silence.

The half-hobgoblin paused besides a clearing. "Lady Hawkswood's children, that way."

Two of the half-Sidhe left, following one of the horsemen. They must be siblings, then. The rest of us continued to walk. From my best estimate—and it was guesswork, because every Sidhe had the ability to use their magic to rearrange their own territory however they wanted—we were circling the outskirts of the main Unseelie Court. Maybe some of the half-Sidhe belonged to the Queen herself, though rumour had it they'd already been claimed. We were just one set of half-bloods from one area of the mortal realm, after all.

As we reached the point where we'd started, the last horseman rode off with three half-bloods on his tail, leaving me and the half-hobgoblin in front. The other half-Sidhe had all gone. So why not me? We were leaving the central part of Winter's Court behind, heading deeper into the trees. The light was reduced to a trickle, the trees forming a sinister canopy of creeping branches overhead. This was wilder territory, according to our guide—the parts of Winter which weren't directly involved with the Court, but were still technically a part of it.

Names were called. Half-redcaps, half-hobgoblins. Some didn't know their names, but gladly fled to the woods anyway. As we continued to walk, the trees grew thicker, we passed more and more territory which belonged to nobody at all, and there were odd... gaps, where smoke filled the spaces between trees. A chill that had nothing to do with the cold breeze raced down my back.

When we re-joined a new path, it hit me that I was the only one left, aside from the hobgoblin guide. "This is as far as I can take you," he said. "This territory lies on the brink between Summer and Winter, and there are other families living nearby. Keep walking in a straight line and you'll reach your new home."

And he vanished into the trees, practically sprinting away.

Heat rushed up my neck, followed by a shock of icy rage. Had I been set up? Had Robin lied? Of all the ridiculous tricks to fall for. Apparently, I was too soft-hearted to survive in the icy Court of Winter.

Fine. I turned around, following the hobgoblin back. I'd bet I could outrun the bastard. Teach him to leave me in the middle of the woods.

"Raine Whitefall?" said a voice.

I whirled around. "Yes?"

A female figure stepped out from behind a tree. A girl—no, woman, half-blood, with pale skin, sharp features and long curly dark hair. She wore dark colours, topped by a long black coat that matched her inky hair.

"Yes. That's me."

"Good. They're expecting you. Come with me."

I didn't move. "*Who,* exactly?"

She blinked. "Why, your siblings, of course, and your —court."

The pause before the word *court* set all my suspicions blaring. "Are you the one in charge of this charade?"

"The ceremony? I'm the servant to the Whitefall family, so that makes me responsible for passing on the inheritance to the rightful heir."

"You mean, heirs. Right?"

She shook her head, beckoning. "Come with me quickly. It's unwise to linger in the forest. There are many who seek to remove the heirs from the competition before you ever lay your eyes on the treasure."

"Treasure." I took one step forward, and blood dripped onto my hand from above. Crimson droplets fell, dotting the path. I looked up, fighting the urge to gag. The body of something human-sized was spread-eagled in the tree above, peppered with arrows. Flies buzzed around the body.

"That was the last person who tried to breach our security."

I skirted around the tree to avoid the steadily dripping blood. "You killed him."

"I didn't need to."

On that ominous note, she turned and walked down the path. Figuring I'd be better off in the palace than as a human pincushion in a tree, I followed. She seemed to know where she was going, striding ahead in a way I'd describe as military—perfect steps, exactly in line, and bloody fast. My breaths came quickly by the time we slowed at a snowy clearing. A gate beckoned, made of solid ice sheared to sharp points. At least there weren't any human heads impaled on the spikes.

Behind were more trees, masking the outline of a large building—a palace which appeared to be made of ice cut into bricks.

"I'm Viola, by the way," she said. "As I said, I'm the servant of the Whitefall family. If you're chosen in the ceremony, I'll become your servant."

Servants. How medieval. I'd deal with *that* after the ceremony. If anyone knew what happened to Lady Whitefall, though, it was her. "Do you know how my mother died?"

"I—I don't know if I'm allowed to tell you yet."

"But she's dead," I said. "She can't give you orders now, right?"

Her mouth went tight, and her gaze dropped. She was scared. Maybe more so than I was. I'd known Faerie had its own rules, and that I was essentially visiting a foreign country for the first time in my life, but I didn't even know where to begin with my questioning. Maybe someone else here had witnessed my mother's death, or knew of the circumstances. I'd find out after this so-called family reunion.

The palace gates opened, revealing an expanse of whiteness. Snow. You never saw real snow like that in the mortal realm, unless a Winter half-Sidhe had thrown a tantrum. It was crisp and perfect and I almost didn't want to tread in it and ruin it. But the child who'd played in the snow was long gone, the part of me who'd dreamed of Faerie had been extinguished years ago, and all I had was the baggage of responsibility and a shit-ton of questions.

"Look," I said, following Viola through the gate. "I'm new to this. Really new. I was, am, a thief in the mortal realm. I had no idea I might be related to the Sidhe. I'm not like them. At all."

Her steps paused. "No. I've heard things about you."

I resisted the impulse to sigh. "Why does everyone know about the dancing thing?"

"What dancing thing?"

My face heated. "Nothing. I thought—the other half-bloods all knew I used to be a... a performer. Just for the mortals, nothing special."

"That sounds great."

"It wasn't," I lied, wishing I'd never brought it up. "Anyway. I'm an amateur at this, and to be honest, I don't know anything about my family. Are there others? Did my mother marry, or have siblings?"

She hesitated. "No. There are no others."

Okay. This whole game had officially veered sideways from 'strange' into 'downright bizarre'. And I hadn't even seen the inside of the palace yet. "Seriously?"

"Let me rephrase," said Viola. "She did have family, but this is all her own territory, and she ruled alone. Many Sidhe leave their parents to start new lives, using magic to build their own territories. This palace has stood for centuries."

"Right." I kept forgetting the way immortality must affect how the Sidhe ruled their territory. Once their kids were grown up, they wouldn't want to spend countless years standing in their parents' shadows. In a world where no one ever died, estrangements could last centuries.

But my mother *had* died. Somehow. No wonder it'd drawn so much attention. Murder of a Sidhe... I'd never heard of such a thing. But neither had I heard of a Sidhe leaving no heirs behind except half-bloods. Had she died recently? Was that why everyone was so disorganised, and my siblings hadn't come to meet me? Was that why I'd been chosen at all? Sidhe heirs didn't have no magic. There *must* have been a mistake.

Viola frowned at me. "Is something wrong?"

"No."

The lie was obvious in my voice, and she flinched. I blinked, puzzled by her reaction. *Oh. Sidhe don't lie.* Well, I'd been raised human, and was a thief at that. Curbing my habits would be impossible.

"I'm good," I said. "Come on. Let's see this palace, then."

She waved a hand, and the obsidian doors swung open. I hung back, reluctant to look inside. I couldn't have felt more out of place. Everything I'd been told said I wasn't worthy to be here. These lands belonged to our superiors. Small though I felt, I'd made it this far. My siblings would be half-bloods, too. Surely they'd be as overwhelmed as me. They wouldn't have grown up here in Faerie either. Until a year ago, none of us would have dared hope we could come back.

I crossed the threshold into the palace.

Even though I'd been mentally prepared, given my knowledge of Faerie, the breath left my lungs as I looked up at the dizzyingly high ceiling inside the entrance hall. You could have fit my whole apartment block into it. The polished marble floor reflected glimmering chandeliers, which shone with luminous light. Surely not candles, because real icicles adorned the banisters of the spiral staircases. Everything was sharp, cold, and entirely typical of Winter—except super-sized. I wasn't convinced the palace entirely matched up with the size and shape it looked outside, but Faerie didn't have to make sense, and nor did this palace of ice, as deadly and uncompromising as the magic that kept it alive.

Magic that might be mine.

Viola kept glancing at me. Oh, right, I was supposed to comment. "Wow," I said, which pretty much summed it up. "It's very… big."

"You'll get the hang of it," she said. "When you have your magic, it'll be easier."

"Uh-huh." I walked forward, wondering where the place even ended. Aside from the spiral staircases, statues filled the space at the back of the entrance hall—mostly fae creatures. They ranged from giant trolls to small hobgoblins, all delicately carved to perfection in a manner that creeped me out. I looked past to examine the murals behind them, which weren't much better. Bloodthirsty and gruesome battle scenes adorned the walls in vivid shades that somehow didn't clash with the beauty of the palace's interior.

"She had a singular taste," said Viola.

"I bet she did." I'd thought the idea that Winter Sidhe were bloodthirsty warriors was just stereotyping, but maybe there was some truth to it. The iron knife weighed heavily at my waist, but Viola didn't seem to have picked up on it yet. Iron wouldn't undo a spell as strong as the one that kept this place standing, but it'd incapacitate anything that attacked me. The palace was all hidden corners and passages and doors spaced in improbable locations that still somehow fit. Viola beckoned me through a side door under the stairs, which sprang open at a touch, revealing another hall with polished marble flooring. A dais at the end indicated some-where speeches might be made, or a court addressed... but there didn't seem to be one present. Chairs were lined in rows, enough to seat at least a hundred people, but the only other people in the room were two other half-bloods sitting on chairs at opposite ends of one long row, and another sitting at the back. My siblings.

They all looked my age, give or take a couple of years. The nearest man was classically handsome, but his clear blue eyes were oddly cold when they studied me. Silver-white hair grew to his chin and his face was equally pale. An elegant sword was strapped to his waist. *Wait. Does he already have a talisman?* It surely couldn't be iron, like my knife. He didn't wear armour, but his black clothing wasn't typically human-style anyway. Maybe they did have more experience of Faerie than I did after all.

"Hi," I said, my voice sounding small when the high ceiling echoed it back at me. "My name's Raine. I'm your sister."

"No, you aren't," he said, in a voice as cold as his gaze. "You're a half-blood."

Well. So much for a warm welcome, even in an icy palace.

"So are you," I said, one hand resting on my knife. His

gaze darted that way, though surely he couldn't sense the iron from where he stood. "Your name?"

"Valour," he said. "I'm the rightful heir of the Whitefall family."

Valour? What kind of a name was that?

The woman gave a short laugh, standing so I could see her properly. Unlike the two of us, she had silky black hair, and hazel eyes that nevertheless shone with Winter magic. That's what the two of them had in common—that unmistakable glow that indicated they had magic.

Of all the luck. Why did I have to be the one to end up with no magic whatsoever?

"We'll see who the talisman chooses." She grinned. "The name's June."

Great. Evil siblings, check. Unwanted inheritance, check. Creepy palace, check. Anything else, Faerie? The man at the back of the room didn't even look at me. With his dark hair and clothes, he looked like a living shadow. I'd bet my stash of stolen contraband that he had magic, too. If I'd ever imagined having siblings, these three weren't what I'd pictured. Not that I'd be seeing them again after today. I made a mental note to ask Viola if there was a shortcut back to the crossing-over point which didn't involve walking for miles through the woods.

The door opened again and Viola came into the room. As she did so, her back straightened, her posture becoming tenser and her expression closing off as she regarded my siblings.

"Now we're all here," she said, "it's time to select the heir. One of you will be picked to go into the chamber first. It's only fair. The sceptre can only choose one of you, so your mother instructed me to do it this way."

"Wait," I said. "Only one of us?"

"There's one talisman," she said, "so it must pick one of

you. You can't all be tested at once, so I'm going to use a test to fairly make the decision."

So just one of us gets to keep the talisman? The thief in me wanted to take it just to spite Faerie for dragging me into this, but the whole scenario made no sense to me.

"I don't get it," I said. "Surely my—our—mother's will dictates who gets what, right?"

"Her final request is that the talisman is given the chance to decide for itself. If the magic picks the first person chosen to be tested, then it stands."

"I know you," said my sister, suddenly. "I've seen you somewhere before. Didn't you live with another family?"

Viola didn't meet her eyes, though her face went slightly pink. "If you'd be so kind as to step up here, all of you. The spell will assign you a random number. The person with the highest number will go first."

My silver-haired brother's long-legged stride reached the dais first. As he stepped up onstage, a serpentine number 3 snaked out of thin air, hovering for a moment. *If it's the best of three, he's already won.*

My sister reached the stage next, to be greeted with a number 7. *Maybe not.*

My steps turned leaden as I climbed behind her, struck by a sudden weird spasm of nerves. Smoke swirled around my head, turning into—

"Nine," said Viola. "Er..." She trailed off, regarding the black-clad man at the back of the hall. He finally looked up at her. "Come and choose a number," she said.

"You choose." His rumbling voice grated on my ears.

"It's required—"

"All right." He sloped down the hall, clambering onto the stage. Twin swords were strapped to his back, and his broad frame made my other siblings look tiny in comparison.

The number 10 appeared above his head.

An angry hiss escaped my sister. My second brother remained composed, but there was a dangerous glint in his eye. The guy leered at us, following Viola off the stage, where a door was open.

"I don't need you there," he snapped at Viola, shoving her back with one hand, and marched into the dark alone.

"Friendly," I said, breaking the awkward silence left behind. Viola scowled, her fists clenching at her sides. I'd bet she wanted to break her role as host and punch him. If he was chosen, she'd be compelled to be his servant by the magic which bound her to our family. Sudden anger—both at him and the Sidhe for forcing this ridiculous ceremony on us—sparked inside me. It'd be the perfect revenge if I ran off with the talisman and sold it in the mortal realm. Then there'd be no treasure for the Sidhe to fight over, so they'd have to go back to bickering about something else instead. And they'd leave me and Dad alone, forever.

There was a horrible scream from the chamber. Loud and high, it echoed through the open door. Blue light followed in sharp bursts, filling the hall with blue sparks. A final, awful scream—and silence.

"I think," said Viola, with a barely concealed grin, "he just failed the test."

My stomach lurched. That scream hadn't sounded in any way like anything living—not human anyway. And I'd drawn the number nine... which meant I was next.

"Raine?" Viola looked at me, her expression softening.

I didn't move. My siblings watched, expectantly. My sister stepped down off the stage, smirking. "Changed your mind? Too bad. I'm going to take that talisman for myself, and I think I'll start by turning you into statues. You'll get to watch me rule this territory for the rest of your pathetic mortal lives."

"You're getting ahead of yourself, aren't you?" I jumped off the stage.

"No," my brother said. "When *I* win, the two of you won't be leaving this palace alive."

"I'll turn you into a hobgoblin," snarled my sister.

At this rate, they'd start a fight before the talisman even picked an heir. Either of them getting their hands on the inheritance would be bad news for the rest of us. At least, that's what I told myself as I approached the chamber door.

Don't, a voice in my head whispered, possibly the self-preservation I'd left behind in the mortal realm. The thief in me, however, wanted to see the treasure for herself, and figure out a way to steal it. I'd stolen from Sidhe messengers before, but there was a world of difference between that and a genuine faerie-forged talisman.

The blue light had died down, leaving the space behind the door in darkness again. A tingling sensation travelled up and down my arms. Magic. Enticing, beckoning, power thrumming in the very air.

Without looking back, I walked into the chamber.

5

Lights flared up as the door closed behind me, illuminating cold stone walls. The rest of the room was empty save for an open glass case in the centre. Inside was a sceptre, white and silver, carved in elaborate patterns. A blue gemstone gleamed at the top. It looked like the sort of trinket you'd pick up at the humans' market, but the power pouring off it was real enough to freeze my breath and send tremors through my whole body.

Speaking of bodies… my brother lay at the side, very dead. Blood ran from his eyes, ears and nose, and his mouth was open in an expression of utter torment.

So that's what happened when you failed to impress a talisman.

The breath stopped in my lungs. Talismans were the strongest of any magical item in either the mortal or faerie realms, because the magic contained within had generally been there at least a few hundred years, gaining strength over time. There were rumours some Sidhe—the exiles who'd attacked the mortal realm—had stolen their talismans by killing the original owners, but such things sounded like absurd stories to me. The talismans, the ultimate source of all a Sidhe's magic, *made* the Sidhe what they were—powerful enough to be regarded as gods.

It wasn't the power I wanted. But its aura of power was more entrancing even than the palace, if it was possible. Strength radiated out from the sceptre in the form of incandescent white light, demanding to be held, wielded, used to conquer. My steps faltered.

If I don't pass this test, it might kill me.

Anyone could technically pick up a talisman, but you needed to be chosen as worthy before you could wield its magic. And talismans weren't meant to be wielded by half-bloods, much less ones without any magic at all. *I'm not intending to wield it. I'm going to get it away from these power-crazy Sidhe.*

I shuffled forward another step. Then another. If it sensed my cowardice, it betrayed no sign. I just had to touch it. That was all. One second, and it'd be over, one way or another.

I reached out. I'd never thought it was possible to see your life flash before your eyes, but in the endless seconds before my hand made contact with the talisman, I saw Dad, looking at me, holding me as a child, watching me as an adult as his sanity crumbled away…

Magic slammed into me, lifting me off my feet. Blue light expanded to surround me in a circle, impossibly bright. My hand locked around the sceptre and I couldn't pry it loose. My skin burned cold, teeth chattering as a surge of energy shot from my palm to my entire body. Every one of my senses flared, highly attuned to every detail—a painful whistling noise like wind trapped in a large room, the brightness of the flare of magic illuminating the sceptre in my hand, the coldness of the metal pressing into my palm, and a metallic taste on my tongue. I gasped as the air rushed from my lungs, my body swaying, my knees buckling. I wobbled down from the platform, clutching the sceptre. My skin tingled all over like I'd trodden on an open switch and had the static shock of a lifetime.

Wait. Can I even put the sceptre down?

I carefully switched the sceptre from one hand to the other. My hands obeyed, to my relief, but the tingling sensation remained. Blue energy swirled around me, the way I'd seen it act around other half-bloods. Winter half-bloods. With magic.

I have magic?

One way to find out. I held up my right hand, the one not holding the sceptre, and imagined conjuring up a handful of blue energy the way other Winter faeries did.

Nothing happened.

I switched the sceptre to my right and tried with the other hand, too. No result. Maybe I could only use magic with the sceptre. That'd do, then. I held it out, concentrating on the power spiralling around it. The light was already fading, and no surge of blue magical energy answered my call.

Then I looked down and gasped again. I wasn't wearing my torn jeans and top any longer, but an outfit more like Viola's—black with silver edges, like battle gear worn by someone in the Winter Court. Where had these new clothes come from?

"At least it didn't put me in a dress," I muttered aloud.

"Raine?" Viola strode in, her face lighting up when she saw the sceptre in my hand. "It did choose you. I'm glad."

"It did?" Obvious question, really—if it hadn't, I'd be lying beside my brother with blood streaming out of my eyes.

"Of course. You wouldn't have been able to pick it up otherwise."

But I can't use magic. I have no clue what I'm doing.

I didn't say the words, because my silver-haired brother strode in behind her, his eyes icy chips of rage.

"You?" he said. "It chose you?"

"Looks that way. Tough break."

"You arrogant human." He raised a hand. Shards of ice rose from the air, aiming at my face like daggers. Viola shouted a warning, too late.

The sceptre glowed in my hand, and on instinct, I jumped, landing on the dais. The icicles shot past, piercing the spot where I'd been hovering seconds before.

He tried to kill me. The thought lasted only a second, because he leaped up to join me, a sword in his hand pointed at my heart.

"Give me that talisman."

I shoved him down the dais with my free hand, holding onto the sceptre with the other. He went flying, to my surprise—I'd never hit someone with so much power before. Was it because of the sceptre? Strength I'd never felt before surged through my bones. Strength, however, wouldn't help me avoid being impaled on an icicle.

As he leaped at me again, I pulled out my knife, slashing at him. The blade caught his palm, leaving a searing line on the skin. I braced myself for another strike, but he fell back, pain flaring in his eyes.

"How dare you."

He lunged again and collapsed halfway. I watched in disbelief as his skin paled to greyish-white, the mark from the iron turned livid red, and his eyes slid closed as unconsciousness claimed him. He must have seriously strong magic for the iron to affect him that quickly. I stared numbly at him for a second, and didn't notice Viola had run back into the room until she beckoned from a passage at the back. I ran to her, my hands shaking.

"He tried to kill me," I whispered. "But he's my brother."

Of course, this was Faerie we were talking about. You'd think family loyalty would matter, though. It did to the Sidhe. But we weren't them. Our mother was dead, and her power—was mine.

Not that I felt any trace of magic inside me, the way it was supposed to be. Just cold, and like I had more questions than I'd started with. I missed Dad. I missed the stable, reliable human world. Sidhe help me, I even missed Denzel. If *he* saw the talisman, he'd probably try to swipe it for himself.

"I'm sorry," said Viola. "I should have warned you. He really wanted the sceptre. I thought—" She flashed me a guilty look that was swallowed up by the dark as we walked into a narrow passageway.

"You thought I wouldn't get chosen."

Silence followed for a few heartbeats, punctuated by our echoing footsteps in the dimly lit stone passage.

"He has a powerful gift for magic. I'm glad it was you who was chosen, regardless. You can ask the others to leave—you can *make* them leave. I've already ordered your sister out."

"Wait, what?" I stopped walking.

"Why aren't you coming?"

"Give me a minute," I said. "I've been here less than an hour and I've already been claimed by a talisman, lost a brother I didn't know I had before today, and had another one try to kill me. I need some adjustment time."

"Fair enough." She kept darting looks at the sceptre. "It looks different when you hold it."

"My mother used it, then?"

How? The word lingered on my tongue, but I was still unsure if I could trust her. She seemed sincere, but not typical of Winter at all. There was something plain *odd* about this whole setup. A dead mother, secret siblings, a talisman which could only choose one of us. I wanted answers, but this was far from the place to put one's trust in strangers.

"She used it," said Viola. "She possessed a great gift, unlike any I've ever seen before."

"What kind of magic can the sceptre do? I—I know it must be different to my own magic." I felt bad for lying again, but she didn't flinch like she did last time. Maybe I'd been convincing.

She bit her lower lip. "It might be different for you, but the Lady's magic was magnificent. She could turn ice to water and water to ice again. Her... her gift was for transformation."

"Shit. Those statues in the entrance hall." I looked over my shoulder. "Please say they weren't... alive."

"Ah. You can use the magic any way you see fit. You don't have to follow in her footsteps."

"Good." *Because I'm not staying here.* And turning people into statues was definitely *not* on my plan. "What can I transform, then?"

"Anything," she said. "Anything that doesn't have magic of its own, that is."

So that ruled out most living things in Faerie. Unlimited transformative power, though—that'd come in damn handy when it came to, say, Denzel's fake amulet operation. It seemed a waste to use a talisman that powerful on petty crimes in the mortal realm, but what else was I meant to do with it? I didn't want a crown, even a metaphorical one. And staying here would tell the Sidhe I'd consented to being part of their games. *No chance.*

"So that's all it does? Why does everyone want to steal it, then?"

She chewed the inside of her cheek. "Because it's unclaimed. That is, it wasn't claimed until you did so. Usually, a talisman without an owner is snatched up right away. Because it's taken so long to find the heir, word got out."

That'd better mean people will leave me alone now I've claimed the damn thing. Aloud, I said, "And can just anyone claim it? What would happen if a human picked it up?"

"A human?" She frowned. "Nothing. Unless they tried to claim it, but that's not possible. As far as regular humans are concerned, they won't be able to see or sense its magic at all."

I could work with that. "Okay, then. Just curious."

The passageway turned left before heading back into the entrance hall. Viola strode ahead in the same military-style fashion as before, then stopped as we reached the hall.

"Here." She handed me a key. "This is for all the doors here. It changes depending on which one you need, but your magic is required to unlock them anyway."

"That's handy. So I can leave, then?"

Her brow furrowed. "Leave?"

"Yeah. You know. Go back to my home in the mortal realm. I didn't know I'd be inheriting a house. My Dad's back there, and—"

I stopped. Her eyes brimmed with tears, to my alarm.

"Hang on," I said. "What—what is it?"

"I didn't know you wouldn't be staying. She—there's nobody else here. The rest of the court left a long time ago."

"Is there anything I can do?"

She shook her head helplessly. "I'm trapped here. My soul is bound to serve the leader of the Whitefalls, whoever it is. I'm just glad it was you, Lady Whitefall."

"Call me Raine." I shifted uncomfortably. "A binding vow… you have to stay here indefinitely?"

In faerie terms, vows took "till death do us part" literally, and that went for anything from a minor promise to a life-time enslavement to a particular family. But most families, as far as I knew, didn't hire half-bloods. That'd changed in the last year or so, but she was clearly familiar enough with this place to have been here a while. My mother had taken her from her family and made her stay here even after she'd died?

Viola nodded, her breathing shallow. "Yes. I'm bound to serve the family until I die. The *family,* not her. That means even when she died, the vow held."

Oh, damn. My mother sounded like a piece of work. I looked at the talisman again and felt an unexpected shudder of revulsion. Never mind the magic—*this* was my legacy. Ice statues that were actually trapped people, and an enslaved half-blood who surely couldn't have lived in Winter her whole life beforehand. Had she been stolen from the mortal realm, like other changelings?

Guilt swirled in my chest, and I walked up to the nearest statue—a hobgoblin—holding the sceptre over it. If I'd used magic to hit my brother, surely I could use it to undo the spell.

"What are you doing?" She wiped her eyes.

"What else? If my mother ran things one way, then I'll run them another. No vows, and definitely no freezing people in ice."

"You can't undo it," she said, back to her brusque self again. "The sceptre's yours, but it doesn't work on spells cast by another Sidhe. I've tried myself."

Sidhe magic was supposed to decay with their death, but the palace still stood. Plainly, my second-hand mortal realm education on Faerie had missed a few pointers. Viola was either too scared to tell me everything, or her vow prevented her from speaking—I'd definitely heard *those* stories. Vows that forbade you to cry out in pain as your body was ripped to pieces, or forced you to watch as your family was tortured to death for angering the Sidhe. Maybe she didn't trust me. I wouldn't, in her position. If the decorations were any indication, my mother had been just like the evil monsters who'd attacked the human realm.

I attempted to relax my features into a smile. "I'm just curious. There's something else, too. I wondered—where's my mother buried? I mean, is there a grave I can visit? I didn't know her while she was alive, but I'd like to know more." Part of me almost suspected one of my newfound siblings had bumped her off, but no half-blood could kill a Sidhe, especially one with a talisman.

"Oh." She hovered anxiously on the balls of her feet. "The Sidhe don't have grave markers like the humans do. Her body was consumed by her own magic in death."

"Is that normal?" I kept forgetting that for all the time I'd spent around half-faeries at home, this realm was literally a whole world away from what I knew, and its customs were alien to me.

She blinked. "No. Nothing about her death was normal. She left on a hunting trip one day, instructing me to clean the palace. While she was gone—I felt it. I'm bound to her, so when she died, my magic reacted, and I was released from any commands she'd given me. I didn't realise what had happened until a messenger from the Unseelie Court knocked on the palace door. Apparently, a number of witnesses had seen Lady Whitefall lying on the forest path, dead. Within minutes, magic had consumed her body and left nothing behind but ashes. The body of a chimera was found nearby, so it was assumed that the beast was the cause of her death."

"But—what about my siblings? They didn't know, right?"

She shook her head. "No. They came here later. Her death occurred not long after the negotiations between the mortal realm and the Winter Court finished."

"What? That was over a year ago."

"I suppose it was."

"You've been stuck here for a year." I gaped at her. "No

wonder—damn. I'm sorry. My mother sounds like a nightmare. I'm going home."

Her face pinched. "I'm not a Sidhe. I don't have the skill to open a way back into the mortal realm."

"Then I'll find someone who can. You can come with me. I can give you permission to do that, right?"

"Yes," she said. "You can. I know someone who can help us get back, too. But… I don't know about this. It might be that my vow keeps me here and prevents me leaving with you."

"Not if I'm the one running the show." There was possibly nothing I wanted *less* than to take on the responsibility of running the damn palace, but if I could use the sceptre to save one life, I would. "One way to find out."

"Hang on." She held up a hand. A door appeared in the wall, leading into a carpeted corridor. "If it's true—I need to take my possessions from my room."

"Oh, yeah. Need any help packing?"

"Don't worry." She disappeared through the door.

I tilted my head to look at the door, which hadn't been there until a few seconds ago. Seemed pretty solid to me. "How did you do that? Does the palace just… answer, whenever you want to go anywhere?"

"One of the few perks of living here," she responded.

I walked down the corridor and opened the next door. Inside was a room plated in gold and white. The furniture alone was probably worth a small fortune. Pity I couldn't carry it out of there. I could, however, take home a few souvenirs. I opened each drawer until I found a stash of golden jewels, and slipped them into my pocket. Then I went to wait for Viola.

There were a few flashes of blue light, a thudding noise, and then she emerged carrying a small bag and a birdcage.

"You have a pet…" I peered into the cage. A bundle of

sparks resolved itself into the shape of a little blue man, made entirely of fog. "Sprite?"

"The most difficult part of being a servant here was hiding him from your mother."

"I didn't even know sprites made good pets."

"This one does." She hoisted her bag over her shoulder, cast one look at the room behind her, and shut the door. "His name's Volt."

"Is that really all you need?"

She shrugged. "That's all I was allowed to bring here when I left my last place."

"Your last place. Not your home?"

She chewed on her lower lip—clearly a nervous habit. "No. Not exactly. It's kind of complicated."

"Speaking of complicated, what am I supposed to do about my brother?"

"The palace threw him out."

"The palace did." Why the hell not, Faerie. I'd possibly never felt more like a clueless human, one who belonged in the mortal realm, where things made sense.

"The territory remains yours, even when you're not living here," Viola explained. "When—if you want to come back."

"My human father's waiting for me back home," I said. "That's why I'm leaving. You probably think I'm out of my mind. I mean, this is a palace."

"No. If you have ties back in the mortal realm, I under-stand." Her gaze dropped, but not before I saw the sadness in her eyes. She'd never be free of this place. Not really. Even if we never saw one another again, the vow would compel her to serve anyone who claimed my family's talis-man. One more reason to get it as far away from Faerie as possible.

"What exactly does your vow say?" I asked her. "You have to serve me. In what way does that… manifest?"

She looked away, not before I saw the sadness in her gaze turn to fear.

"I'm just curious. I've never seen a vow in action, and I don't want to use it by accident if we part ways in the mortal realm. Honestly, I've never needed a servant. I'm fine being alone. If it isn't obvious, making friends isn't my strong point."

She took in a breath. "The vow dictates I can't betray you, even under duress. I belong to your family, so I'm forbidden to join another, in either realm. If you give me a command, I have to obey it."

"Everything I say to you?"

"No, only if you say it's a command. Language can be flexible, and I can wriggle out of a command if I really don't want to follow through on it. With your mother, it was rarely worth the risk."

"Ah." Faerie mind games. Definitely not my area of expertise. I held up the sceptre. "If I can transform anything, can I undo vows using this?"

She shook her head. "No. Vows are a different kind of magic which doesn't belong to a particular Court. Usually, if the person who you make the vow to dies, it's invalidated. But in my case, the vow will hold as long as any member of the Whitefall family survives. I also can't repeat the exact wording myself, which you'd need to know to even begin undoing it, *if* it were possible."

"You can't?" Then I'd have to guess, when I had about as much experience with real faerie vows as I did with scuba diving. That is to say, none whatsoever. "Then you can go free in the mortal realm. I won't give you any commands. I've no interest of playing whatever other game my delightful mother left behind."

A tentative smile formed on her face. "Thank you. I don't know how I'll repay you."

"I can think of a way," I said. "You know how to get back to the mortal realm, right? Can you take me there?"

"I do," said Viola. "I should warn you, he has a tendency to ask for a price, and I never know what it'll be until I ask. I've been back twice since she died, both times to scout out your siblings."

"Oh." I nodded in understanding. "I was worried you'd been stuck here completely alone. So you have somewhere to stay in the mortal realm, then?"

She dipped her head. "There are others who frequently pass between realms, who live on half-blood territory."

Good. I dared let myself hope we'd work this out—then opened the door to find a decapitated hobgoblin on the doorstep. To be precise, the one who'd led me here.

"Ah!" I jumped back into Viola, my heart thumping against my ribcage. He'd been brutalised, his body shredded with a sharp instrument. "Who did that?"

"I—don't know." Viola grimaced.

"Not my brother, right? Maybe my sister." How in hell was this suddenly my life?

Viola waved a hand at the body, and the earth rose up to swallow it. A coating of snow fell on top, covering up the blood. Here, it'd never melt.

"You're not so bad at magic yourself," I said to her.

"One perk of serving your family." She dusted snow off her clothes. "Let's go."

6

We'd only walked ten metres before Viola stopped so suddenly, I nearly left her behind.

"What is it? The vow?"

She shook her head. "The vow isn't forcing me to go back. I think we're okay."

"Good." I resumed walking. "Whereabouts is this person? I take it there's a shortcut back to the paths where I came in?"

"Someone dragged you here the long way?" She walked briskly ahead, apparently over her hesitation. "There's another path just down here."

"That hobgoblin did. Guess walking back that way didn't work out so well for him." I was doubly glad she'd mentioned there was another way, because I didn't particularly want to run into whatever had attacked him. Assuming it wasn't one of my own siblings.

The forest swallowed us up in a wave of branches dripping snow onto our heads. I shook it out of my hair, wishing my new clothes had a hood. Viola marched on without stopping, forcing me to run to keep up. Within a couple of minutes, we veered down a side path covered in smoke instead of snow.

A screeching noise came from the bushes, followed by a heavy beating of wings. A giant bird flew at us, talons clawing at my eyes.

I raised the talisman automatically in defence, though hell if I knew how to use its magic. Viola, however, jumped up to meet it, blue magic flying from her fingertips. The bird fell head over heels and toppled onto the path.

"We're friends of the Little People," she shouted at the creature.

The bird shook itself and turned into a young woman with pointed teeth and wildly long black hair. "Viola. Didn't recognise you with her. Thought someone stole—" She shrank away as I pointed the talisman at her.

"Don't attack me on my own territory," I said, to cover up my surprise. In human form, she resembled a half-faerie girl I'd dated once, but she definitely hadn't been able to transform into a bird. Few half-bloods could fully shapeshift like that.

"Technically, you're between territories," said the girl. "I'll tell him you've come."

"Now isn't a good time to be standing outside," said Viola, beckoning me to follow. The girl plunged into the undergrowth, and we went after. Thick smoke masked our view, and brambles caught in my hair and snagged my clothes. We emerged in a clearing, where a small cottage sat nestled between the thick oak trees.

"Visitors!" called the girl.

An old man walked out of the cottage. *Faerie...* but what sort, I wasn't sure. He was older than any faerie I'd seen, his dark red skin apparently hewn from bark, and a beard down to his knees. His eyes fixated instantly on the talisman in my hand, and I wished I'd had the sense to put it away.

"You're the one?" he said. "The new Whitefall heir?"

"We'd like to go back into the mortal realm," said Viola. "Now, if possible."

"And what will you give me for that?" He eyed the sceptre. *You want it? Take it.*

A different voice in my head whispered, *no. It's mine.*

No, it bloody well wasn't. But I planned to sell it in the mortal realm, not here. I tucked the sceptre into my belt pointedly, and shook my head. "You tell me. I'd like to go home today, if you don't mind."

He laughed a little. "I like this one. Maybe she'll last out here, after all. What do you want with the mortal world, girl?"

"I live there." *And it's none of your business.* "What kind of trade are we talking about?"

Viola trod on my foot, a warning.

"A deal," he said. "One favour. To be collected whenever I choose."

Not if I never come back here. Whatever he was, he wasn't Sidhe. He couldn't cross between realms. "Sure, why not."

"Done."

Vows and promises didn't require fancy language—a word was enough. Which was why you had to be careful what you said. I hadn't been nearly cautious enough, but once I got home, it wouldn't matter.

"Cheers," I said, turning away from the house. The bird-girl waved at me, now smiling in a deceptively innocent way that didn't quite hide her pointed teeth. Viola walked stiffly out of the clearing, and I hurried after her. "What?"

"You shouldn't talk like that to the Little People."

"Little? He was the same height as me."

"It's just their name. They live in the cracks between realms. If we hurry, we can catch the next rift."

At the end of the path was smoke, and not much else. A gap between the trees filled with nothing but swirling grey. It looked vaguely familiar to me. "What's that?"

"The rift," she said. "This part of Faerie is closer to the mortal realm, and there are certain places like this which overlap. But they're usually claimed by someone. Lucky you didn't offend him too much."

"Does he have a name?"

"Little People don't. The girl's called Frances, though. She's half-blood—wandered in here years ago and never went back."

"So half-bloods did come to Faerie before. I thought it was a new thing."

"For the main Courts, it is." She stepped forward. "Here, though, we've been coming through for years. Hang onto my arm. Sometimes it likes to spit you out somewhere else."

"Hold on," I said, but she was already moving forward. Not particularly wanting to be left alone with the creepy cottage, I grabbed her arm and jumped after her. The smoke engulfed us, then a flash of white light swallowed us up.

The next second, we lay on a hillside. Viola let go of my arm, getting to her feet. "Not too bad this time."

I stared around. We'd landed in the mortal realm—where, I had no idea. The sky had darkened already, which seemed odd. Either the day had gone by faster than I'd thought, or some weird time lapse had happened while I'd been in Faerie. *Of course... you can be there for hours, and come home to find whole days have gone by.*

"Viola, how do I get home from here?"

"Walk it." She ran down the hillside, and once again, I had to run to catch up. At least we were on steadier ground here.

"What if the rift throws you into the middle of the ocean or up a mountain?" I asked, my breath coming out in puffs.

"That doesn't happen. You can only exit Faerie through what the humans call a liminal space—a place where the two realms meet."

'Liminal space'. The phrase had an echo of familiarity. "Hang on," I said, slowing to stop myself from skidding down the hillside. "Isn't that how the faeries attacked Earth?"

"Sort of, but they did it on the Ley Line. That's a long line where the two realms meet at certain spots. It's easier to cross over in other rifts. Less traffic."

Panting, I caught up with her at the bottom of the hill. "Traffic. You're speaking like people cross over all the time."

"They do now," she said. "But only if you know where the crossover points are. Most people don't, especially half-bloods."

"Yeah, there'd be a stampede," I said, thinking of the gathering of half-bloods that morning. I hoped they'd had better luck settling into their new families than I had. "So... my mother never married, never had any pure-blooded children... and left the sceptre to me. What would have happened if there'd been no heir?"

She didn't answer for a long moment, but a clicking sound signalled the cage opening, and her sprite flew free with a yell of delight. Volt spun down to land on her shoulder.

"My vow would have been cancelled," she finally said. "I knew there was an heir when her magic didn't cease to function after she died. The palace would have collapsed, without her magic to hold it up. And the sceptre—it'd have decayed eventually, but she put years' worth of power inside it. Someone would have come to steal it eventually."

"Hmm." I thought of the hellhound that'd attacked my flat. "It sounds like people are after it anyway."

Her steps faltered. "Only in Faerie," she said. "Here, it's worth nothing, but might still draw attention."

"I'll hide it," I said. "But what about you? I can't undo the vow. I don't know anyone who's an expert, aside from the Sidhe, and they're not very talkative about things like that. Ruins the mystery, I guess."

"Most people don't understand how vows work. They're both flexible and inflexible at once. Words can mean more than one thing at a time, and it's important that both parties know what they're getting into. That's not to say some faeries don't make vows and regret them anyway. Even a human can work around a promise made to a weak faerie who didn't consider all their words' possible meanings."

"It seems to me that's impossible."

"Nothing is absolute, though some Sidhe would have you believe otherwise." She skipped on, breaking her usual military walk. At least someone was cheerful. More so than I'd have expected—but then again, who wouldn't want to escape after so long trapped in a snowbound palace?

A twinge of guilt wormed through my chest. I paid it no attention. I had no ties to Faerie, not anymore. It felt wrong to be glad my mother was dead, but at least she hadn't put a vow on me. At least, not that I remembered.

We'd walked for ten minutes before we reached somewhere I recognised, and another ten before it struck me that we should have taken the bus... if I'd had money. Which I didn't, because my coat had disappeared. I dug my hand in my pocket, withdrawing a handful of shredded leaves. The jewels I'd taken from the palace apparently didn't stay that way when I carried them into this realm. So much for selling them.

"Any idea where my clothes went?" I asked Viola, as we neared half-blood territory.

"Ah. If her magic did it, then... nope. Unless you know how to use a transforming spell?"

"No, I don't have the slightest idea. I can't walk home looking like this. Every half-blood will know who I am."

"Take this." She rummaged in her bag and handed me a jacket. A human-looking one, plain black. "I'm going to half-blood territory."

I hesitated to take it. "Are you sure?"

"It's the least I can do for getting me out of that palace."

"Will you be okay?" I asked.

She smiled and nodded. "Yeah. I'll come and find you if your family's magic starts messing with me again."

"Hope it doesn't." Here, the sceptre looked like a powerless trinket rather than the talisman it really was. I returned it to my belt and carried on walking.

The mortal realm looked different. I'd expected it, after the dazzling colours of Faerie, but the contrast still hit me. It was so… grey. Winter was carved with precision, while the mortal realm seemed like a haphazard mess that stank of car exhaust fumes and sewers and *people*. Winter smelled sharp and cold, while Summer was like a perfume overload. I wondered how the half-bloods who'd gone to Summer had fared. And the other Winter ones. *Bet I'm the only one who came back.*

Time to go home to Dad. No—get rid of this incriminating artefact first. It barely glowed now, drained of the power it possessed in the faerie realm. Here, it'd be worthless. Except to human collectors of rare items, who'd have no idea of its true value. I might covet it, but I didn't *need* it. The more you had, the more you had to lose. I'd take it to a human market and say it was the lost staff of a fictional faerie queen. It's amazing how gullible humans can be.

Another splinter of guilt twisted inside me at the thought, which made no sense. I didn't have any attachments in the human world. I was a thief. I wasn't supposed to have a conscience about these things. Who cared if I fooled someone into taking this damned sceptre off my hands? Rich antique dealers were everywhere, and the supernaturals coming out into the open had brought in a whole network of illegal trade in magical objects. The sceptre would probably be halfway across the country by tomorrow. Problem solved.

Except for the people who'd tried to kill me for it.

Please. Like they'd ever guess I'd sell it to a mortal. Nobody would. It was the perfect way to dispose of a so-called treasure I didn't want. My siblings would think I was happily ruling over my kingdom, and wouldn't find out I'd left unless someone told them. Then they might come looking, but by then, the sceptre would have long disappeared. I'd never found out who'd sent the hellhound, but surely even they would have known I'd gone into Faerie with the others. It wasn't like I'd been conspicuous during my return to the mortal realm.

I walked with my head down, holding Viola's jacket tight to hide my too-shiny new clothes. I needed to change, but going home would mean bringing the sceptre into the flat. After the last attack, I didn't dare risk it. So I headed for the market instead.

The affectionately named "goblin market" was staffed by half-blooded ogres attempting to prove to the humans that they weren't all bloodthirsty killers. In fairness, the guard, named Ug, was as harmless as it was possible to be for someone nine feet tall and as wide as a shed. Green-skinned and hulking, he gave me a cheery wave as he spotted me.

"Not come to steal anything, thief?" He spoke in affectionate terms.

"Nah. Not worth it with you watching." Since the doors to Faerie had loosened a little, markets like this one had begun to crop up all over the country, selling genuine—and fake—

items and trinkets from Faerie itself. Harmless—anything otherwise was instantly shut down by the Mage Lords.

My target was Twill, a leathery-skinned old human man who was more avaricious than me and Denzel put together.

"Raine," he said. "I thought you'd gone into That Place." He was one of those older humans who still felt superstitious about speaking the names of Faerie and its inhabitants.

"Nope," I said. "Not enough to steal there. I do have something cool, though. The half-bloods are upping their game." I presented the sceptre with a flourish.

"Oh. That's pretty."

"Yep. Human-style faerie replica. Tell them it can cure warts."

He peered eagerly at it. "That a real stone? What sort?"

"Make up a fancy name. That's more your thing than mine." My free hand twitched as though to snatch the sceptre back.

It's mine.

Yeah, along with the title I didn't want, the legacy I wasn't equal to, and the murderous siblings. *Forget it, Raine. Find something new to covet.*

As Twill peered at the stone, I glanced down and saw my own reflection glinting back, unusually clear. The mark on my neck had brightened, and for a brief second, I saw someone else reflected back at me. Older. Taller. Bone white, sweeping hair, and bright blue eyes. Holding the talisman, which radiated blue light. My brother's scream from the chamber echoed in my ears. That's what the talisman could do to anyone who tried to claim it.

What am I doing?

I jerked my hand back, pulling the sceptre out of reach. He raised an eyebrow questioningly.

"I've changed my mind," I said. "I—I don't want to sell it. Sorry."

"You can't do that," he said, his calm demeanour abruptly changing. "You've already made me an offer."

"It was a mistake. I don't have anything else to sell."

His nails dug into my arm. "Too bad."

"Hey!" I twisted my arm, teeth gritted in pain and surprise. I wrenched myself out of reach and backed away. "Don't touch me like that."

"Sorry, I've no idea what came over me."

There was nothing remotely apologetic in his tone, and the gleam in his eyes appeared downright sinister. I stumbled away, and he moved after, faster than I'd expect of someone his age. Again, his hand locked around my upper arm, the one carrying the talisman.

"It's worth a lot, little Raine. Give it here—" He choked off, letting go with a snarl of pain as I rammed my elbow into his throat. He roared in rage, but I'd already pivoted out of reach, pulling my knife out. I ducked sideways down the nearest path between stalls, keeping an eye out for other attackers. I'd made a mistake coming here.

I was too busy looking for threats on my level when a gnome ran under my feet, nearly knocking me over. I righted myself, accidentally kicking it in the process. The gnome yelled at me and tried to grab my leg. I stepped out of range and walked smack into someone else. "Ah! Sorry."

"Not to worry," said a low male voice, as the speaker caught my arm. "You should watch your step. Accidents happen alarmingly often around here."

"Yeah, I know." The speaker was a male half-faerie—Cedar, the guy who'd helped me carry the dead hellhound out of my flat. I hadn't taken him for the sort to frequent the markets, with his well-made clothes and obviously polished demeanour. I sidestepped him, ignoring the gnome's indignant yelling. I'd let far too many people see me here, when I was supposed to be keeping a low profile. I didn't have my hair covered as I usually would, and under Viola's coat, the new clothes were all too visible.

"Allow me to escort you from the market, so you don't tread on any more customers," Cedar said, his hand still resting on my arm.

I pulled away. "That won't be necessary."

I walked fast, but he kept pace with me. The market had reached the stage where getting in and out required using elbows and knees and hoping the person you hit wouldn't turn you into a frog. I could move quickly when I wanted to, but apparently Cedar could, too. When we reached the edge, he turned to face me.

"I didn't expect to run into you again… Raine, was it?"

"Yes, Raine. You shouldn't talk to me."

He arched a brow. "Why?"

"I'm a magnet for trouble." I backed away. "Besides, you don't know me."

"You're right, I don't. But I'd like to. We didn't get a chance to talk the last time we met."

Someone being this forward with me wasn't new, even coming from a half-Sidhe as handsome as he was. Being a performer—for a mortal audience, at that—resulted in a dozen propositions a night, at least. I'd learned to school my face into a smile when I turned them down, but couldn't summon up the energy now. Sure, he'd helped me out before, but he was also far too pushy for my liking.

"Sorry to disappoint you," I said. "You'll probably never see me again." I wouldn't normally be so rude to a complete stranger, but I needed to get *home*.

"That would be a pity," he said, but I'd already turned my back.

"Bye," I said, walking swiftly away, even more conscious of the attention I'd drawn. What if Twill told other people about the sceptre? If he did, then my siblings might hear and work out where I was. If my brother had woken up yet…

Panic jolted through me, visceral and unexpected. My hand jumped to my belt—which suddenly felt lighter.

The sceptre had gone.

7

"Thief!" The irony of the word coming from me of all people wasn't lost on me, but I didn't care. Cedar had been trying to distract me on purpose. He'd wanted the sceptre all along.

I skidded to halt, almost colliding with a short guy with furred legs and hooves.

"Whoa! Calm down, Raine." Denzel wheeled around. "Any reason you're yelling *thief*? Because that includes both of us."

"Someone just stole from me." I paced back to the road's end. Of course, Cedar—if that was really his name—had vanished by now. "I need to find him."

"Someone stole from *you*?" Denzel cracked up laughing.

"It's not funny," I snarled, pushing past him.

He stared after me. "Wait—"

Too late. I was already running. My feet pounded against the pavement, carrying me to the market—I doubted the thief would backtrack there, but it was as good a place to hide as any. And I needed witnesses. A shop near our encounter sold fake troll skulls—that'd do. Luckily, the gnome had gone, and so had Twill.

"Hi," I said to the human male owner. "I wondered if you saw a guy—a half-faerie, with long black hair and a scar on his face? He just walked this way with me, but I didn't see where he went."

"With you?" he said. "Your friend?"

"No. He stole from me, actually. Do you know where he went?"

"Who? I didn't see anyone."

Had Cedar being wearing glamour? Humans were generally unobservant anyway. Thanking him, I left for the next stall. Same result. It was hopeless. I'd never find him like this. He'd picked the perfect place to disappear. In fact, it might not even have been Cedar who'd taken it. So many hands had brushed past me when I'd had to elbow my way out. But only one person had stood that close. Damn it all. I'd wanted to be rid of the talisman, but nobody ever got the best of me.

After ten minutes of questioning everyone from passers-by to a wandering piskie, I'd almost given up when Ug the ogre wandered over to me.

"What's up, Raine?" he asked.

"I'm looking for someone," I told him. "Half-blood. Fancy clothes. Stole something from me."

"You stole from him?"

"Unfortunately, no. He robbed *me*. Have you seen him?"

He frowned. Ogres' memories weren't the most reliable, but he could at least see through glamour. "Might have done. Went to half-blood territory. That's where they all go."

"Damn." Half-blood territory… with that information alone, I might not find him, but there were people coming and going all over the place what with the new arrangement with the Courts. It was the next likely place for information, though the odds of finding one individual were low, considering how many years it'd been since I'd regularly been there. "Thanks."

I headed for half-blood territory anyway, since it was on the way home to Dad. Raucous cheering reached my ears, and I stopped to stare at the gathering on the front lawn through gapes in the hedge. Delicious smells drifted on the breeze—a barbecue. The half-bloods were celebrating being accepted back into Faerie. This must be the new group, the ones going in tomorrow. Or the ones like Viola, who used those liminal spaces to hop between realms. Maybe that's why Mr Charming Sceptre Thief dressed like a noble—he was one.

Damn the Sidhe, who the hell have I let get his hands on the talisman?

For a moment I stood there, staring at the half-bloods dancing and laughing on the other side of the hedge like they hadn't a care in the world. I hadn't eaten since before my sojourn to Faerie. A free meal sure looked tempting, but the guards outside suggested there were conditions to entry. I'd rarely seen so many half-bloods in one place. Surely one of them must know the thief. Stealing a Winter Sidhe's talisman might just be the most foolish, attention-grabbing thing it was possible to do. Actually, it was the sort of thing *I* would do. Which made it all the more insulting. *It's mine.*

Now I was in the shit. I had no money, no talisman, and I might have unintentionally let the enemy get hold of something with enough power to terrify even the Sidhe.

I hesitated for a second, debating, and made for the gate.

The armoured Seelie guard moved smoothly in front of me. "Name?"

"Raine."

"Ticket?"

"I lost it," I bluffed. Damn, it looked like I'd have to play that card after all. "You know who I am, right? I used to—"

"Perform for the Chief. It's Lady Whitefall's heir."

A dozen people looked my way. So much for making a

quiet entrance. At least he stepped aside to let me pass. I scanned the growing crowd, and nearly walked into Viola.

"You're back?" she asked.

"Apparently," I said. "What's this celebration in aid of?"

"Does there need to be a reason?" She grinned. "Want to join me at Winter's table?"

"Sure, why not."

There were a number of half-faeries sitting at both tables, and I studied them as unobtrusively as I could, looking for a familiar face. The table closest to the entrance was made of what looked like several tree stumps fused together, with creeping vines growing over it and piskies hovering over the baskets of fruit. The second table had a similar food selection but was carved out of ice. So were the chairs. I sat down and immediately slid onto my back. Ow.

"Whose ingenious idea was this?" I climbed onto the seat more carefully this time, casting a look around. I'd picked a seat with a good view, but there were too many people, and I still wasn't a hundred percent sure which Court the thief had been from.

First, though, I was starving. Faerie food tended to range from normal to downright weird, so I ignored the fried insects and grabbed a handful of grapes instead. As I tossed them into my mouth, I scanned the Winter table, searching for long black hair, a scar, noble clothes.

I glanced sideways to see Viola watching me. "Something up?"

"I didn't think you'd come back."

I shrugged. "I don't turn down a free meal."

"Where's the… you know." She dropped her voice.

"Gone," I told her.

"I knew what you were doing," she said. "You never wanted it—it was obvious the second you stepped in the palace."

"I didn't give it away," I whispered. "Someone stole it."

Her eyes rounded. "*Who?*"

"That's what I'm here to find out. A half-blood took it. This guy at the market—I don't know *how* he did it, but it was missing right after I talked to him."

"Are you sure? What did he look like?"

"Like a half-Sidhe. He had shoulder-length black hair, and he wore fancy clothes, kind of like a Court noble…" I trailed off. "You know, it might even have been a glamour. This is hopeless."

"No, it isn't," she insisted. "You'd know him if you saw him again, right?"

"Yes. I want to skewer him. I can't even believe this." I made myself keep eating even though the thought of the sceptre sent my appetite fleeing. I needed some rejuvenating energy, so I could impale the thieving liar on my iron knife. "Oh—he has a scar on his face. It's pretty noticeable. But he might have glamoured it, or used a disguise. And I don't know which Court he was from. He had hazel eyes and his clothes weren't decorated with symbols. Said his name was Cedar, but it might be an alias."

"Doesn't ring a bell." Viola scanned the crowd, tapping her fingers on her knee. "I'm sure he's here somewhere. Fancy clothes? That sounds like a noble. And glamour's easy to see through."

"I don't see why a noble would steal from me."

"Depends on his family," said Viola. "I didn't have chance to explain before, but the situation in the borderlands at the edge of Faerie isn't quite like in the heart of the Seelie or Unseelie Courts. The border families, like ours, don't answer to the main Courts but to the leader of their own family. If he's a half-blood, he's probably acting on someone else's orders."

"You can't steal a—" I cut myself off before I said the word *talisman* aloud. But it was true. The Sidhe punished such things with exile, the worst possible punishment a faerie could suffer. But then again, that applied to stealing a talisman from someone important. I might be well-known here amongst the half-bloods, but I didn't have the faintest idea about reporting crime in Faerie. Worse, if the thief had come from Summer, I'd have to convince both the Seelie *and* Unseelie Courts that he'd robbed me. I'd never heard of a half-blood ever getting an audience with either, even one related to a noble family. And that was assuming I wanted to go into Faerie again. Which I really, really didn't.

Viola rose to her feet. "All right. I'll go and look around. There must be someone who's seen the thief. What he stole isn't exactly inconspicuous, either."

"Wait—"

I cursed under my breath, glancing back at the Winter table to find a half-dozen people staring at me. *Did they hear?*

"Aren't you Lady Whitefall's daughter?" someone asked.

"Yes." I hadn't seen either of my surviving siblings yet, but that didn't mean neither of them had been the one to send the thief after me. But then again, the thief hadn't tried to kill me. Unlike my brother.

I wanted out of here. I'd sell my soul to be back home with Dad, watching trash TV, contemplating my next theft, scheming with Denzel. I hadn't wanted to leave him in the lurch, but there was no way he'd help me without at least trying to snatch the sceptre for himself.

Maybe I was as shit at choosing friends as I was at keeping hold of my own treasure collection. Some thief I'd turned out to be.

Irritation prickling my spine, I rose to my feet, and paced towards the Summer table to get a closer look. I kept thinking I caught glimpses—silky dark hair, a mischievous smile—but the only uniform-wearing half-bloods present were the guards at the gate, and he definitely wasn't amongst them.

Okay. Time to pick someone gullible to question.

I found a half-hobgoblin I'd seen at the market. "Hey," I said. "You were at the market, weren't you? Did you see a man with long, dark hair, and a scar on his face?"

He gave me a blank look. "No."

I moved on, nearly tripping over a gnome. "Sorry—"

"It's you again." The gnome bit my ankle.

I yelped as his teeth sank in. Damn, that stung. "Get *off* me. I said I'm sorry." I kicked out and he went flying a good five metres into the air. The gnome crashed into a tree at the side and leaped at me with his bloody teeth bared.

I dropped abruptly to my knees, whipping out my knife. He froze, eyes bulging, as I reached out and grabbed him around the neck. His gaze darted to the knife. "Iron. You human scum."

"I'm not human," I hissed, hauling him away before we drew any more attention. "That man at the market, the half-faerie guy who talked to me right after I saw you. Did you see where he went?"

"With you." He wriggled in my hand, but I tightened my grip.

"Not then. Where did he come from? Was he here?"

"How should I know?"

"He was next to you. Did you see where he came from, or where he went afterwards?"

"That one? He was already at the market, watching you."

Ugh. He would be. I dropped him. "Never mind."

Standing, I re-entered the festivities, circling the Summer table from the back.

"What're you looking at?" demanded a hulking half-troll. "Your table's over there."

"I'm searching for someone."

I walked along the table, but nobody would speak to me. Three threats later, plus a wine glass thrown at my head, I returned to the Winter table to find Viola beckoning me into the shadow of a thicket of trees. In her hand were two glasses and a bottle of blood-red liquid.

"What the hell did they put in the water?" I muttered. "Everyone's being even twitchier than usual."

"Well, Summer doesn't want us near their table. Also, they know who you are."

"Figured as much. Get any clues about our guy?"

"No, but I did swipe some of their elf wine." She passed me a glass and downed the blood-red contents of her own in one. "You look like you need it."

"Damn right." I dragged a hand through my hair and tipped back the wine. It tasted sweeter than I was used to, and a thousand times stronger. My head fizzed with bubbles and the world swayed. "Whoa."

"Any better?" She poured another glass and clunked it against mine. "To freedom."

"To the thief's head on a platter." I drained the rest of the glass and put it down. The sound of faerie music drifted on the breeze, and my foot began to tap of its own accord. Music might loosen up the crowd and make them stop being so hostile, so I could actually get some answers.

Viola grinned and started dancing. Her sprite appeared and joined in, flying around our heads with a group of piskies like a horde of bluebottles on crack.

"This is real elf wine." I laughed, suddenly light-headed.

"Isn't it?" Viola giggled. "Sidhe's blood, I didn't know it was that strong, I swear."

The party had turned rowdy further down Winter's table, and a conga line danced in our direction. The rational part of me kept yelling that this wasn't my plan, that I needed to find the sceptre, but the thief might be somewhere in the crowd, and Summer and Winter had begun to merge into a single group. As a bunch of half-Sidhe joined the line, I moved to get a closer look at them, and someone yanked me into line.

Next thing I knew, I was dancing with the crowd on Winter's table, any self-consciousness gone with the remaining elf wine. Shrieks of admiration followed the path of my feet, caught in the rhythm of a dance I thought I'd forgotten. A nagging part of me said I wasn't wise to draw so much attention, but when my head cleared enough to see everyone had tried to copy me and instead caused a pile up on the improvised dance floor, I figured I couldn't have created a better distraction if I'd tried. I finished with a bow, turned down the advances of a half-blood girl with a shimmering snake's tail, and slipped off the table into the crowd. It now resembled a mosh pit more than a dance floor, a chaotic mess of shimmering wings and glitter and couples making out with abandon, apparently oblivious to the danger of being trampled. Half-faeries sure knew how to throw a party. Who cared about the bloody sceptre? I ought to be glad it was off my hands.

The problem was, now I wasn't drunk on the high of performing for the crowd, some all-too-sensible thoughts began to come back. And I kept thinking I saw him, as every half-Sidhe in the crowd stuck out like a sore thumb. I followed a pretty male half-Sidhe to the crowd's other side only to realise he was from Winter, not Summer, and he must have swiped the crown of thorns he wore from someone else. Also, he had a tail. Turning my back, I wove into the crowd again.

Viola appeared at my side. "To freedom!" she yelled, waving her glass.

Damn the Sidhe, she was worse than me. I grabbed her arm and hauled her away from the crowd before the overly rambunctious half-trolls knocked one of us over. We stumbled onto the grass near the tree thicket again. "C'mon. We're going…" I trailed off. "Where *is* home?"

"Gone." She made a noise between a sob and a laugh, her eyes damp.

"Are you okay?"

She hiccoughed and waved the wine glass, spilling its remaining contents all over her wrist.

"That's enough of that." I grabbed the glass from her. "Seriously. You can hardly walk."

"You can," she slurred, wobbling over to the trees and falling into a bush. "I wish I could dance like that."

I pulled her out of the bush with one hand. "It's nothing to be proud of, believe me. Did you live in the mortal realm?"

"No… not for a while." Her expression sobered a little. "My mortal family… they were killed in the invasion."

"I'm sorry. So were my grandparents." And most of Dad's extended family, too, he'd told me. "But I'm confused. I didn't know any half-bloods were allowed into Faerie at all."

"My original family allowed it, because they needed soldiers to defend their palace."

"Soldiers?" So that was why she walked like she was in the military. Not that I was one to talk, because I walked like a thief.

"Yes," said Viola. "I'm a hybrid half-blood—both my parents were half-faeries. My father was a soldier working for a powerful family over in Faerie, and he owed them his life. That is to say, they owned him." She pulled a face. "Anyway, my parents grew up here in the mortal realm. When I was born… after I turned eighteen, the Sidhe decided to call on whatever debt he owed them, and insisted that they send their only son to join the army. That's when I decided to break the news to them that I wasn't a son. They already had four daughters, who they'd managed to keep safe from Faerie, and when the Sidhe came, I didn't want any of them to be caught up in the vow. So I chose to enlist of my own free will. I spent a few years in the army, and then—then I met her." She paused. "Sidhe's blood, it sounds ridiculous. She was—is—a servant girl. And there's no leaving the Sidhe's army without a price."

"And I thought I had family drama," I said. "So how'd you wind up in in the Whitefall palace, then?"

"Your mother offered me a way out. She replaced the vow I'd sworn to the army with her own. Now I belong to your family instead."

"And the person you left behind? The… servant?"

"She's still there. As long as I'm trapped under this vow, I can't go back."

Sobriety crashed down on me, dampening the effects of the wine. "I need to undo the vow. That means I need my…" I lowered my voice. "Talisman. Surely I should be able to track it, if it's mine." I stood, looking around. The racket from the party pounded in my head, though the music had faded.

Wait. That wasn't celebrating. Someone was screaming.

Viola and I exchanged alarmed looks, then ran back towards the party.

Screams ensued as arrows fired into the crowd. I spun on the spot, trying to pinpoint where they came from, and one hit the ground inches from my foot. Another hit the half-faerie next to me, embedding itself in the back of his neck. He dropped to his knees, howling in pain. The arrow was crudely cut, deadly sharp—and iron.

The worst weapon you could use on a half-blood.

I backed away from the crowd, instincts telling me to leave, but the revelry had turned into a panicked rush away from the danger zone. Caught in the middle of the crowd, I was swept along with them, and I'd lost sight of Viola.

At my side, another half-blood fell under an arrow. If I'd

moved the slightest bit forward, I'd have been hit. It couldn't be a coincidence.

I'm the target.

An arrow whipped over my head, and I ducked. *Yep. They're aiming at me.*

With no weapons save for my knife, I elbowed my way in the direction the arrow had come from. This probably wasn't wise, but the moment I turned around, I glimpsed a figure slip away into the shadow of the same tree thicket Viola and I had been in. *Aha.*

I leaped onto the table above the others, oblivious to heads turning in my direction—my aim was to stay on a higher level than the crowd and stop any of them getting hit by the arrows, while simultaneously avoiding them myself. It was a dance of death amongst shattered glasses and broken plates. Another arrow whipped past my face. Some of the less sober crowd members started dancing again, thinking it was the second part of my act.

Within seconds, I'd cleared the edge of the table in a flying leap, aiming at the figure hidden in the shadows.

Either they didn't see me coming or thought they could outrun me. I smacked into the figure, sending both of us crashing into a heap. My knife blade met the assassin's throat, drawing blood. I tore off the mask, revealing a male stranger's face.

"Who put you up to this?" I hissed. "Tell me."

He tried to push me off, but the knife nicked the skin of his neck. Grey spread where the iron touched, and a pained gasp escaped him.

"Did my brother send you?" His eyes were pale brown, which suggested Summer rather than Winter, but he hadn't used magic. "Did he?"

"She—" He choked, his face paling even further. Damn, that iron acted quickly. Speaking of—why the iron arrows?

I'd *never* had one used against me by another faerie. It was considered disrespectful at the least.

"Raine!" yelled Viola. "We have to get out of here."

I looked down at the faerie, who was either unconscious or dead. I didn't particularly care which. Shouts filtered through from behind the trees.

"What're they shouting?" I asked Viola.

"Your name," she whispered.

"Oh, no." I'd made a complete spectacle of myself. So much for never hitting the stage again. I'd done so twice in a night, and now everyone knew my face. *No more elf wine. Ever again.*

The ground trembled, and a half-dozen trolls rampaged in our direction, led by the one who'd been hit by the iron arrow. Apparently they'd decided to blame *me* for the attack. I backed up and ran, which turned into a sprint as the assassin's body was buried beneath the crowd. At least the effects of the alcohol had faded a little, thanks to the shock. Faeries have fast metabolisms anyway. We pelted past the guards through the gate onto the road, ignoring their shouts, and ran down the street until the roar of the crowd had faded behind us.

"What a day," I gasped, pausing to catch my breath at the street's end. "You holding up okay, Viola?"

She vomited into the hedge in answer. I hovered, looking out for attackers, and a whistling noise was my only warning before an arrow nearly hit me in the ear.

I spun around to face the new threat. A knife came up, and I ducked on reflex, grabbing my own weapon. A slim figure wearing a mask and carrying a crossbow over one shoulder staggered away as I cut at him with the iron.

"Who the hell *are* you people?" I stabbed at him again, aiming for his wrist or arm—honestly, it didn't matter where I hit him. His rugged appearance was enough to tell me he was half-blood, and they all reacted the same when pierced with iron.

Viola emerged from the hedge with outstretched hands, and a blast of Winter magic hit him in the arm, making him drop his weapon. The half-blood cursed and dropped to his knees, and I kicked him hard in the chin, stopping him from retrieving the knife.

"Thanks," I said to Viola. "That's better. Now, you tell me where—"

Our assailant grabbed my ankle, but I danced out of reach, kicking the knife away from him into the gutter. Then I stamped on his wrist hard enough to break the bones. He yelled aloud, and I hauled him up by the scruff of his neck. "Who the hell sent you to kill me?"

"I did," growled a voice near my ankle, and sharp teeth jabbed my foot. That bloody gnome. I kicked at him again, forced to drop my prisoner as his teeth sank in deeper. I kicked him sideways into the hedge.

"*You* can't be behind it," I said to the gnome. "You're not smart enough."

He backed away from my knife. "They were looking for you anyway, mortal. You're dead."

Another arrow shot past my head. Two figures appeared from the hedge, positioning themselves in front of us. Then two more.

Damn. They'd set us up. We were outnumbered.

8

A knife flew at my head. I dodged easily and met the first guy in battle, trading blows with my own knife. He was good, I'd give him that—moving as fluidly as me, catching my attacks on the sleeves of his jacket to avoid the iron touching his skin. Losing patience, I kicked him in the knee then slashed his palm. As the iron effect took over, Viola let out a shout of dismay.

She'd knocked out the second assassin, but the new arrivals had her backed up against the hedge, and an arm locked around her throat from behind. I couldn't watch three of them at once. She choked, her breath cut off, and I lunged at the hedge to take out the person strangling her.

An arrow brushed my back and a second zipped over my head, but my knife found its home in the hand around Viola's neck. As the hand let go, I whirled around to face the other adversaries.

Two arrows pointed at me. Before I could move, a swift figure jumped from the hedge and met the first assassin before the arrow left his bow, snapping the instrument in two. The second assassin tried to get past the new arrival but stopped with a choked cry of pain, dropping to the pavement. The whole thing had taken maybe ten seconds. I gaped at the stranger, but a rustling noise and a yelp drew my attention to the attacker in the hedge I'd stabbed. He leaped out of the hedge, bleeding heavily from his left hand and holding a knife in the other. Human. *Twill.*

"You," I growled.

An ugly sneer twisted his mouth. "You didn't expect me to let a treasure like that slip through my grasp, did you? Give me the sceptre."

"I don't have it," I told him. "It's gone. Someone else took it."

"Liar."

"I'm not lying." I held the knife up in warning. "Since when did the likes of you employ faerie assassins?"

"They're not with me. You have many enemies, girl."

"Hope you didn't need that hand for anything." I'd dealt a shallow wound, but it wouldn't incapacitate him the way iron did half-bloods. Backing up, I used every ounce of inhuman speed I possessed to launch myself at him—

Sparks exploded in my face, followed by a burst of smoke. Blinking frantically, I barely deflected a knife blow. Crap. He could use witch spells, which meant he was a supernatural of some kind. The smoke stung my eyes and made me move slower than usual, and his knife cut through my sleeve, missing the flesh by a fraction. As he raised the knife again, Viola jumped in.

"Take that!" She hit him over the head with a tree branch. There was a tremendous *crack,* and he crumpled onto his front.

"Thanks," I gasped. "Now—"

Blood sprayed across my path, and I sprang back as yet another body fell from the hedge, his throat cut. And behind him was the stranger who'd arrived to help us before. With the faint light of a streetlamp on his face, I now saw who he was.

Cedar. The thief.

Fury burned in my veins. "You. You rotten stealing—"

"You're welcome." He was already turning away, past the bodies, when I tackled him. The move should have knocked him over but he'd anticipated my attack, bracing his feet on the pavement. I held the knife against his throat, and he laughed. He really was handsome. Too bad I was about to carve his pretty face in. Though from the look of the scar on his cheek, someone had tried to do the same once already.

"Give it back," I told him. "Now."

"I have nothing of yours."

"It's bad manners to lie," said Viola, who'd worked it out. "You're from one of the families, aren't you?"

He raised his hands in surrender. "I don't have anything that belongs to you. Honest."

"You robbed me at the market," I snarled. "*Don't* deny it."

A rustling sounded in the bushes. Again. How many people had followed us?

An arrow whistled overhead, and the thief broke free from my grasp, knife in hand. *Iron.* Apparently I wasn't the only one who used mortal weapons. The assassins did, too, though… and now another three had joined their dead buddies.

I ducked another arrow and ran towards the assassins. It'd have been a bad idea if they'd been prepared for my speed, but they weren't. Arrows whipped past on either side, but they were too slow to draw. Viola threw a handful of magic at them, causing enough of a diversion for me to knock the bow from one's hand. My knife sank into his arm, through his armoured sleeve, and he collapsed under the iron. The other two lay at Cedar's feet. As one stirred, Cedar waved a hand and green light shone around the hedge, branches reaching out to catch the assassin's arms and lock them into place.

Aha. So he was from Summer, then. And he wouldn't be getting away from me again.

He turned to Viola and me. "You fight well."

"I'm army trained," said Viola. "I can put a knife through your eye at ten paces. Maybe more. I'd hate for you to find out the hard way."

He laughed, to my surprise. "Maybe they won't kill you after all. But it's too late. You really shouldn't have come back into this realm."

"And you really shouldn't have stolen my talisman."

I jumped at him, grabbing his weapon hand, but apparently he'd seen me coming. We crashed into the hedge, which immediately moved, its branches forming a shield in front of him and pushing me out of his way. Bloody Summer magic. When it wasn't making things grow, it was manipulating the natural world to use as a weapon.

"Hey!" I yelled, dodging the grasping branches. "You snake."

"My purpose here is done," he said, from behind the wall of branches. "I helped you kill those assassins. I don't think there are any more of them, but you never know. Be careful."

The branches dropped, and he sprinted away. Disentangling myself from the hedge, I pelted after him. "Give back what you stole from me."

"I have nothing of yours, I told you," he called over his shoulder.

"You're a coward and a thief."

"I can deny neither of those things, but you're wasting your time." He pointed at the hedge, and branches extended to grab my feet. Viola and I were ensnared immediately, our ankles bound in thick branches.

Damn, he was good. But he'd forgotten one Summer

faerie was no match for two Winter ones. And I still had my knife.

I crouched down awkwardly, hacking at the hedge with the iron blade. I cut one leg free, and Viola broke away first. She ran after him in a blur of blue light, but he'd already broken into a run. Cursing, hopping on one leg to keep the hedge from grabbing my other foot again, I freed myself and caught up with Viola. "He climbed over the hedge."

"Back into half-blood territory?" I swore. "Right. Come on." I ran at the hedge, clearing it in a high leap. At least we were at the opposite end of half-blood territory to the place where the trolls had rampaged after us. Tall apartment blocks housed half-bloods who wanted to live here on the territory, interspersed with holes in the ground that belonged to wild fae. There were two large buildings between us and wherever the thief had disappeared to. *To hell with this.* I took a step back, then a running leap at the building's side. Like a lot of Summer half-bloods' places, it was built close to nature, with a giant tree wrapping the whole apartment block inside its roots. Perfect for climbing, and to give me an aerial view of the territory. Even that daredevil thief wouldn't run into the witches' forest at the territory's end, so he must be somewhere here amongst the half-bloods' houses.

I climbed swiftly onto the roof and kept running, searching below—*gotcha.* Cedar had taken a path between this block and its neighbour, and if I moved fast enough, I could waylay him.

As I dropped one storey down, using the tree's thick roots for balance, he looked up, eyes widening. I let go and dropped two more storeys, catching another root above the ground. I hung from the building's side, close enough for him to hear me. "Get back here."

He raised a hand. "You're persistent, aren't you?"

The tree root *moved,* and he smirked a little, revealing the glow of green faerie magic in his hand.

I leaped from the tree to the building opposite, clearing a distance which no human could jump, magic or none. As I did so, Viola closed in behind him on the ground, unseen. All his attention was on me, and his escape. I climbed another storey, then performed another death-defying leap, this time landing directly in front of him on the ground. He was trapped between Viola and me.

Cedar ran for the nearest wall—the one covered in a tree root, which moved to catch him as he climbed, faster than I'd expected. I had enough experience of broken bones to know how tricky it was to balance so far above the ground. Of course, having plant-controlling magic helped him. With the tree's roots still moving, I climbed the opposite building to avoid being grabbed. However much advantage he had with Summer magic on his side, I was faster. I reached the roof first, and waved at him as he used the tree's movements to boost himself on top of the building opposite.

"That's cheating," I called to him. "Try making the jump without using a tree for help."

He kept moving without answering. Whatever he wanted the talisman for must be urgent. Too bad he'd never reach his goal.

I ran parallel to his path, reaching the end of my own building first. Then I jumped again, clearing the gap between the two blocks, and slammed down in front of him. A brief glance below showed Viola stood underneath us, both hands glowing blue with Winter magic.

"It's over," I told him. "Nice try, but—"

He jumped off the roof.

That, I hadn't expected. The tree roots caught him and slowed his fall, but between that and Viola's magic, I didn't dare jump down myself. Instead, I moved closer to the edge, and paused. Cedar hung upside-down from a tree root which had frozen in the air, glowing with Winter magic.

A grin split my face, and I leaned over. "Need a hand?"

He looked at the sheer drop, his eyes widening. "Damn."

"Changed your mind about stealing from me?" I leaned further. I couldn't make the jump without leverage, but Viola had apparently frozen the entire tree. Note to self: learn to use Winter magic.

"No," he said, breaking free of the branch. He fell several feet and caught another frozen branch, using it to slow the drop to the ground. Viola waited for him. Surely he knew he wouldn't be able to run from both of us.

I climbed down after him, in time for Viola to throw a handful of magic right in his face. His grip on the branch slackened and he fell, landing face-down in front of her.

"Oops," said Viola. "Might have overdone it."

"At least he didn't fall that far." I jumped the rest of the way down, grabbing the back of his coat and yanking him upright. "Oi. Don't pass out. You have something of mine."

"What?" His voice slurred. "I told you, I don't—"

Viola waved a handful of magic threateningly at him. I pulled my knife out.

"We can do this the easy way or the hard way," I told him. "Viola, is there somewhere close by we can take him to question?"

"My flat's over there." She pointed in the direction we'd run from. "If you wanted to avoid drawing attention, though, you might be too late."

"Ah." I looked up. Sure enough, several sleepy faces peered from windows. The half-bloods who hadn't been at the party didn't look pleased to have been woken up. "All right, then. We'd better move."

9

In the end, we had to drag Cedar between us, who recognised a losing battle. Good, because I had a raging headache by now, and would rather go to sleep than run an interrogation. But I wanted that damned sceptre back, however much trouble it'd caused me. Luckily, Viola lived on the ground floor of one of the blocks a five-minute walk away, and we persuaded Cedar to march with us in that direction until we were safely inside her flat.

Despite clearly being neglected, it was in surprisingly good condition. Plainly decorated, with no signs it belonged to a Winter half-blood, let alone one who worked for such a powerful family. Viola and I deposited Cedar in one of the bedrooms, and she used magic to freeze the window shut. He scowled at us.

"What?" he said. "I really don't have anything—"

I marched into the room so we stood nose to nose. Then I grabbed the front of his coat. As expected, I found the shape of the sceptre beneath my hands, and pulled it free. He didn't resist, waiting until I held it up to the light.

Even without much to see by, it was clear this talisman

wasn't the same as the one I'd held before. The blue gem looked like it was made of glass, and no surge of magic accompanied my touch.

"The talisman is a fake," he said. "Does that look like a real talisman to you?"

I lowered the sceptre. "What did you do with the real one?"

"I didn't take it. Whoever did must have got you in the market. I told you to watch your step."

"A likely story. Someone hired you to steal it from me. My brother, by any chance?"

Confusion clouded his features. "I don't know your brother, but I'm not going to deny I wanted to take the talisman. You're a thief, too."

"By necessity."

"Then you ought to understand."

"No. I work for myself, not other people. And I'd never steal a Sidhe's talisman. Not even from a half-blood."

I'd almost said *from a half-blood with no magic,* but caught myself in time. Disclosing that information would be very unwise. I had the upper hand because he assumed I had power as great as the rest of my family, *and* that it worked with or without my talisman. If only.

"I work alone," Cedar said, "and I want to destroy the talisman, not use it."

I stared at him for a second. "What? You can't destroy a talisman. Why would you even want to?"

"For the same reasons most people want to steal it, I imagine," he said. "You seem to be getting on fine without it. Most faeries who've never lived in the mortal realm have no clue about hand-to-hand combat."

"I've lived here all my life, so trust me, this is my area of expertise. And you're changing the subject."

"I suppose I am."

I punched him full in the face. The satisfaction at seeing his head snap back was worth the bruised knuckles.

He lifted his head, his mouth bleeding. "All right. I deserved that."

"And this." Viola kicked him in the kneecap.

His eyes widened. "What did I ever do to you?"

"I just really don't like thieves. Except her."

"Ah." He moved suddenly, jerking away from the iron knife in my hand. "Don't poke me with that."

"You use an iron weapon yourself, right? Is that a new trend in the Seelie Court?"

"I'm not from the Court," he said. "The *Court* has no need of your talisman, because they have enough power of their own. The assassins were sent by one of the border families."

"The what?"

Viola's sharp intake of breath made me whip my head around to face her. "You know them?"

"Of course I do. We're one of them."

This was getting too weird for me, too much for my tired brain to keep up with. "You," I said to Cedar. "Tell me what you want with the talisman. What's so special about it?"

He started to speak, then all the colour drained from his face and he made a choking noise instead. Even though I hadn't seen one in action yet myself, I knew the effects of a Sidhe's binding words. Someone had put a vow on him—a powerful one. If his words were bound up in a vow, he wouldn't be able to answer no matter how we phrased the questions we asked. Which meant we needed to try a new strategy.

"You're bound?" I said. "So you can't talk about the talisman. But why help us fight off the assassins? You thought *they* had it?"

"No, I just have a bad habit of betting on the underdog." He shrugged nonchalantly. "The playing field is entirely too uneven, and if anyone else claims the talisman… let's just say it's better for all of us if you stay alive."

"It's better for *me* if I don't die, but I really don't see what's in it for you."

His gaze swept my body. "Maybe I don't want to watch you die."

"Lucky for both of us, it won't happen." I folded my arms. "Did you think I had the talisman when you showed up at my house?"

His brow furrowed. "No. How could you? You hadn't even been to Faerie yet."

"So it was just a coincidence that you appeared right after a hellhound tried to rip out my throat."

Understanding flashed in his eyes. "You think *I* sent that monstrosity? Hellhounds are Winter beasts, and besides, if I wanted you dead, I wouldn't have stuck around to help you clear away the evidence. You should be more concerned with who sent the assassins. They carried the emblem of a powerful family. Your neighbours, if I'm not mistaken, and one of the major Winter families in the borderlands."

"The Darkwaters," said Viola. "I should have guessed. They had an army, the last time I checked."

"They've fallen on hard times in the last couple of years," Cedar said. "Since the arrests."

The emphasis he put on the last word, and the way Viola stiffened, set my suspicions rising. "Arrests?"

"Some faeries were found guilty of working with the renegades who attacked this realm," he said. "The Sidhe punished them brutally. The Darkwaters were stripped of their main talisman when the one who owned it was exiled, so it makes sense that they're trying to steal another."

"But—why send assassins?" I said. "I thought you couldn't steal a talisman unless the magic inside it declared you worthy. Don't they know that?"

"So you *do* know how all this works." He flashed me a knowing smile. "Then you'll know that some would sacrifice anyone to avoid getting their own hands dirty. If they take the talisman while you're still alive, it makes little difference to them, because magic is perfectly capable of transferring its allegiance if it finds someone more worthy."

Wait. So that means my siblings could steal it back? Or anyone else? I'd thought the choice was absolute, not that the magic might abandon me again at any time it wanted to. Maybe it already had. I mean, I'd tried to sell the talisman to a human. Not exactly a model example.

Dread curled around my spine. But... that meant they'd keep trying to kill me, whether I had the talisman or not. I'd done my best to escape them, and all it'd got me was a useless prisoner.

Fine, then. Maybe if I killed enough of their assassins, they'd fuck off back to Faerie.

"Too bad for them. And you. I'm not handing it over to the enemy."

Cedar raised an eyebrow. "You don't have an army hidden somewhere, do you?"

"No, but she has me," Viola added.

"Who even are you?" he said. "I swear I've seen you before."

"I'm Viola. Servant of the Whitefall family."

"And my general badass-in-chief," I put in. "So don't underestimate us. We'll get that talisman back. And it'll never be yours again."

"I never had it," he said. "The thief must have struck beforehand. Maybe even before you left the faerie realm."

"No way," I said. "I *held* the talisman, not a minute before I ran into you. Unless that bloody gnome took it, or someone pickpocketed me in the five seconds it took me to reach you."

"It can happen," he said. "The best thieves move fast."

"I know. I *am* one. Doesn't mean I'm egotistical enough to think I can steal a talisman right from its owners' hands." The fake was actually a fairly convincing lookalike, if I hadn't seen the real thing. "Tell me you haven't done it before. Not stealing from the *Courts*. Isn't that punishable by death?"

That's enough, Raine. Curiosity was one thing, but he'd already proven he didn't know anything useful.

"In certain circumstances," said Cedar. "Stealing another Sidhe's magic is frowned upon at best, but the reason most talisman thieves are exiled or killed is because most duels between two Sidhe result in one of them being killed. That doesn't have to be the case. And with the border families, the Courts never come interfering if a talisman happens to end up in someone else's hands. As for *you...* your mother died without a pure-blooded heir. In their eyes, that makes you, and your talisman, fair game."

Oh. Now I get it. I'd figured there must be some rule I was missing, but it all came down to that pure-blood-versus-half-blood nonsense I'd faced a hundred times before. Except these border families apparently had no qualms about murdering a fellow family head if they happened to be half-blood. And I'd bet the Courts wouldn't recognise it as murder of an equal.

My nails cut into my palms as I glared at him. "So the Sidhe think half-bloods are good for nothing and the talisman should have gone to a pure faerie. Blame my mother for that one."

"If your mother still owned the talisman, it'd be a different story. She was feared by even the other family heads, and they're all watching with interest to see if you live up to her."

My stomach twisted with dread. "Can nobody tell me why the hell I wasn't told this at any point before I was summoned into Faerie?"

"Because the talisman was never meant to pass to a mortal," said Cedar. "You're going to have to revise your attitude, fast, if you're to maintain control over that territory of yours. It wouldn't surprise me if someone had already tried to claim it."

"Screw you," I spat at him. "You wouldn't know the first thing about being hit over the head with a future you never wanted, and the alternative being death."

"You can always walk away," he said. "I wouldn't make assumptions about what I don't know, either. I'd like nothing more than to walk away myself, but I made a promise to destroy that talisman, and I stand by it. I'd rather you didn't die in the process."

"I'd rather that, too," I said. "So I'm going back to Faerie tomorrow morning, and you'll be staying right here."

"Agreed," said Viola. "And I'm going to find an incentive for you to stay."

She walked off, leaving me between him and the door. I moved pointedly, not putting my weapon away, in case he tried anything. He didn't move from the bed, though.

"She means tying me up, doesn't she?" he said.

"You deserve worse. One last question. Why were you really at my house? To steal from me?"

Ice shot down my spine. Dad. What if he'd—?

Apparently seeing my alarm, Cedar said, "I haven't hurt your family, and that kid who you were with is in Faerie, as far as I know."

"Kid… right, Robin." I'd have laughed if the situation hadn't been no laughing matter at all. Robin himself would have no clue this was happening—though he was the one who'd convinced me to go into Faerie in the first place. "You never said you wouldn't take the talisman from me again if we found it."

"I didn't," he said, "but I hope you'll come around to my

viewpoint by then. The talisman is dangerous, and the realms—both this one and Faerie—would be better off without it."

"I'll be the judge of that, considering it's *mine.*"

He smirked and shook his head. "You should know that the next group heading to Faerie leaves at dawn, which is in only a few hours. And if you'd like my assistance—"

"No chance. I'm not accepting any help from someone who's openly admitted he wants the talisman for himself."

"To destroy it," he corrected.

"Yeah, yeah." Viola returned, eyeing the frozen window. "Can't find the ropes. I can seal the door, though."

"Do it," I told her.

He sat upright. "Wait—"

I closed the door, and Viola used magic to create an icy barrier in the gap between the door and the wall, as she'd done to the window.

"Good enough." She yawned. "I don't have another spare room. You'll have to sleep on the sofa."

"Okay." My body felt wound in knots, my mind too sharp to shut down. "We need to leave early to catch the next messengers to go into Faerie." I moved out of earshot of the door. "We can't leave him in here forever, though."

"I know," she said. "But even bound by a vow, he's capable of giving us information. I think he *is* with one of the families. I also think he's pretending to be a lowly thief, and is actually someone more important. He wouldn't have access to that level of information otherwise. Which makes getting rid of him a challenge, because the families tend to pay back the deaths of their own in blood."

"And even if he's telling the truth about wanting to destroy it, he's still working against us," I said. "He's seriously been waiting a year for this?"

"They all have. After she died, the others expected a free-for-all. But the palace kept them out. Now you've claimed the talisman—and it's missing—rumours will spread quickly."

"Thanks for that, Viola. I think I've had enough brutal honesty for one day."

"Sorry."

I walked to the kitchen to pour myself a glass of water in an attempt to ease the likelihood of a hangover. "I really don't get what makes the border families different to the rest of Faerie. They belong to both Courts, right?"

"They're a group of families from Winter and Summer bound under a shaky allegiance but with a tendency to declare war on one another every few years. The Seelie and Unseelie Courts ordered them to form their own territories and live peacefully, on the divide between Summer and Winter's main territories. Now, they don't wage open war, but there are constant incidents. Mysterious attacks. Monsters set loose on a rival family's territory. You get the idea."

"So families belonging to the same Court would still attack one another? Like the one who sent the assassins… Darkwater?"

"Right." She nodded. "Their family and ours have never been allies. In the borderlands, we view even our own people with suspicion. And the Courts rarely bother to intervene with borderland disputes. Generally, if a transgression takes place, punishment is left up to the one wronged. The territory in that part of Faerie is neutral, which means it can technically be claimed by any of the other families, Summer or Winter."

"This just gets more and more pleasant," I said. "So where does Mr Charming Sceptre Thief fall into this?"

"I'd say he's from one of the other families—a Summer one—but I've never seen him before. And I've seen most of the other families' armies at one time or another. There are certain nobles who stay out of sight and work undercover. I'd guess he's one of them."

I looked at her. "So it was your job to spy for her—right? That was part of your duty?"

Wariness crept into her expression. "The vow makes speaking of it tricky, but now you've already guessed, I can talk more openly. Yes, I was a spy. She knew my past as a soldier and she exploited my abilities for her own. It wasn't a terrible life."

"But you said you left someone with the other family you served."

"Damn that elf wine. Yes, I did, but she and I haven't seen one another since before Lady Whitefall died. It's a little complicated—my relationship with the last family I served is even more so." Her fingers tapped nervously on her knee. "We weren't allowed, technically, in the army. It's worse now I belong to the Whitefalls."

"Is it frowned upon to be involved with someone from another family?" I asked.

"It depends if they're currently fighting."

"Oh." Considering what I'd heard of the situation in the borderlands, sneaking off to meet with someone on another territory must be risky to say the least.

"Exactly." She grimaced. "Let's just say things have been a little fragile since Lady Whitefall's death, what with soldiers all over the woods, and assassins coming to the palace."

"How'd they get enough half-bloods for an army?" I asked. "That's a lot of people, even for an extended family."

"You're forgetting they're immortal, and half-bloods have been crossing to that part of the realm for generations. My parents grew up with knowledge of Faerie. When the families began recruiting for their armies from amongst the half-bloods living in this realm, many were happy to move into Faerie, even if they could never return to the mortal realm.

My parents didn't, but… I was in the army when they died. I wish I'd been able to come home sooner."

I frowned. "You mean in the invasion? But that was over twenty years ago. You're not that old."

"Ah. Didn't you know time passes differently in Faerie? There, it's only been six years since the invasion."

"I did, but… crap. I forgot." Today, I'd lost several hours. If I stayed longer, I might lose days. Weeks. What would happen to Dad then? "Wait. How long have you worked for the Whitefall family?"

"Three years. My first few attempts to leave the army didn't succeed. In the end, there's no breaking a vow, and Lady Hornbeam forbids anyone to desert their post—on pain of death."

"Damn." I winced. "So you waited…"

"I'd given up hope when Lady Whitefall offered me a way out." She grimaced. "Anyway, we need to work out what to do tomorrow. He's right—the thief won't walk openly carrying the sceptre."

"What if they use the rift?"

"Do you really think the Little People would let someone who stole a Sidhe's talisman through?"

"I don't really trust anyone over there, to be honest. But if the thief's waiting to go back into Faerie with the next group, I think I have an idea."

Catch me letting on that my faith in my abilities had taken a major hit lately.

"All right," said Viola. "Tell me the plan."

10

I sure as hell didn't feel like a master thief after an hour's sleep on the sofa, and leaving Cedar behind felt like a monumental mistake. But the dawn chorus and Viola's shouts roused me from slumber.

"They're leaving early! We need to move."

I groaned and threw an arm over my head. I'd removed Viola's coat, but had fallen asleep wearing the outfit my talisman had transformed my original clothes into. And obviously, I didn't have any spare ones with me. "What time is it?"

"Five in the morning. They're leaving in ten minutes."

"Crap." I didn't have time to shower, so I compensated with a quick wash in the bathroom. Despite the exertions of yesterday, my new clothes showed no signs of wear. That was magic for you. I put my knife into place and paused by Cedar's door. No sound came from behind. Either he was asleep, or...

The ice had melted. "Damn. Viola, I think he got out."

Viola appeared behind me with her pet sprite clinging to

her coat. "I knew I should have double-sealed the doors. My magic doesn't work as well in this realm."

"He didn't steal anything, did he?"

She shook her head. "Nothing to steal here."

"Then we'll go."

A commotion drifted over from the main part of half-blood territory. *Here we go again.* After last night's rampaging trolls, I was even less eager to draw attention, so I walked with Viola around the outskirts of the flats, alongside the hedge bordering the territory. I paused when we came within sight of the field, hanging back to avoid being spotted.

Then I saw the lone human standing apart from the crowd: Dad.

My heart plummeted. His gaze travelled over to me and he walked in my direction. Viola moved in front, heading towards the crowd and masking us from view as Dad came over to me.

"Dad," I whispered, taking his arm. "What are you doing here?"

"I had to see you before they took you away again." He must be having one of his more lucid days, but this wasn't the time.

"I'm sorry," I whispered. "I'm really, really sorry. They threatened me—they threatened to kill both of us. You have to leave. It's not safe here."

"I was hers, too, and I remember..." He trailed off. "I have to remember. I have to go back."

"No. She doctored both our memories, but—she's not there." I wanted to tell him the truth, but the words stuck in my throat, and we were in too public a location. "You can't come to Faerie, Dad. Besides, I'm not going back permanently. I have something I need to do, then I'll come home."

"I never should have let her leave us behind."

"It wasn't your fault, Dad. She took you against your will,

and it wasn't fair. Neither of us belong in Faerie. It'll be okay —just let me do this one thing." My heart broke to see his face crumple, then he seemed to pull himself together. "C'mon. I'll take you to the gate." I fervently wished he'd hurry, not wanting to miss Viola's cue. We were supposed to arrive before everyone had got here. The hobgoblin had started speaking again, which captured everyone's attention, at least. I hurried Dad to the gate, which was open. "Hurry," I whispered. "I promise I'll come back for you."

"Raine, I—I'm sorry for everything."

He turned his back and walked away, and I sagged with relief. Footsteps behind me announced the arrival of a guard and I swiftly moved to the side.

Behind me, light flared in the middle of the field, blinding green this time. My timing was off, but being beside the hedge had put me behind the green flare, hiding me from view. When the horsemen stepped out of Faerie, they were between me and the crowd. I crept around the edges and trod lightly past the crowd, scanning for a familiar face—or rather, the pull of a familiar magic. *I should be able to sense it. It's mine.*

Nothing called me, though, as the jumble of magical auras around the place made it hard to pinpoint a specific one. I scanned the half-bloods, dismissing those who had no possible hiding place for the sceptre. I'd expect the carrier to be a half-Sidhe, someone powerful. But maybe that's what they wanted me to think. Maybe they'd put the sceptre into the hands of someone who'd skim under the radar because they looked powerless.

My gaze snagged on a half-hobgoblin carrying a sack over his shoulder. I edged closer, peering at the bumpy shape inside the sack. The top might have mimicked the sceptre—if I got within a few metres, I'd be able to see.

At that moment, someone else appeared behind the

hobgoblin in the crowd—a tall human-shaped figure with silky dark hair and a scar on his face. *I knew he planned to steal it.*

The crowd, enraptured by the appearance of the Sidhe on horses, didn't even notice him. But that meant they wouldn't notice me, either. I crept in, melding into the crowd immediately. Now the thief and I were equally distant from the hobgoblin. As a large half-ogre in front shuffled his feet, I saw an opening under his arm and ducked, gracefully navigating the crowd without bumping into anyone. My path clear, I readied myself to grab the sceptre—

Summer magic surged, and the grass rose around my feet, covering my shoes. *Hey!* I leaned forward, but my feet remained locked to the grassy carpet. *You cheat.* Gritting my teeth, I attempted to walk forward, but my feet stuck, pushing me into the path of the half-ogre. He roared in anger and aimed a punch at me. I ducked, he hit his neighbour, and all hell broke loose.

I wrenched one foot loose from the grass, only to be knocked flat onto my face by the ogre's meaty hand. Fists flew, yelps of pain split the group, and I crawled forwards, yanking my other foot free, shielding my face with my arms. The hobgoblin had disappeared beneath the crowd.

A flash of silky dark hair and a sideways smile. *Gotcha.* I elbowed my way past the flailing half-ogre and vaulted over a group of gnomes, crashing into Cedar as he attempted to approach the gap into Faerie. My hand locked around the wrist that held the sceptre, and blue light washed over me.

Power surged through my hand, but either he didn't feel it or it wasn't enough to make him let go.

Eyes turned in my direction, and I growled, twisting his wrist, attempting to pry his hands loose. A jab to his ribs with my free hand, followed by another, had no effect. His uniform, whatever it was made of, was an effective shield.

"Let go," I growled, and felt a rush of the same preternatural strength I'd had when I'd hit my brother. My grip tightened, squeezing his wrist hard. At the same time, the gap into Faerie widened, and the half-bloods who weren't brawling hurried forwards in an unstoppable tide. It took everything I had to keep hold of the sceptre.

And then Viola crashed into him from the side, sending all three of us sprawling in a heap. Cedar recovered first, gripping the talisman, and I leaped after him into Faerie.

We fell onto the path, landing in the undergrowth. A wave of green light swept me aside, and my back slammed into a tree. Viola appeared behind him, trapping him between us.

"Give it to me," I warned. "Or else."

He looked to the left and right, then ran directly at a tree at the side of the path, throwing green energy from his palm. The tree split down the middle to let him jump through, immediately sealing the second I jumped after him. Branches smacked me in the face and tangled in my clothes, and I fell onto my face in the undergrowth. *Damn you.*

Pulling myself upright, I ran, leaping over bushes and dodging more trees as he wove deeper into the forest. Being a Summer faerie meant he was in his element. But magic answered to me in this realm, especially with the talisman so close.

I caught up at a clearing, running as fast as possible when impeded with so many obstacles. He picked up speed, trees and bushes moving aside when he ran at them. But I was fast —maybe faster than he was. Reaching out a hand, I called on the magic inside the talisman. The same way I'd tried to call magic to me ever since I could remember, no matter how many times it didn't work.

Blue light surged from my fingertips and the air froze in its path, sending icy shards raining down on him. As he ducked, I launched myself at him and grabbed the sceptre. Immediately, a sense of *rightness* settled over me. *It's mine.*

Cedar lifted his head and grabbed my ankle, trying to unbalance me. I twisted free, holding the talisman high above him. "Don't you even think about doing that again."

Blue light radiated from my palms, especially the one holding the weapon. Viola caught up and stopped a few feet away, staring at the light, too.

"You don't know the first thing about that weapon," he said, his tone harsh. "Give it to me before I have to do something I'll regret."

"Oh, will you?" I pointed it at him. As he jumped to his feet—whether to run or attack, I didn't know—I waved the talisman, and sent a current of blue light surging in his direction. The light smashed into the air, and which froze in front of him, wrapping around his legs. Now that was more like it.

Viola walked to my side. "Raine… what are you going to do with him?"

"Depends if the spell's permanent or not."

"It isn't," he said, knocking against the ice with one hand. A piece broke off the ice, but his attempts to free his legs were useless. *Ha.* I took a step or two closer, checking the ice. It'd solidified from nothing, as though my sceptre had conjured it into existence. A muscle ticked in his jaw and his furrowed brow betrayed the strain as he fought to free himself. As a Summer faerie, he'd probably lost all feeling below the knees by now.

It'd be easy to leave him here. So easy. The mortal realm was where I belonged, and if I got back before the door closed, he wouldn't be able to follow.

Oh. I whirled around, beckoning Viola, and ran back through the trees. I'd come further chasing him than I'd thought, and lost track of the path where the door opened.

"It's closed," he called after me. "The path will be shut by now. You can't go back into the mortal realm."

"Damn." I turned to Viola. "Will the rift—?"

"Not twice in two days," she said, looking stricken. "Oh, no."

Soft laughter made my fists clench. "You're the one trapped in ice," I told him. "I wouldn't push me." I turned the knife over in my hand.

Viola gave me a sideways look that seemed to communicate, *don't kill him.* Why? He was too unpredictable to be an ally, to say nothing of the fact that we were all stuck in Faerie now. Maybe she still thought he might be a noble in disguise. Actually… that was a good point. What if we left him to die, only to find out he was heir to one of the most prominent Court families? It'd hardly be the weirdest thing to happen this week, or even today.

I took one step forward. A dangerous, almost feral glint appeared in his eyes, a flash of green across each hazel iris. If he was trying to goad me into a fight, I'd be more likely to draw attention with my magic. No… there were enough beasts in the forest to take him off my hands.

I took a step back. "I'd like to say it's been a pleasure, Cedar. Good luck."

Rustling in the bushes drowned out a warning shout from Viola, followed by a flurry of footsteps. Then the nearest bush moved, growing tentacle-like appendages. Shadowy fae—death stealers. We must be way out in the outskirts, in the wild forest that belonged to neither Court. A chill raced over my skin. I'd seen this type of faerie before, but only in the mortal realm. Here, it was wrong, out of place.

At least iron worked as well on these fae as any. I grabbed my knife in my free hand, holding the sceptre in the other. Immediately, the blue light noticeably dimmed. *What's wrong now?* Was it reacting to the iron? I wasn't about to let go of my other weapon, so I waved both at the new threat.

"Go," I told the shadows.

They moved around Cedar, sensing easy prey. My heart sank. Being suffocated by one of these things was a horrible way to die. I wouldn't wish it on anyone, not even him.

I jumped, slashing at the creature. It fell away beneath my knife, allowing an easy strike to the tentacle—I didn't know where its head was, but hitting it once with the iron did the trick.

Viola yelled behind me. She'd been caught in another tentacle. I used my knife to make sure my attacker was dead, then ran to help her. Blue light shone from her hands and the beast flailed away. Once again, my knife bit through shadowy flesh.

"Oh no," said Viola. "The thief—"

He'd almost disappeared beneath another beast. The death stealers were more like giant worms with tentacles than anything else, making a valiant attempt to latch onto Cedar's head. He fought one-handed with a short blade he'd pulled from his pocket, his other hand trying to free himself from my icy trap.

I jumped before I could consider whether I was making a mistake. The beast shrank away from the iron in my hand, giving me the chance to cut it away from Cedar's face. He inhaled sharply and stabbed, slicing several tentacles clean off. The beast half-slid off him, onto the ground, and I checked it was dead. Cedar cursed behind me, trying to break free from the ice.

A knife flew past, followed by a delighted shriek. Redcaps couldn't resist a battlefield. Cedar attempted to dodge, but the ice held him still, and the knife struck him side-on.

"Hey!" I yelled at the redcaps, brandishing my own blade. Viola got there first, throwing a handful of icy energy that sent one flying into another. I raised my talisman to do the same, and they pointed at me, jabbering and shrieking. As one, they fled into the woods.

A tentacle-like arm wrapped around my throat from behind. I hit out, but my elbow bounced off its hide. Waving the sceptre wildly, I fought for breath.

The tentacle slipped, then dropped. Blood splattered me from behind. I spun around to see Cedar had lunged forwards, his legs still imprisoned in ice, and sunk his iron knife into the creature. Shuddering, I pushed its lumpy body off me.

"You're welcome. Again." Cedar's tone was more abrasive than before, and his gaze was flecked with pain and anger as he kicked at the ice from the inside.

"Don't do that. You'll make the bleeding worse."

He took in a pained breath. "I thought you planned to leave me here."

"I thought so, too. But you owe me now."

Saving a faerie's life meant they owed a debt. I didn't know whether the same applied to him—a half-blood who'd probably been raised here in Faerie—but to my surprise, he laughed.

"Playing our games already, Raine," he said. "Yes, I suppose I do owe you a favour."

"Assuming you don't bleed out."

"I won't. I have healing magic. And your ice is melting."

He hit the ice with the side of his iron knife, and it shattered enough for him to free one leg. Cedar fell forwards, swearing in what I assumed was the faerie tongue, and half collapsed onto the ground. Blood dripped a steady beat onto the earth from his wounded side. He was lucky the weapon hadn't been made of iron. Unlike his own. He'd helped me. Why? So I'd owe *him* a debt? Surely not—after all, he'd thought I planned to leave him to die in the forest.

And I'd thought it was just the Sidhe who were masters at playing mind games with one another.

Viola hurried up to me. "Raine, what are you doing?"

"He owes me for saving his life," I told her. "It'd be a waste to leave him out here to die. Doesn't the palace have a place for prisoners?"

An indefinable expression passed over her face. "Yeah. She kept a lot of prisoners in the dungeon. If you're sure."

"We're going back to the palace," I told him. "You're going to be my prisoner until I decide your fate."

11

It was a good job Viola knew the way back to the palace, because we'd wandered so far off track that the path had disappeared. Faerie liked to change directions just to mess with you, and my own magic apparently didn't extend to rearranging the world to make it easier to find my way back to the palace. I wasn't sure whether the Sidhe screwed with directions to deliberately confuse human or half-blood stragglers who wandered in, or if they just got bored, what with being immortal.

"You'll be able to do that soon," said Viola, when I mentioned this. "The sceptre should contain the power already. Essentially, you can move the paths, but only on your own territory. Once we get back, you ought to be able to move the path so it leads directly to the palace."

"Good. If we're going to make a habit of coming here, I might as well find the shortcuts."

Carrying Cedar between the two of us was awkward, though I finally had chance to relieve him of his weapons. He carried a nice carved iron blade that I'd have pinned as faerie work if I didn't know better. Almost too fancy to be a mortal weapon, but he couldn't have got it anywhere other than the human realm.

I became less convinced by the second that capturing him was a good idea, but considering his ability to sneak up on me, it'd be best to keep him somewhere I had the key to. The wound was worse than I'd thought, despite his self-proclaimed healing abilities. His golden skin had drained of all colour when I checked up on him. The winding forest path finally led into familiar snow-covered ground.

I held up the talisman, and the path *moved*. Trees shifted, and the palace was suddenly in front of us.

"Open sesame," I said to the gate, which didn't open. "Worth a try."

"You need the key," said Viola, an amused undercurrent to her voice. "Also, hurry up. My arms are killing me."

"Let me carry him once we're inside."

Through the gates, I walked to the palace and unlocked the oak doors with the key, glad I'd left it in my pocket from last time. Viola staggered through, dropping Cedar over the threshold. He groaned and pushed to his knees, and Viola swiftly grabbed the back of his coat, pulling him upright.

"Have you seen the dungeons yet?" she asked.

"No." I paused. The word 'dungeons' conjured up images of screaming humans trapped behind bars, and the presence of those ice statues brought back memories of my dad's panicked, terrified rants about being trapped in the Unseelie Court. Trapped here, and tortured by the Sidhe. "You've been in charge of prisoners before?"

She nodded. "Lady Whitefall was fond of keeping people who angered her in the dungeons. Is that where you want me to take him?"

My chest tightened. She was so open and friendly, I kept forgetting she'd likely committed crimes on my mother's behalf. Maybe even murder… of humans. Family loyalty—and vows—didn't give you much choice.

"I think I want to check this dungeon out first." It'd be a good way to test the sceptre's magic. I waved it at the floor and a trapdoor appeared in front of me. I unlocked it using the key, and spun around at an angry hiss from Viola. Cedar had broken free and staggered towards the palace door, leaving a trail of blood behind him.

Viola tackled him, slamming him face-first into the floor. His head made a *thunk* noise that echoed throughout the hall. "That'll hold him for a bit. What do you think?"

"The dungeon?" I looked down into the dark. "It's bloody creepy." The narrow stone corridor below the trapdoor, just visible in the darkness, was a screaming advertisement for a horror flick, complete with cobwebs and dismantled skeletons. *Humans?* I recoiled as something brushed my outstretched hand, but it was just a spider. The size of my fist. "Nope," I said to it. "You're going to run away and I'll pretend I never saw you."

"Who are you talking to?" Viola came up behind me. "Oh, Horace. He's okay. I can bring Cedar after you if you like. The lights should come on in a second."

"Horace," I said. "You named the spider, too. Of course."

Lights ignited below—candles, but without flames. Leaning closer, I found they were actually alive, flame-shaped insects with luminous wings. Stone stairs led from the trapdoor down into the creepy corridor.

Evil once inhabited this dungeon. I felt its traces, like icy blades under my skin. Her magic, warped into darkness. Transformations intended to torture enemies into submission. All that and more had occurred using the magic of the sceptre in my hand.

I backed away, hit by a spasm of nausea. "Yeah… nope. He might be a dick, but locking him down there…"

People died down there. What with my life upheaval, I hadn't yet faced the other uncomfortable truth—my mother had kept other humans than my dad here, and they hadn't all been fortunate enough to escape.

"Okay," Viola called. "We have to put him somewhere, though. I think he hit his head too hard."

"You mean *you* hit my head," said Cedar, not sounding incapacitated at all. "Such manners for a servant of the Unseelie Court."

"Watch it," said Viola. "I'm still not convinced keeping you alive is a good idea, and Raine didn't say I couldn't stick a knife in you if I wanted."

"No, I didn't, but he does owe me a favour. Besides, if he dies, I don't want his ghost stuck in the palace forever."

"Ghosts don't exist in Faerie," Viola said, her voice sounding like it came from far away.

I backed up the stairs and waved the sceptre, and the trapdoor vanished. Turning around to Viola, I found myself faced with another door in the wall. Blood still streaked the polished floor where Cedar had been.

"Viola?" I called, assuming she'd gone through the door.

"I put him in a guest room," she called back.

I opened the new door and walked into a corridor identical to the one my bedroom was in, lined with wooden doors and carpeted in light blue. Quick glances into the rooms confirmed they all appeared to be for guests, decorated with elegant fittings and an absurd level of extravagance. I could have slept in a different room every night of the week and still not used them all.

Viola's voice came from behind one of the doors. "You probably have a concussion. Don't move."

I didn't hear Cedar's response, but pushed open the door to find the two of them nose to nose, Viola holding Cedar's knife. "I'll be keeping these," she said. "Nice weapons, by the way. Oh, and you can't escape the palace. Not if we don't want you to."

"That would depend on how quickly you'd like that favour." His gaze moved over to me, entirely too steady for someone who'd just hit his head on a hard surface. Healing abilities must come in handy here.

"I'll think about it."

Viola backed away as he shrugged off his well-made coat, which had barely the slightest tear from the wound. The slashes on his ribs were half-sealed, but he'd been through the wars already, by the look of it. Pale gashes marked his chest and arms, long healed over, and darker band-shaped scars circled his wrists.

I frowned. Few things could cut deep enough to leave a permanent mark on a faerie with healing abilities, even a half-blood—except iron. Maybe he'd come off worse in a fight with a human, but given how quickly he fought, that seemed unlikely. Was he really a thief, or something else? Perhaps he was a soldier, like Viola. His lean athletic build was fairly typical of a half-blood male, while his well-made clothes suggested a background as noble as mine. Then again, he might have stolen them.

I looked away, but not before he caught my gaze. "If you wanted me half-naked in your room, the stabbing wasn't necessary."

"Oh, please." I rolled my eyes at him. "Looks like it's a common scenario for you, if those scars are any indication."

He didn't take the bait. "My job would be more pleasant if it frequently involved being a guest in a beautiful lady's palace, but I can't say this has ever happened before."

"By 'job', you mean 'thief', right?" I let the compliment slide right off me. If he wanted to divert my attention from questioning him, he'd have to try harder than that.

"Naturally. You still haven't said what you'd like as your favour."

So he's a professional thief? If such a thing existed in Faerie. He might be a noble, or he might be a nobody. In Faerie, anything might be an illusion. I'd learned that lesson well enough in the mortal realm.

"That's because I'm still thinking about it," I said to him. "I take it this vow of yours is going to make talking about certain subjects difficult. There's no time limit on our favour."

"Correct, but keeping me here won't stop those assassins from coming after you."

"No, but it means one less enemy to keep track of."

He arched a brow. "Enemy? I helped you, in case you've forgotten."

So he had. "Because you want the sceptre. That doesn't make us allies, Cedar, so you can stop flirting with me."

"You're the one who keeps staring at me. Unless… you don't prefer *humans,* do you?"

"No, I prefer people who don't *steal my family heirlooms.* Or nearly get me killed running into a nest of Unseelie fae. Where were you even running away to, anyway?"

His eyes narrowed. "If you—" He choked on the words, pushing away from the wall. One of the slashes on his ribs began weeping blood again.

"Don't do that, you fool," said Viola from behind me. "You'll make it worse."

He heaved a breath. "I didn't think you had a vested interest in keeping me alive."

"I do," I said. "Provided you don't wriggle out of repaying the favour."

"I'm true to my word." He took an unsteady step backwards, towards the bed, but remained upright, chest heaving, arms trembling. "Are you sure you don't want that favour now? My presence here won't help matters."

I put a hand firmly on his shoulder and pushed him back onto the bed. "Lie down and stop being ridiculous." His skin was warm to touch, almost fevered, and the thrum of magic underneath his skin was unexpected. Not in an unpleasant way, but I'd never felt the buzz of someone else's magic so intensely from brief skin contact. *Of course. It's because you have magic yourself now.* His smelled like scented candles and woodsmoke. I lowered my hand, hoping only I had picked up on the surprising intimacy of the brief moment of contact. This was Faerie: such things were probably normal here.

"So," I said. "Who are you worried about finding you? One of the families, by any chance?"

"I'm here on my own account, Raine," he said. "As to the families, they will all want my blood when I destroy the talisman. So don't think I'm doing this because it's mere entertainment to me."

There was a flash of something furious in his gaze before it slid away from mine again.

"You're planning to betray them," Viola said quietly. "Right?"

His gaze shifted to her, a furrow appearing in his brow. "I'm sure I know you."

"If you're with the families, you probably saw me at Gatherings," she said smoothly. "I don't know *you*, but I can guess which family is yours."

"Not necessarily," he said in an offhand tone. "My allegiances are mine alone."

"Then give me a clue," I told him.

"Are you calling in your favour?"

"No," I told him. "I think I'll save that for something important. You stay here, and try not to injure yourself again."

He bristled at my tone, which mimicked the exact condescending way he'd spoken to me at the market. There was something drained in his expression when he leaned forwards. "Raine—"

I shook my head, backing out into the corridor.

"Well, that made no sense whatsoever," I said to Viola after I'd closed the door. "Will the room stay locked?"

"As long as I have anything to do with it," said Viola. "I still think we should have used the dungeons. If he *is* with the other families, we need to make a show of strength to prove we don't invite known enemies in here and give them the VIP treatment."

"He's bleeding," I said. "He also has some pretty nasty scars. Looked like iron. Are you sure he came from here and not the mortal realm? His weapon was iron, too." But he knew the families of Faerie better than I did. Right?

"Some of the families… they use iron to punish half-bloods," she mumbled. "Mine did. Not on me, but there was always the threat if you did anything to anger the family's leader."

The image of the marks circling his wrists flashed into my head again, followed by the dungeon I hadn't been able to bring myself to take him into. Iron used to punish half-bloods? I'd never seen such a thing even in the mortal realm. Certainly not from other faeries. My stomach turned over. "Damn. I think he might be telling the truth."

She looked sideways at me. "What do you mean?"

"He said he's not exactly working for a family, but they clearly have some kind of hold over him. I think you're right, and he's betraying them. And he's a half-blood, so it's not like he'd have a position of importance in the family, right? I mean, unless they're all like mine and have only half-blood heirs. If he's a noble, will anyone come looking for him?"

"It depends on how important he is. If he's acting on his

own account, as he claims, then perhaps they won't. On the other hand, capturing another family's heir… let's just say it wouldn't reflect much better on either of us than leaving him to die in the forest."

My hands dropped to my sides. "Great. I suppose that's in the guidebook to Faerie everyone forgot to give me when I showed up here."

If my mother had expected the talisman to stay in her own family's hands, she ought to have at least left me a clue about why everyone wanted it. A transformation talisman wasn't that unique, right? Lots of faeries could alter their appearance or shapeshift, at the very least. And my conjuring those ice spikes wasn't so unusual for a Winter faerie.

Viola looked at me. "I can help, if you have questions."

"Honestly, I don't even know where to start." I considered the most urgent. "Firstly, my talisman. All I've managed to do so far is summon up ice. If someone stronger than Cedar attacks me, I'll need to know how to wield it as a weapon without relying on guesswork."

"I understand," she said. "I have some of her magic myself. She gifted it to me when she accepted me into her Court."

"Wait. I thought you had your own magic. I didn't know you could give part of your magic to someone else."

Her smile faltered. "Yes, it was part of our vow."

"Okay. Can't you tell me anything else?"

"No." She looked down. "I was afraid this would happen. When I was her servant, I was forbidden to even mention the sceptre to anyone else, including her own Court. I hoped that I'd be able to tell you more, as the heir, but my vow—" She broke off, as though struggling to find the right words. "All I can say is that now you're the talisman's wielder, you alone can unlock its secrets, if it chooses to share them with you."

"You talk about it like it's… alive, or something."

"They do say talismans possess a type of consciousness no

other item in Faerie does. They're forged from the hearts of our ancient trees, after all."

"Hmm." Maybe that accounted for the weird sense of not being completely in control of my own body when I'd first picked it up. "But you can't tell me what makes it so powerful, so deadly, that everyone wants me dead for it."

"I suspect that's precisely why I can't speak of it," Viola said. "She must have anticipated that the heir would be hunted, and many would lay their hands upon it. But you won the power. That alone proves you're worthy to unlock its secrets."

"Assuming it decides I am." I exhaled in a sigh. "Okay. I'll bet if I *do* guess, then you'll be able to tell me everything, right? But then, I'd already know. Seems a major flaw in the way these vows work."

She smiled faintly. "If you ask me, it's deliberate. On the Sidhe's part, anyway."

"Of course it is." I rolled my eyes. "All right. Can you at least give me a crash course in the families? I don't even know how many families there are, which ones might be targeting me—anything."

"We know it's mostly the Darkwaters who are responsible for the assassins," said Viola. "That family is possibly the biggest threat, because its leader has always coveted Lady Whitefall's power."

I nodded. "And the others?"

An echoing boom rang through the corridor.

Viola jumped. "Someone's trying to get in."

12

I ran ahead, readying my sceptre. If one of Cedar's friends had come to rescue him, then I'd have another prisoner *and* a means of getting answers. If it was an assassin, they shouldn't have been able to get through the gate, but I wouldn't rule anything out.

There was another knock on the door as I approached it, Viola at my side.

"Yes?" I asked sharply. "Who is it?"

"Are you Raine Whitefall?" called a male voice from outside.

"Yes." I opened the door, revealing the same sprite wearing the tuxedo who'd come to my flat. At least, it appeared to be the same one.

"The other border families would like to invite you to attend their Gathering, traditionally held to welcome a new family's leader. I trust you've already completed the necessary procedures."

I lowered the sceptre. "What?"

He arched a brow at my impolite mortal exclamation. I

should have probably prepared a verse or something. "Have you claimed your talisman?"

"Yes, not that it's any of your business."

"Then you're leader of your family, and you're invited to the Gathering. It takes place at sundown tonight, at the clearing where the territories meet."

"Yeah, I don't know about—"

"Tonight," he said, and vanished. Glitter fell where he'd disappeared, forming a piece of paper on the doorstep. Another invitation.

I closed the door on it, turning to Viola. "What's this Gathering?"

"An informal… well, gathering. Of all the families in the borderlands."

"Sounds delightful. By any chance, might it be a setup for someone to find a creative way to assassinate me?"

"The seal looks official." She picked up the invitation. "Don't forget none of them want the other families to get hold of the sceptre. They'll hide their hands until it's convenient. They wouldn't dare openly attack you at a Gathering, because it'd expose their strategies to the other families. Half of their games are head games."

"And I'll look weak if I don't show up?" If the rest of Faerie was anything to go by, I'd say yes. But if all the families were present, maybe I'd be able to figure out who was responsible for sending a legion of assassins after me. And which family Cedar belonged to, assuming it wasn't the same one.

Viola turned over the invitation in her hands. "Yes, unfortunately. I won't lie, going to the Gathering might put a stop to the rumours that we're an easy target."

My hands curled into fists. "Every family will be there, right? So is it on Summer or Winter territory?"

"The Gathering will take place in a neutral area that belongs to nobody in either Court."

Then I'd be able to openly confront the person responsible for screwing with me without trespassing on their own territory—but still be able to use magic. Opportunities like this one probably didn't come along very often.

"All right." I glared down at the invitation. "Fine. If they won't take no for an answer, maybe they'll listen with an audience. Will the Unseelie Queen or anyone be there?"

"Oh, no," said Viola. "Just the border families. We're not exactly friendly with the main Courts."

"I'll bet my mother alienated all of them." I sighed. "Great. Is there nobody who might be a potential ally? As Cedar helpfully pointed out, we don't have an army, and it looks like the rest of the court is frozen in the entrance hall."

"The Gathering might provide the chance to make new alliances, but bear in mind that your mother spent many years ensuring that none of the other families dared to approach her."

I raised my eyes to the ceiling. "Seriously?"

"It's what the Sidhe do, Raine," said Viola. "They forge alliances only to stab one another in the back. They kill, steal, and hoard power. That talisman is the only thing standing between certain families and total domination of the borderlands."

"Well," I said loudly, "they can just fucking try." I dropped my hand. "Firstly, where's my room? I want a shower and a change of clothes."

"Just use the sceptre." She waved a hand, and a door appeared in the wall. "You have to imagine clearly where you want to go, and the magic will follow."

"Let's see." I pointed it into the corridor beyond, and another door appeared on the opposite wall. I walked into the corridor and opened the new door I'd created, which led back into the entrance hall. With one wave of the sceptre after another, I created a whole row of doors. Each opened to the same spot in the entrance hall. "How's that possible?"

"Magic," said Viola, with a grin. "Let me show you the rest."

She did, taking me on a circuitous route that covered every room. I stared into ballrooms the size of mansions, sitting rooms with sofas big enough to seat an elephant, and a dining hall large enough for a banquet. Endless doors lined more corridors than could possibly fit into one building.

"I'm pretty sure this place isn't the same size on the outside as it is on the inside."

She spoke her default answer—"Magic"—and waved a hand, conjuring another door. "Same as this. There have never been any kitchen staff here—the food just appears. Check this out." She opened the door, which led into a spacious kitchen.

Plucking an apple off the sideboard, she took a bite out of it while showing me around. I grabbed one, too, suddenly starving. It'd been a hell of a day so far. "You ask it for what you want?" I asked, biting into the fruit.

"Yeah. To do that, you have to be specific, like with the doors."

I chewed on the apple. Sure tasted real, anyway. "I'll conjure up another birthday cake later."

"It's your birthday?"

"Two days ago." I took another bite. "I nearly got killed by a hellhound and found out I'm Sidhe. If I've had worse, I don't remember."

"I'll throw you a party," she said.

"I think I'll pass, thanks." I walked around eating snacks and examining the shiny kitchen. Everything seemed to run on magic here—or specifically, my mother's magic. "So there aren't any staff here at all?"

"Nope," said Viola. "I am, technically, but my job mostly involved spying on the other families and keeping our defences up."

"And what does this Gathering involve, exactly?"

"Remember the celebration in half-blood territory? That, but run by the Sidhe."

"We ended up nearly getting hit by arrows at the half-blood one." I stopped pacing. "Right. If I have to go to this party, I'm taking a shower first."

———

I didn't intend to sleep the day away, but a knock at my bedroom door woke me. I groaned, lifting my head blearily from the silken covering on the giant four-poster bed in my room. Viola had admitted she didn't actually know where my mother's suite had been, only that she wasn't allowed in, but the bedroom I'd selected was extravagant enough by itself. A thick white carpet covered the floor, while the walls were equally flawless, as white as freshly fallen snow. The furniture was carved from honey-coloured wood, and soft lights shone from stones built into the walls. Magic, most likely.

"Raine!" said Viola.

"Yes?" I rubbed my eyes, swinging my feet over the edge of the bed. I'd changed outfits and showered before collapsing onto the bed, and my hair had dried in clumps resembling a bird's nest. "Coming."

I opened the bedroom door to find her standing in the entrance hall.

"We have an hour." She waved a hand and another wooden door appeared. "Time to make you presentable. Do you have the talisman?"

"Of course." I'd fallen asleep with it next to me on the bed.

On the other side of the new door, floor-length mirrors covered one side of the room, and on the other were wardrobes bursting with what looked like the entire contents of a giant department store. "Don't I have enough clothes in the wardrobe in my room?"

"Not like this. C'mon. You don't want to go to the Gathering with your hair like that, do you?"

"Not sure I really want to go at all, to be honest."

Viola paused, one hand on the wardrobe door. "If you like, I can send a note saying you're too busy with your new court duties to attend."

"Can't imagine that'll do me any favours." I sighed. "I'll go, but I'm intending to find out who's responsible for sending assassins after me. There's no rule against using magic there, right?"

"No, but it's unwise to openly attack anyone."

"Good enough." I grinned. "I have the ability to transform anything. I don't need to hurt anyone to threaten them."

"At this rate, just looking at you will give the Sidhe a scare," Viola said wryly.

"Ha ha." She had a point, though. The floor-length mirrors showed what a mess I looked like. Bags under my eyes, white hair like a scarecrow's, and generally like I'd stolen the talisman in my hand, not claimed it. If I wanted to make an impression at the Gathering, I'd have to try harder to look like one of them.

Viola pulled the wardrobe door open. "Transforming your clothes is easy," she said. "Just direct your magic to them, and imagine what you'd like in their place. Whatever you choose is probably here."

"Wait," I said. "Faerie really needs to stop stealing my clothes. It's not like I have a ton of them."

"These are faerie-made clothes, so they can be switched

out at any time," she said. "You won't lose any of them. They'll just reappear in the wardrobe."

"Awesome. I'll never have to lift a finger again."

"It does save time," she admitted. "But takes the fun out of it. Will you at least let me style your hair?"

"Okay, but only because I'll probably freeze it if I use the sceptre on it." I tugged at a limp white strand. "It doesn't do much anyway."

"Oh, wait and see."

Ten minutes later, I stared into the floor-length mirror in disbelief. I didn't look like a scruffy human thief. Okay, I wasn't quite a faerie princess either, but Viola had somehow managed to make my poker-straight hair wavy, and in such a way that it looked natural, not that I'd applied a pair of curling tongs until I'd nearly burnt my hair off. An elegant blue dress swirled around my legs, not long enough to tread on, and compact enough not to get snagged on branches. Faerie was even more hazardous than the mortal realm. Though with the sceptre, I could probably transform the dress into something more practical if I ended up having to kill someone.

I looked nothing like me. Some part of me might have been pleased with that, but this was just another costume. Another performance. I thought I was done with it all.

I turned my back on the endless mirrors. "We should probably check on the thief before I go, in case he's plotting anything."

"He won't get out," Viola said. "The room's locked with magic, and I took his weapons away."

"Has he made any trouble?"

"He woke up an hour or so ago and asked for a snack." She shrugged. "We can't keep him here indefinitely, but he's being suspiciously polite."

"He was like that when I first met him. It's one of his acts."
I waved my sceptre at the wall. A door appeared, leading into
the corridor of the guest rooms.

"First on the left," she said.

"It'd help if these rooms were numbered." I pushed the
door, remembered it was locked, and stopped. "What did I do
with the key?"

"It'll appear in the pockets of whatever you're wearing,"
she said. "Unless you lose your clothes outside of Faerie.
Don't do that."

"I wasn't planning to." I found the key in the pocket of the
light jacket I wore over the dress.

Viola retreated into the dressing room. "Don't be too
long. And please don't start a fight with him and ruin your
hair."

Cedar cleared his throat. "What was that about losing
your clothes?"

I spun around, and he rose to his feet, eyebrows disap-
pearing into his hairline.

"Yeah, I know I'm playing faerie princess," I said before he
could speak. "Don't comment."

"I was going to say you look stunning, actually." His
throat moved as his eyes drank me in. This was hardly the
first time I'd been the object of scrutiny, but for some reason,
I didn't voice an objection. The echo of his magic's touch on
my skin shivered up my arm even though we were nowhere
near one another, accompanied by the scent of woodsmoke
underneath the perfume Viola had insisted I wear. *That's
what you get for bringing a Summer faerie into a Winter palace.*

"Thanks," I said, before remembering I was supposed to
be angry with him for wanting to destroy my talisman. "I
take it the wounds are better?"

He'd put his torn coat back on, which sort of surprised

me. I'd have expected him to steal clothes, at the very least, considering his own were covered in blood.

I was also certain, however, that in Faerie, Sidhe didn't look at members of the opposing Court the way he'd looked at me. I looked down, deliberately breaking eye contact.

"More or less." He shrugged, the movement a little stiff. "What's the occasion?"

"Faerie apparently requires fancy clothes for formal events."

He arched a brow. "Aren't I the only guest?"

"Dream on," I said. "I'm going out, actually. I've been invited to attend the Gathering of the border families. I'm told it's compulsory."

"What?" He looked alarmed. "There hasn't been a Gathering in over a year."

"Since before she died, right? Well, the Whitefall family has a new heir, so apparently it's my duty to go. Since they'll think I'm a coward if I don't. So I figured I'd ask if you could tell me what to expect. Specifically—those assassins. Who exactly is commanding them, and will they be there?"

"I've told you my suspicions," he said. "At least two of the families have already proved they want you dead, and if you go, I can guarantee at least one of them will attempt another attack on you. You'll never get near Lady Darkwater, if she is indeed the one commanding the assassins. The Sidhe— they're not like half-bloods. They expect you to be as ruthless as they are, or perish."

"You could make a fortune in theatre in the mortal realm. *Or perish.*" I rolled my eyes at him. "Unfortunately, you're not fooling anyone here, so drop the act and sit still like a good little prisoner. Unless you have something to say that's actually useful."

He sat up straight, anger flashing in his eyes. "I'm not acting."

"You pretended to be someone you weren't, Cedar. That's basically the same thing."

"When did I—?"

"Hello?" I said sharply. "*Oh, I'll come and help you carry that hellhound, like I'm not plotting to steal from you the moment your back's turned.* You make me sick."

His face paled. "I saw someone who needed help—"

"And robbed her. Don't bother, Cedar. Whatever your excuses are, I've probably heard them all before."

"I'm not making excuses. You've never been bound to a vow, have you?"

"No, but I've been screwed over enough times not to take a word you say at face value. Just try to imagine what it feels like to know you're nothing more than a means to an end to someone."

"I know exactly how that feels, Raine," he said. "I caught the hellhound's trail when I went into the mortal realm, but I didn't realise you were the target until I reached your house. By then, it was too late to hide myself. I spent the whole night patrolling in case they tried it again."

I folded my arms. "If you think that makes up for the stunt you pulled at the market, you're mistaken."

"Perhaps not, but at least hear me out. I wasn't the only one watching you at the market. There were others. And your magic is particularly potent. My own magic isn't powerful, yet I still sensed the talisman when you tried to sell it. The reaction would have reached everyone with Sidhe blood in the area. If I hadn't tried to get it away from you, the others would have. Unlike them, I didn't want you dead."

So he could sense my magic the way I could his, after all. It must be second nature to him, like everything else in this world. His excuses might actually have worked if his intentions had been honourable from the start, but they hadn't been. He was a fake, whichever way he tried to spin the story.

"The assassins already knew who I was," I said. "You knew they'd shoot arrows at me with or without the talisman."

"I didn't know they were after you when I was at the market. After the hellhound, I figured there was a lone Sidhe with a grudge—few others have the skills to command one of those creatures. And whatever you've learned about the talisman isn't enough for you to survive in battle against a Sidhe."

Maybe he's right... or not. "It still wasn't your decision to make."

"No, well. I apologise for that."

I shrugged. Words meant little, when he could twist them as well as any Sidhe. "If you think I'll consider letting you out, it won't work. You're acting on someone's orders, and I intend to find out who. After this farce of a Gathering, I'm coming back to question you." And if it turned out he really was nobility in disguise, I wondered if his trigger-happy Sidhe overlords would accept his life in trade for leaving me the hell alone.

"Raine!" said Viola urgently. "We have to leave. We're running late."

I hadn't heard her reappear behind me. "On my way." I stepped back.

Cedar pushed to his feet. "If you go, you'll forfeit the sceptre to whoever bests you first."

"Thanks for your unwanted input. I'll see you later."

I shut the door in his face, locking it for good measure. His words whirled through my head, threatening to distract me from my mission. He might have lied, but he wasn't an outright enemy. I was about to walk into a whole crowd of them, with nothing but my wits and a talisman I could barely use. But I wouldn't back down.

"He'd better not get out," I said to Viola. "Unless we take him to the Gathering to trade back to his family?"

"Considering we don't know which it is, it's probably not wise," Viola said. "To most of them, one life isn't worth that sceptre, especially a half-blood's."

I grimaced. "Well, *this* half-blood isn't going to take any shit from them. Let's get this over with."

13

The dress swirled around my legs as we walked outside. "Is there a shortcut to the Gathering?" The cold breeze ruffled my newly curled hair. I didn't particularly want to show up looking like a windswept human. The Sidhe must have some exclusive magic to constantly look pristine, because I sure as hell didn't have it.

"Sure. I'll do it."

Viola reached out her hands and made motions like she was opening a pair of double doors. The snow-coated path contracted and expanded, turning into another shadowy path, flanked by tall oak trees. Cold, but without the snow.

"There are a few shortcuts like that on the territory," she told me. "I can show you them later."

"Sure. Might come in handy." Assuming I stayed. Leaving Cedar in the palace while I went back to the mortal realm wouldn't be a good move, but I wasn't even certain *how* to get back, short of begging my way through the rift again. I still owed the Little Person a favour, and I wasn't looking forward to delivering on it. Bringing every half-faerie here when none of them had the ability to walk out under their own power had seemed inconsiderate of the Sidhe, but now, the notion took on a sinister edge.

In fact… it meant we were all effectively prisoners here.

A chill raced down my back as I recalled Cedar's words. Was I walking into a trap? *Considering it's Faerie, I'm gonna say yes.*

I just needed to keep my wits about me, not let the sceptre out of my sight, and resist the impulse to transform this blasted dress into jeans and a T-shirt.

Luckily, the path was sheltered enough that the wind didn't get through, and I reached the end without incident. Eerie darkness and shadows wrapped around the forest, opening to reveal a clearing that was at least the size of a football stadium. Moonlight reflected on a raised platform, and as I drew closer, it became clear that there were several of them. One for each family? I definitely wasn't ready for this.

"This is our family's area," said Viola, confirming my guess.

"Speaking of," I said, "where's the rest of the family? Is it really just the two of us? They left after she died?"

She nodded. "Yeah. It's pretty common—there was no heir, after all. But it won't help the situation."

"Maybe I'll transfigure some of the trees into people."

"You can't create a person," she whispered. "Even magic has its limits. When it comes to that sceptre, you can't turn something into a living being."

"What about when I froze Cedar in ice?"

"You transformed the moisture in the air."

"Nice." Unfortunately, I wasn't a hundred percent sure I could repeat the performance. My iron knife was a heavy weight inside the inner pocket of the short coat I wore over the dress, in case the sceptre didn't work. I kept the talisman in my hands, though instincts told me to hide that, too. *I need to let them know I'm not afraid to wield it.* Keeping the talisman within sight would reduce the chances of losing it to another thief.

Maybe now I'd find out which family had sent that hobgoblin to steal it. And which had sent the assassins. Perhaps the same one.

Viola hovered next to me. She'd dressed in a stunning silver-and-white number that glimmered whenever she moved. She was better at playing the part of a faerie princess than I was. I looked like a kid who'd stolen her mother's wedding dress to play in. Viola appeared poised and confident, but her hands were shaking. *Why?* I was the one who had to take centre stage when I'd rather hide backstage forever.

"So I have to… stand on the stage?" I asked. "Why is nobody else here?" Had I been stood up by an entire group of Sidhe?

"They'll be here. They like to make a performance out of their arrival."

"Great. Well, I won't be dancing."

"I think it'd impress them if you did the same dance as the Gathering," she said. "But we need to show we're a force to be reckoned with. Especially to the Hornbeams."

Viola had listed the major families, and the Hornbeams had been one I'd actually heard of—because Robin had said they'd claimed him.

"The Hornbeams have a split territory, right?" I said.

"Between Lord and Lady Hornbeam, yes," she said. "One owns each half."

"So they live on opposite ends of the territory? Sounds like a happy marriage."

"A thousand years is a long time."

I couldn't argue there, but her words reminded me how

out of my depth I was. The Hornbeams had ruled their territory for a *thousand years*. I'd barely been here a day.

"Don't worry," she added. "They're ruthless, but it's the Darkwater family who sent those assassins. They're who we need to watch. Of course, the family leader herself will deny ever being involved. They never actually *admit* to wanting to steal power from one another. This family is seen as the weak link."

"Not for long." I wished I could believe the words as easily as I spoke them.

"I hope you're right. It's hard to sleep through people trying to knock the palace down."

I glanced down at the sceptre. It looked so innocuous. "As long as it's claimed me, they won't make a direct challenge on it, right?"

"I wouldn't have thought so, but you never know. Out here away from the main Courts, especially with some of the families weaker than before…"

"You're not helping."

"Sorry. I just wanted to warn you not to *ever* let the talisman go. Especially near any Sidhe. They might not even waste time killing you before they claim the power. Or they might challenge you to a contest, and the winner gets the loser's talisman. Of course, by making a display that blatant, they'd be running the risk of being publicly rejected by the talisman."

"And it might kill them," I added. "But I think my brother, at least—he'd risk it. Hope he doesn't come here. Though at least then I'd have more of a showing." I looked at the stage again. "I'd like to know how she managed to lose everyone else in the palace. They weren't bound by vows at all? I mean, aside from the ones she turned into statues."

"No. I was her only servant or spy, and she hired me when there was hardly anyone left."

"Weird." The circumstances of her death were odd, too—and there was an obvious question I hadn't asked. "When she died, why didn't someone steal the talisman right away?"

"Because she didn't have it with her when she died."

I blinked. "Seriously?"

Viola nodded. "She left it in the palace, and all her magic was contained inside it. That's why some of the families thought *I* killed her, at first. I was nowhere near where her body was consumed in magic, and because it was clear the talisman hadn't chosen me, they stopped. But it made tracking the heirs down more difficult than I'd have liked. I had to keep throwing the other families off the trail."

Music rang through the trees, vaguely like harps and pianos mixed in with a drumbeat that made the ground shake.

"Someone's here." I walked up to the stage, hesitating with my foot on the bottom step. "You're not coming?"

"I can't stand there with you."

"Why?"

Distress clear on her face, she said, "Because my former family are going to be here. If they see me beside you… it wouldn't help the situation for either of us."

"It's not the Darkwater family?"

She shook her head. "No. But they'll be watching. You'll have to be careful. Just try to pretend you're there in the sceptre's room again. Don't show any weakness. They'd kill you for it."

"I figured as much."

She hugged me quickly, careful not to knock my hair out of place. "I'm sorry you had to do this so early on."

"It was bound to happen eventually, right?"

But the timing—the Sidhe knew I was here, in Faerie. Who'd initiated it? Which family wanted my attention?

The music grew louder. "Best get onstage," said Viola. "If

you stand here, it'll look like you're hiding. I'll put on a glamour, and I'll be close by."

"Okay."

It's a performance, I told myself, climbing the steps on shaky legs. I imagined a curtain in front, ready to lift when the audience appeared. Except I was both player and spectator, waiting for whatever show Faerie threw at me next. I didn't used to mind the spotlight—I'd lived for it. But the stage lights painted over truths, created a new reality. I'd pretend to mortals that I was there for their entertainment, that I existed only for them, and Robin had acted like the same applied to him.

Why in hell was I thinking about him now? Probably because of the music. The source wasn't obvious—it seemed to come from all around us, an eerily beautiful symphony that sounded like faerie music designed to ensnare mortals. Part of me was tugged towards it, my legs itching to dance of their own accord, but I planted my feet firmly apart, my hands clenched around the sceptre. It glowed blue, maybe in reassurance. *You won't get me so easily.*

Sure enough, dancers appeared in rows—winged Summer faeries, moving in the space between the stages in an alluring pattern, dressed in leaf green and shining gold. I lifted my gaze, determined not to get swept up in a spell. A burst of green light flared up over the stage directly opposite mine, the one Viola had pointed out as the Hornbeam stage. The leading borderland family of the Seelie Court was about to arrive. Green banners flew high, and more Summer faeries circled the stage, glittering piskies floating above carrying lights. Flashes of green conjured up clouds of multi-coloured birds, which fell in a coordinated curtain over the stage.

A crowd appeared upon it as though they'd been there all

along. Rows and rows of them, filling the entire stage in a sea of green and gold.

Their leader stepped forwards. His face was hard to see from this angle, though it was probably down to him being Sidhe. The more powerful the Sidhe, the less human they seemed—though if anything, they were far too much. A screaming exclamation point in the middle of the universe that demanded everyone pay attention. In this realm, more even than in the mortal realm, Sidhe appeared made of a substance not quite solid, but like angels cloaked in flesh that barely contained their radiance.

The mortal part of me shrank away, repulsed and entranced all at once by the raw power pouring off both him and the woman at his side. Of course—there were two of them, husband and wife, both leaders of the Hornbeam family. They stood side by side, not looking at one another, though their green-and-gold finery matched. Not every faerie chose a permanent partner, and from what I'd heard, a fair few Sidhe found the concept of spending a literal eternity with the same person tedious. Their habit of hoarding magic and growing paranoia with age probably didn't help.

Half-bloods filled the space in front of them, ranging in age from teenagers to adults. So one or both of the Hornbeams had had affairs with mortals. The half-bloods were clearly placed in an inferior position, and with two ruling Sidhe, they'd never be allowed to ascend to a leadership position. But there were so *many* of them. My own stage felt bare by comparison. I held myself upright, knowing that any second now, Lord and Lady Hornbeam would notice me.

The dancers' performance reached its peak, and a crescendo of applause struck up from Summer's side. If every family put on a display like that, I couldn't be more unprepared if I'd come in my pyjamas. Apparently I should have brought an entourage. The dancers bowed, then glided to the front of the stage. That formation was awfully famil-iar. *Wait a second.*

I picked him out two rows from the front. Robin had *told* me he'd been claimed by this family. I hadn't known they'd let him organise the entertainment. He hadn't mentioned bringing his entire performance group here, either. Now he was allowed to perform for royalty? He wore his confident pose, the way he had when we'd brought the house down together. When everything made sense.

Nothing about this made the remotest amount of sense. Why bring half-bloods from a mortal theatre here, even a well-known one that attracted the richest clientele in the city? Not money. The Sidhe didn't care for mortal trinkets, even though they found our fragility entertaining. As my gaze travelled across the performers, and the audience, understanding clicked into place. This was where we belonged—performers, and soldiers. Lesser. Not standing up here on a stage meant for a Sidhe Lady in everything but name. They *hated* that I was here, like an equal.

Had someone brought in Robin on purpose, wanting to get to me? It seemed a petty and vindictive thought, yet the situation was oddly suspicious all the same. With all the mortal realm at their disposal, why pick him? He was nobody special, not compared to the Sidhe.

But... if he's here, then he'll know a way home. Surely the family wouldn't allow him and his performers to stay here in Faerie. They'd have a way back into the mortal realm, and if they did—that was my ticket home.

If I swallowed my pride and asked him, obviously.

Movement in the bushes signalled the arrival of another family. Hobgoblins ran through the gaps between the stages, and rows of half-blood soldiers followed. Flanking the Sidhe approaching the stage were two great hulking trolls, the largest pure-blooded ones I'd seen, filling the entire back of the stage. Between them walked three Sidhe—no, one Sidhe and two other faeries. Winter. They passed underneath a rippling curtain of water that didn't leave so much as a splash. The Sidhe Lady leading the show wore a dress that resembled water, too, though as she drew closer to the crowd, the water flow ceased and the dress froze in ice, coating her body.

The Sidhe really needed to tone down the special effects. Once you got over the brightness, though, there weren't actually that many people on her stage compared to the Seelie contingent. The soldiers, though... maybe this was Viola's family, though their uniform looked similar to the assassins' and she'd already said they weren't from the same family. No performers or dancers came with them. Just a handful of soldiers... and my brother.

My brother stood beside the leader of what I suspected must be the Darkwater family. The family which wanted me dead.

His gaze connected with mine, and a cruel smile tugged his lips.

I attempted a cold stare, but the betrayal hit harder than I'd expected, considering I'd *known* he was working against me. But to side with another family? That was low.

His gaze lingered for a second, filled with contempt and hatred that took my breath away. I did my best to glare back. *You're no brother of mine.* Attempted murder outweighed blood, even here where blood mattered more than anything. And for all his position next to the Lady of the Darkwaters, he was still half-blood. The talisman had picked me instead.

I sure as hell didn't feel superior, though, standing alone on the stage. I didn't *want* to rule over a kingdom, or even a piece of one. The Sidhe might be the reason I existed, but they'd wrecked Dad's sanity and abandoned us. This wasn't a burden any half-blood should have to bear. We weren't made to rule.

Do you really believe that? Is it right? I'd never wondered. I mean, the Sidhe were immortal. That fact alone made them superior to the rest of us. But while our blood might be inferior, a talisman had chosen me regardless. No wonder they wanted me dead.

Others began to appear on the stages, some with a performance, some without. Loud music and voices filled every inch of the space, but I stood in a pocket of silence, painfully aware of how alone I was even with Viola hidden behind me.

Finally… all the border families were here.

Lord Hornbeam spoke first. "I'd like to formally start this Gathering. The families have not met for quite some time—and certainly not with all of us present."

All eyes flickered in my direction. Great.

"Indeed," he remarked, "I hardly saw our newest heir over there, hidden in the shadows. Alone."

Laughter rippled through the Summer contingent, and my face heated. I wanted to point the sceptre at him and turn him into a walrus. All Sidhe sounded similar, their voices like achingly beautiful melodies even when they were insulting you. I preferred half-bloods with their slight imperfections to perfect, cruel creatures like him.

"That's hardly a nice welcome," said Lady Hornbeam. She turned to face me, and my eyes burned like I'd looked directly at a supernova. A force of nature, brimming with power strong enough to shake the earth. No wonder they never came to the mortal realm. They'd crack it in two. "Welcome, Lady Whitefall."

I didn't smile, nor did I expect to receive anything other than contempt disguised as a welcome. A quick glance at the crowd confirmed my suspicions. The others' expressions barely concealed ambition, anger, lust—probably for the sceptre. What could it contain that would surpass even their magic? They *had* power. Maybe they'd never have enough to be satisfied. But the idea of having power for the sake of power made no sense to me. *At least that probably means I'm safe from turning into one of them.* I couldn't read the Sidhe's expressions, though—they were too far away, and too unknowable.

Once they'd finished their pathetically deferential welcomes, Lady Hornbeam turned to me again. "Do you have anything you'd like to say, Lady Whitefall?"

I knew the right words to say, even if they didn't sound like me. "It's a pleasure." My voice came out more confident than I sounded, amplified almost as loud as the Sidhe's. Had my sceptre amplified my voice, or the general magic in the air around here? "I'm delighted to join you here for this Gathering. May I ask the occasion?"

"Merely to celebrate finally having a representative on the stage for the Whitefall family again," said Lord Hornbeam, and there was a murmur of similar comments from the other Sidhe. Everyone seemed to follow their family's lead, I'd noticed. So the Hornbeams were the big deal around here. And complete pricks. As long as I knew where I stood, I'd deal with this.

Lady Hornbeam stepped forward. "If there's nothing more to say—let the celebrations commence."

Summer's dancers leaped into performance again, while the air between the stages rippled and distorted. Suddenly there lay two tables where there'd been nothing before, stacked with enough food to feed an entire city.

I hung back, reluctant to join in. Here, they could spike the food with anything and pretend it was part of the fun. Considering I didn't know where it'd come from, I wouldn't touch a thing. This was the real, Faerie version of the meeting in half-blood territory. I definitely wouldn't be dancing on any tables this time.

Viola stepped up behind me. "I wouldn't eat anything."

"Figured as much," I muttered. "How long do I have to stay?"

"Not long. They aren't expecting you to."

"That's not a good thing."

"They don't actually want to be here," she said in a low voice. "The ceremony is so they can see what you're capable of. And get the measure of you. You did great, by the way, considering how they tried to intimidate you."

"Yeah," I said out of the corner of my mouth. "Lord and Lady Hornbeam hate each other, don't they? They're both obnoxious, so I get why."

She stifled a laugh. "They are. Everyone knows none of their heirs are biologically related to both of them, but it won't change who inherits the power. The chosen heir is the one with the strongest magic."

"Assuming they die."

"They're both over a thousand years old. I wouldn't hold your breath."

I shook my head imperceptibly. "I'm glad to be mortal right now. I think a family that extensive would be a nightmare to keep track of. What do they do at Christmas... you don't celebrate that here. Right?"

"No, but your mother knew I did, so she let me put up a tree."

"That sounds weirdly nice."

"I said she wasn't all bad."

"Unlike my brother."

She stiffened. "Oh."

"Did you know?"

"Of course not. But it explains where he got his training

in magic. And his knowledge of this realm. He's been rejected by the sceptre once already. He won't try to steal it now."

"Someone else might." I thought of Summer—of Cedar. Did he belong to the Hornbeams? Obviously, he'd know about their designs on the sceptre…

"Someone's coming this way," said Viola.

I peered over the crowd, my heart sinking. Robin. The fool. Did he know the risks of confronting me here? I debated slipping away or pointedly ignoring him… but maybe he knew when the Sidhe messengers would next visit the mortal realm.

"Viola, can you leave me for a second? I have to talk to him alone."

"Sure. I'll be right behind you."

Viola vanished, and Robin stopped next to me.

"What?" I asked sharply.

"I—I thought I'd offer you an explanation."

"Looked pretty obvious to me where your loyalties lie."

"I couldn't not perform for them," he said. "They're—you know who they are."

"Yes, I do. I also know you probably shouldn't be talking to me. But—tell me. Do you know if anyone's going into the mortal realm? I have to get back. Tomorrow, if possible."

He bowed his head. "I'm leaving tomorrow afternoon. I can come and find you first."

I wanted to believe him. The part of me who'd followed him around for years, who had given him everything, wanted to believe. He was my only link to the mortal world. To escaping this madness before it was too late.

"I'll think about it," I said. "Go. I can't be seen talking to you." I put on my iciest expression, certain that if the Hornbeams had spotted us, one of us would face the consequences.

He stepped back, hurt and indecision etched on his face, but bowed his head and ducked back into the crowd.

A faint whistling noise came from behind me. Only my thief's ears, trained to the slightest sound, could pick up on it. Swiftly, I moved to the left, as an arrow embedded itself in the ground beside me.

I whipped around, swinging the sceptre in an arc, and sent a blast of magic at the trees behind me. Ice spread up them, coating their surface—but no assassin appeared.

Silence. The music had stopped, and I felt all the others' eyes on me. Slowly, I swivelled back to face them. The arrow protruded from the ground in plain view. Everyone watched —each family head included—waiting for my response.

This was the real test.

I reached out and picked up the arrow, holding it so that everyone could see. "Is anyone going to admit to firing this at me?"

Silence spread through the crowd. I turned to the Darkwaters, first, then let my gaze travel across all the families, not allowing anyone to escape it. Some looked uneasy. Some looked falsely concerned. The Sidhe, of course, wore blank, beautiful masks impossible to see through. They didn't lie— *couldn't* lie—but I doubted they'd fired on me themselves. No —if a Sidhe was behind it, they'd ordered one of their people to shoot at me instead.

"It's very lucky for you that it missed," said Lord Hornbeam.

"Fortune shines on you tonight," added his wife.

Yeah, right.

I glared at them. "Good, because whoever shot this is going to get something more painful than an arrow through the head, when I catch them."

Silence reigned. Nobody started the music again, and it hit me that I'd won myself a chance to leave on my own terms. I turned my icy glare to full blast, then took a deliberate step back, away from the crowd.

My hand went numb, pain tingling up my arm. *Huh?*

Oh no. Oh shit, no. The arrow must be poisoned.

Sweat trickled down my forehead. I kept my head high, trembling, my body rigid, not daring to move in case I gave away my weakness. I was sure my knees would fold and my body pass into unconsciousness, but I managed to hold on as I addressed the crowd. "Clearly, I'm not welcome here. If the person who fired this arrow doesn't admit they did so, I'll have to use this."

I held up the sceptre. The prize everyone here wanted. A collective intake of breath rippled through the crowd. Its magic pulsed through my hand, dulling the numb effect. But not enough. My head swam, and the Sidhe's faces looked distorted.

Viola came up behind me and whispered, "Raine—we need to go. You'll be dead in ten minutes if not—"

I held up my hand to silence her, using the other to point the sceptre at the gathering crowd. Blue light shone over my head, enveloping the low-hanging branches of the nearest tree.

Every single leaf dropped at once, transformed into powder the instant it hit my magic. The fragments spiralled to the ground.

"The next person to try to kill me will get a worse fate than that," I said.

Then I walked away.

As the trees closed in, the world swayed.

Just... a few... steps.

Viola spoke my name, and I was falling...

14

The Sidhe's faces followed me into my dreams, morphing into terrifying monsters beneath their stunning exteriors. Every time I tried to run, the arrow stuck to my hand, locking into place, and hideous creatures tore at me, screaming words I didn't know. At the centre was a woman with a gaping hole where her head should be. I recoiled in horror, clutching the sceptre—which had also turned into an empty hole. The dark swallowed me up, and I kept falling.

No pain awaited when I woke. A dazzling display of lights blurred my vision, until they resolved themselves into the absurdly over-decorated bedroom. Viola hovered beside the bed, relief flashing across her face when she saw I was awake.

"You slept through the night. It's morning."

"I'm alive."

"I managed to get you back here in time to slow the poison."

I sat upright, surprised nothing hurt. *I need to get home. Sidhe knew how long had passed this time around.* "I have to go… find Robin."

"I don't know who you're talking about," said Viola. "I patched you up the best I could, but I've never been a good healer. Your own magic should help, though."

I cursed, sweat trickling down my forehead. "The performers. I need to meet with them. They're all half-blood and live in the mortal realm, so they'll be going home today. If they haven't already."

"You know the performers?" I could almost see her mind ticking.

My cheeks burned. "Yes. I was with them. A long time ago. I don't know why they're suddenly dancing for the Hornbeams, but there's no way they live here. Robin said they didn't."

"Weren't they claimed as half-bloods?"

"Robin was. He—he belongs to the Hornbeams, but it must be distant. He's not that important."

"Oh, the guy from yesterday? Old lover?"

"You could say that. I'd rather sell the bloody sceptre than ask for his help, but I just wanted to see my dad again. That's all."

"You will." She held something I hadn't seen before—a single white flower, which she turned over and over in her palms. I watched the movement, putting two and two together.

"You saw her last night, right? That's where you disappeared to."

She nodded. "The Gatherings are the only time the families come together, and there hasn't been one since before she died. Besides, your mother didn't know about us."

"I suppose she didn't check you had any attachments at your last home before hauling you off to the palace." Once again, I was reminded that my own mother had been part of these sickening games. Maybe she'd killed members of other families in a similar manner.

"No. It's my fault for breaking the soldier's vow in the first place. The rules were a little complicated."

I frowned. "A little? I thought humans were confusing. Were you not allowed relationships at all?"

"No, not even with each other. Our mission was to defend the territory, nothing more. Service was for ten years, minimum. I was a teenager when I signed up."

"That's ridiculous."

She shrugged. "I can't say I didn't know what I was getting into." She paused and sighed. "I never thought—it sounds so melodramatic, but have you ever met someone you just *clicked* with, as if you knew one another forever when it's only been five minutes? Even though you're acting against your better judgement just by thinking about it?"

"Sure." Once. None of my other relationships had had that *spark* Robin and I had, as much as I'd tried to bury my feelings by pursuing people who were utterly unlike him. Amongst others, these had included a shapeshifting half-faerie who turned into a wolf when she was annoyed, and a selkie girl who couldn't leave the water. After a kelpie had taken a liking to her and almost drowned me, I'd called the relationship off. Robin didn't have a monopoly on my history of bad romantic decisions, but Viola didn't need to know all of it.

"If she's waited this long for you, it must be worth it," I told her. "It's cute, actually. You hereby have my permission to sneak off and visit her as long as it takes me to figure out how to undo this vow."

"Thanks." She brightened. "I'm more worried about her family, really. Nobody likes the Whitefalls."

"Of course not. They tried to poison me at my own welcome meeting." I grimaced. "I need to be ready to leave. Robin's going back to the mortal realm this afternoon. I might not get another chance for a while."

"I'd have thought he'd want to stay here. Running away from the Hornbeams—it's not a good idea."

"I don't think they see him as that important." His nervous behaviour at the Gathering didn't add up with the way he usually acted towards the Sidhe. He and the others had probably come here expecting to be showered in riches. Instead, they'd been paraded like outsiders brought in for entertainment. Not worthy of standing onstage even with the other half-bloods. He'd had to take the only offer he'd been given, otherwise he'd have been forced into it.

My throat closed up, and my hands trembled in my lap.

"Are you okay?"

"I don't have healing magic, right?"

She shook her head. "It's common, but your mother didn't have it."

"There's something I haven't told you," I whispered.

"What is it?"

"Magic. I don't have it. Well, I didn't. Not before I picked up the talisman. Other Winter faeries can summon a snowstorm at twelve. I've never managed a single snowflake. Even with the talisman—I'm not as strong as they are."

"Raine, it doesn't matter what your magic was like before. The talisman chose you. You're amongst the most powerful Sidhe in this part of Faerie. Maybe even stronger than Lady Hornbeam—*don't* let her find out…"

"The bloody Hornbeams." I groaned. "They saw me fall, for sure."

"No, they didn't. You covered your tracks."

I sagged against the bed. "Thanks. If they know I'm weak…"

"They don't," she said. "I was afraid something like that might happen. I didn't know they'd poison the arrow, though. That was underhanded. The other families won't be talking about the Darkwater family in a favourable light now."

"You think it was them? The Darkwaters?" I rubbed my forehead. "My brother. Why would a rival family take him in to begin with?"

"Because they're weak," Viola said. "They have an endless supply of assassin half-bloods, but very few Sidhe remaining."

"Oh." I frowned. "Do I really have no other relatives? How's that possible when Sidhe can't die?"

"I don't know. Lady Whitefall never told me. I knew there was no heir, but she expected to live forever. They all do. The heirs are all for show. They don't actually get to do much, especially the half-bloods. Just stay here, as long as they say so." Her eyes were haunted and sad. She wasn't free, and neither was the woman she loved.

I closed my eyes then opened them again. "Sorry. You have it worse than I do."

"Nobody shot me. I'll be fine." She forced a smile. "I feel like I'm tainting your mother's memory."

"Oh, it's already tainted," I said. "I was born here, actually, but she erased all my memories of her, like she did to my dad."

"She did?"

I scrubbed a hand over my face. "For all I know, she took my magic away herself."

"I… wouldn't have thought she'd have done that," said Viola. "She might have been ruthless, but she treated me well, and would have treated her children like royalty."

Hmm. "I don't know. But she wrecked my family, and now she's doing a spectacular job of screwing up my life, too. If assassins are gonna keep coming after me, I need to at least get my dad somewhere safe. *Where*, I've no idea."

But there was only one possible place: here. I could barely

stop him from wandering off and ruining the neighbours' property, and I dreaded to think what Faerie would do to him.

Not to mention I'd have to break the news that my mother was dead.

But staying here would mean staying a part of the families' games. They'd already lured me away from the palace once. I couldn't hide here forever. Their stunning facades covered attempted murder, and they were probably already concocting their next excuse to get me out into the forest, away from the protective boundaries of my own territory.

"You know… it wasn't always like this," she said. "It used to be possible for members of rival families to be friends with one another. In the time I served in the army, we were only ordered to fight against beasts crossing the boundaries into our own territory, not assassinate people."

"Hmm. But you served another family? I didn't see an army on Winter's side."

Her gaze dropped. "A lot of families replaced soldiers with assassins, from lesser families, or half-bloods without any fae family."

"And my brother."

"If he lived with the Darkwater family before, they'll be angry with him if they find out he tried to claim the sceptre. I doubt he wants to stay with them."

"Nope, he just wants to steal the sceptre. They probably offered him a deal. A shot at me in exchange for eternal servitude, or something. You know, for all the power they have, the Sidhe seem downright miserable."

"Isn't that the curse of immortality?" Her lips twitched as if in amusement.

"Guess it is." I climbed to my feet, reaching for the sceptre on the bedside table. Its glow brightened at my touch. "Right. I'm going to change, then I'll see if Robin shows up."

I looked down at myself. I didn't wear the dress any longer, but the same outfit I'd been wearing before I'd transformed it. Like Cinderella at the ball, it'd transformed back to how it'd been before.

I felt more like myself after a shower and something to eat, but sifting through the impossible variety of clothes in the wardrobe seemed like a monumental task. I wished I could donate them to charity in the mortal realm, but knowing my mother's tricks, I didn't dare let them near humans. I selected a simple pair of trousers and shirt, made of fine materials which were soft to touch. My knife had survived the transformation, at least. I tucked it into my waistband, and put the key to the palace in my pocket. Closing the wardrobe, I looked around for a clock, but there didn't seem to be any in the palace at all. It'd be useful to know what time Robin would appear. The lack of a connection with the mortal realm was even more annoying. I wanted to know if Dad had made it home. Not to mention how much time had passed since I'd last been there. I never had figured out how to turn anything in the palace into a source of money to pay our looming rent bills, and at this rate, I'd end up missing the deadline.

A door slammed outside my room, and Viola yelled, "He's gone."

I ran to join her, finding she'd opened a door from the guest room corridor. "What?"

"He's gone. Cedar got out."

"Shit. When?"

"I don't know. It might have been in the middle of the night. By the *Sidhe*," she cursed. "Don't move. He might have left a trap. Or stolen something."

Behind her, the guest suite lay open. I walked into the room, my heart sinking. Bloody bandages lay on the floor, but other than that, it was as though nobody had been in here.

I looked at Viola. "Where could he have gone?"

"Surely not far. He doesn't know the way around."

"I shouldn't have brought him here." Or rather, I should have pushed my misgivings aside and shut him in the dungeon. "How'd he get out?"

"No clue."

Viola and I walked down the corridor, checking every room, opening doors to each area of the palace. Surely he'd have got hopelessly lost wandering around alone, unless he'd found an open window. He was certainly good at climbing on roofs and scaling buildings, even if his magic wouldn't work quite as well on my territory as it would in a neutral zone. As for his own territory—

Oh, yeah. "Did you get any clues at the Gathering as to which family he belongs to?"

"I didn't," she said. "I'm not so convinced he's important now. Surely he'd have been mentioned at the Gathering, or someone would have come looking for him by now. Even if he is acting alone."

"Hmm." The image of those band-shaped scars on his arms flashed through my head again. Someone had hurt him. Someone powerful… and from Summer.

As we reached the end of the second corridor, magic buzzed through me without warning, and my talisman glowed blue. "Whoa. What's that?"

"A reaction." Viola's eyes widened. "There's someone outside."

She opened the way into the entrance hall, next to the statues. They really were creepily life-like, and a reminder that even Viola hadn't been entirely honest with me. What'd my mother done, turned her entire court into ice? Was that where they'd disappeared to? I didn't know how to undo *that* spell, let alone deal with whoever'd knocked on the door. Hopefully it was Robin.

"All right." I hurried over and opened the door, holding my sceptre in case it was an enemy.

"Raine," Robin burst out, eyes wide. "Go. Run. You should leave this realm."

I blinked at him. "What?"

"I said you should leave. This realm. Now."

I laughed, more perplexed than anything. "Er, Robin, wasn't I supposed to meet you this afternoon to go home anyway?"

Green flashed in his eyes, and he took another step forwards. "My Lady insists."

My heart sank. "Not you, too. Is it the Hornbeam family? They want the sceptre?"

"If I don't deliver, they'll punish me." He held up his hands, giving me a glimpse of a pair of iron bands circling his wrists. "I need the sceptre, that's all. But you can escape if you go into the mortal realm. Just give it to me, and you'll be able to go. I swear I won't hurt you."

My heart raced, and Viola tugged urgently at my arm.

"I can't." I looked at him, feeling more pity than anything. His whole performance had been about sucking up to the Sidhe, and look where it'd got him. "If I go with you, we'll all probably die. If I give you the sceptre, do you really think she'd let a half-blood stay in control of the Whitefall family indefinitely? Do you think she won't chase us both out, or turn us into servants?"

"Sorry, Raine."

Green energy shot from his palms at me. I raised the sceptre in defence, and an arrow flew over Robin's head.

"Assassins!" yelled Viola. "Get away from here, you scum."

Robin lunged at me and grabbed for the sceptre. I kicked him away, as another arrow shot past. Across from the palace, the path led to the neutral area where we'd been last night. I hadn't rearranged the territory after the Gathering because I'd been unconscious, and I'd forgotten the path straddled several territories. The enemy was firing at me without actually leaving their own territory. I could stay inside until they ran out of arrows—or hit Robin—or teach them a lesson.

The two assassins moved closer, skirting the territory's edge, crossbows in hand.

Blue light surged from my palm, stirring up the ground in front of me. I'd never tried transfiguring a person, but if these two wanted to volunteer to be guinea pigs, they could be my guest.

My attack hit a tree instead—but the tree *moved*, branches reaching out like arms to hug the assassin from behind. He let out a startled cry as the tree's branches cut off his path, caging him in. Even his partner watched for a disbelieving moment until the *snap* of finality as his neck broke. The tree had formed a cage of bark—a deadly trap.

The second assassin roared in fury and ran forward.

Big mistake, thought the part of me not momentarily stunned by the sheer brutality of what my magic had done.

Cedar ran forward in a blur, a knife flying from his hand and burying itself in the enemy's neck.

"Hey!" I ran after him towards the trees.

"I'm just getting my weapon back." He dropped to his knees beside the assassin to retrieve the blade. "You need to up your security."

"Your family needs to stop sending people to attack me."

He eyed the dead men, confusion furrowing his brow. "They're not mine."

"I meant the one who knocked on my front door." I spun around. Robin had apparently made a run for it. "My list of double-crossing bastards is out of hand." I jerked my head in the direction of the palace. "C'mon. Get back inside. Where've you even been?"

"Where else? Your territory didn't take kindly to my attempts to leave."

"I thought you left already. I wondered what you stole."

"There's nothing here I need." His expression turned dark as it passed over the tree I'd used magic on. I hadn't known my sceptre could kill people *that* fast, though it was hardly worse than anything I'd seen the faeries do to one another. And the assassins deserved it. Surely the Darkwaters would run out of people eventually.

"Get back inside," I told him. "Prisoners aren't allowed to wander the grounds."

He moved in the same direction as me, but kept his eyes on the forest. "I was under the impression you planned to leave for the mortal realm."

"I do. Doesn't mean I'll let you sneak up and steal the talisman from me when my back is turned."

"Am I so predictable?"

"Yes." I glared at him, and he shrugged and walked back into the entrance hall. Then he paused, looking at the ice statues at the back.

"Those statues," he said. "Don't they look too lifelike?"

Viola and I looked where he pointed.

A gasp escaped her. "That's Volt."

She jumped at Cedar, magic flaring from both hands.

He barely dodged, raising his own weapon in defence. She stopped inches from the iron blade, her face a mask of fury.

"Hang on." I moved between them. The sprite had been frozen solid. "Cedar can't have done that. He's from Summer."

Her furious expression didn't fade. "He did it. Somehow—"

"Don't be ridiculous," he said. "Why would I freeze your… pet?" He sounded like he wanted to laugh, which was possibly the worst thing to do in the circumstances.

"Because you're what she said—a double-crossing bastard. Set him free."

"I can't, because I didn't do it. Didn't you have enemies knocking on the doors a second ago?"

"Robin?" I asked. "He's from Summer, too. Only Winter magic could have frozen someone."

"Whoever did it is here in the palace," Viola said. "But—there's only the three of us. I swear I didn't see…" She trailed off, eyes darting to a piece of paper on the floor. "Did you see where that came from?"

"Robin," I said. "Must be… it's that invitation, the one to the Gathering."

Except the words on the paper had changed. My blood chilled.

It's in your interest to come to meet with the Lord and Lady Hornbeam, Raine. Your father would like to see you.

My father. The Hornbeam family shouldn't know about him… unless Robin had told them.

A rustling sounded by the door, followed by a *thunk*. I turned on the spot, my heart lurching. Blood sprayed across the entryway from where a soft feathered body had fallen onto the doorstep.

"Wha…?" I gasped.

"Frances!" Viola ran to the door. "She's—she's dead."

It was the half-faerie shapeshifter who'd been with the Little People when we'd been through the rift.

With trembling hands, Viola lifted a bloodstained scrap of paper. "It was in—in her mouth," she said, handing it to me.

Scrawled on the paper were the words, *This one tried to stop me bringing the mortal through the rift. If I don't see you before noon, Raine, your father will be next.*

The paper slipped from my hands, and the world tilted. "The rift—they went through the rift, and found him."

"What?" said Cedar, alarm in his voice. "What happened?"

"Summer has Dad. The Hornbeams kidnapped my father."

15

Anger flared, and the talisman glowed in response, vivid blue-white. My hands trembled, and the mark on my neck tingled.

"I get the message," I growled. "I'm coming."

"Hang on!" Cedar said. "You can't just march over to the Hornbeams' territory—Sidhe's blood, they want you dead."

I whirled on him. "Tell me," I hissed. "They're your family. Right?"

His mouth thinned. "Yes. I said I have no allegiance to them, but if they find out I'm travelling with you, that will change."

"And you'll turn against us?"

He didn't need to answer for me to read the truth in his eyes. "No favour I owe you can contradict a faerie vow," he said in a low voice.

"Damn the Sidhe." I looked at Viola desperately. "Might it be a trick? How'd the spell that trapped Volt even get in here? I thought the security was airtight."

"It *was*," she said, her eyes wide. "But the invitation must have contained a small amount of magic, enough to trap a sprite. I'll have it destroyed." Her gaze snapped onto Cedar. "You'll pay for this."

"I had nothing to do with the invitation," he said. "I thought they'd leave you alone after the Gathering."

"You're the one who *told* me they'd never leave me alone until I was dead," I snarled at him.

"I hoped I was wrong." His words were clear, masking an emotion I couldn't name. "This was *exactly* what I hoped to avoid."

"By destroying the talisman. Sure. That's the truth, you traitor."

"I'm not a traitor, Raine," he said. "I've never pretended to be anything other than what I am—someone acting on his own terms."

"This has *nothing* to do with my dad. Nothing. He doesn't even belong to the Whitefall family."

"Tell them that, not me," he said, but the strain in his voice betrayed panic. "Sidhe help me, I'll be slaughtered for this, but I can help. Call your favour in if necessary. It won't cancel out the vow that binds me to the family, but maybe I can give you advice."

"You might regret offering that information," I told him. "You didn't say we couldn't use force."

"All right." He smiled, for some inexplicable reason. "You're learning. I hope you're ready. The Gathering was proof enough, but the Hornbeam family must have a reason for using such brutal force this early."

"Aside from wanting the talisman?" It struck me as weird, actually. Why would they take my father? Weren't the Darkwater family the ones sending assassins after me? "I don't know, but—someone I know from the mortal realm is with them. Quite a few people, actually, including the guy who just tried to kill me." Maybe *he* had taken Dad. *Of course he did.* He'd used me before, and he'd have traded me in for power without a second's thought.

I might have pitied Robin, knowing how manipulative the Sidhe were, but the notion of him kidnapping my father made me want to brain him with the sceptre.

"That kid? I saw him. He's under her control. I know the signs."

"Yeah. He ran away."

"He'll come back. He has orders. It looked like a compulsion spell rather than a vow, but it wouldn't surprise me if she used one of those on him, too. She likes to be thorough."

"You seem certain it's Lady Hornbeam."

His head dipped. "I know them. It's her."

"All right, since you're the expert, what do *you* think we should do?"

"What would it take to make you trust my word?"

"Not belonging to the enemy would help. Unless you're willing to take me to their territory. You know the way, right?"

"Yes," said Cedar. "I will give you my word that I won't lead you astray."

"Then swear on it." The words came out before I was aware I intended to say them.

He blinked. "Excuse me?"

"I want you to swear to tell me only the truth. On the honour of your family. That's my favour. Make a vow."

"Watch out," he said. "Vows have a tendency to escape the unprepared, and I'd guess you've never used one before."

"Stop screwing with me and say the damn words."

His face went blank. "I swear to tell you only the truth."

An unexpected current of energy ran through me, and an odd sensation tugged at my chest as I took a step back from him.

"That was unnecessary," he said. "I don't like to lie as a general rule. Most half-bloods raised here in Faerie don't."

"But you *can*," I said. "Right. If you come with me into the forest, I want you to swear never to take the talisman again."

"I can't do that," he said. "If the vow I'm under contradicts yours, either I'll be forced to act anyway, or the combination of both vows might literally kill me, or both of us. The same would happen if two completely different vows came into conflict. There's a reason we rarely use them."

I gave Viola a questioning look. "Is that right?" It sounded like it, unfortunately.

"Yes," said Viola. "It's the truth."

"So you left the Hornbeams on a mission to steal for them," I asked Cedar. "Then you decided you'd rather destroy the talisman instead?"

"I've wanted to destroy it since I became aware of what it's capable of, but don't expect any more information from me than that," Cedar said in a low voice. "I can walk with you up to their prison, and no further. As I said—if they catch me, we're enemies."

"Good enough. We need to move."

"You're going there dressed like that?"

I looked down at myself. "What's wrong with my clothes? If you'd prefer the dress, that moment has passed."

He blinked. "That's not what I meant. I was going to suggest choosing something with more protection built into it."

"All right." I waved the sceptre, and a knee-length coat wrapped around me, black and thick, armoured yet breathable enough to move freely. Modelled on Viola's, except with an extra pocket for my iron knife. "Let's go."

Cedar walked alongside me towards the trees. "I prefer this outfit," he said in a low voice. "It's more you."

"You don't know me." The words were less heated than

when I'd said them last, but I didn't care what he thought. I had a mission: get Dad back, away from the families and their games. One small part of me, though, wondered who Cedar really was. Someone the Hornbeams trusted? Surely not, if he'd betray them so easily. Yet important enough to be tasked with finding the sceptre in the first place. Or rather, ordered to find it, with a vow he intended to break. And I thought *I'd* been playing dangerous games.

"Raine," Viola said. "I think someone *wants* you to leave. I'm half sure this whole thing is a trap."

"I can't risk Dad's life," I told her. "The talisman's on my side now. If the Hornbeams want to directly challenge me for it, then they're risking their own lives by trying to claim its magic."

"Exactly," Cedar muttered. "I'm not convinced that's their plan."

"Can you tell me what it is?"

"No, mostly because I don't know," he said. "Lady Hornbeam… let's just say she's unpredictable."

Viola stepped forwards. "I can scout ahead and see if I spot your father, and if there's a chance to get him away from them without having to face either Lord *or* Lady Hornbeam." Blue light shone from her hands, and a plain black armoured coat replaced her jacket. Like Cedar's. They all wore similar uniform, actually. Maybe to disguise which Court they belonged to so the enemy wouldn't anticipate their attacks.

"You're turning yourself into one of their soldiers?"

"Summer's, yeah," she said. Obviously, if she used magic, she'd give herself away, but if she kept her distance, she might get away with it. "I'm going to head to the jail and see how many guards they have. I'll see if I can create a diversion. Wait for me at the border. There might be an ambush."

And she vanished into the trees.

I kept walking with Cedar until we met the path splitting

the territories, where Viola had told us to wait. He remained in tense silence while I ran a hand over the hilt of my knife. "I owe her for this. Big time."

"Isn't she chained to your family by a vow?"

"You could say that," I said, reluctant to get into another discussion with him, and equally reluctant to move any closer to him now we were alone so close to enemy territory. Except this wasn't enemy territory for *him*, and if he turned on me, I'd turn him into a tree this time. His magic was even more present here, a hum in the background, flickering against mine like a candle flame. "You never said how you escaped your room." I spoke more to dispel the silence than anything.

"Through the window. I used magic on one of the trees around the back of your palace so the branches knocked into the window, and I managed to get it open."

I shook my head at him. "So you were outside all this time? Waiting to take the talisman?"

"The thought did cross my mind. Your security is fairly extensive."

"If it wasn't, someone would have taken the talisman sooner." I tapped my foot on the ground impatiently. Where was Viola? She'd gone to check out the *jail*—a word that conjured up images of that awful dungeon, of humans trapped behind bars. Images that had haunted my dreams ever since I'd been old enough to grasp the weight of the ordeal Dad had gone through.

I'd never forgive myself if I let him endure it again.

Cedar paused before saying, "It's not your fault. I respect why you decided to hold onto the talisman."

My hands clenched. "Why I chose not to give it up to a thief from an enemy family?"

"If I'd destroyed it before Lady Hornbeam played her hand—"

"Then what would they have done to you? Exiled you? We'd both be dead one way or another. Just how badly does Lady Hornbeam want the talisman?"

He took a step closer, his eyes gleaming with that strange, feral light I'd seen before. "Badly enough not to care if you're dead before she rips it from your fingers—and yet that pales in comparison to what she will do *with* the talisman."

My pulse raced fast, the impact of his words hitting like a thousand tiny stone. Dad's life… or mine? Or the talisman? Nothing was worth this.

"You haven't been able to tell me about it until now. Did I guess close enough to get around your vow? Or part of it?"

A nod told me all I needed to know. I'd got around part of his vow… for all the good it did. I was still walking into the heart of an enemy's territory.

"Raine," he said softly. "The chances of me escaping the vow's effects are low, but it should be me who goes to the jail to get your father out. I'll help you get into the mortal realm, somewhere they'll never find you or him. I'd help you disappear." He moved to stand in front of me, his magic close enough to brush against me, and that odd tugging sensation pulled at me again. He was telling the truth.

I took a step back, shaking my head. "No. I'm saving my dad. No other option is on the table. Maybe they're less likely to catch you, but if they do… you'll have to kill me. Right?"

The forest suddenly seemed very quiet, and the area we were in more like a bubble containing only the two of us. He met my gaze, but the light seemed to go out of his eyes as he spoke.

"Yes, unfortunately. I've never lied to you about my intentions. I'm just not always acting under my own power."

"And are you now?"

I didn't mean the words to slip out. I just felt so lost, scared for Dad and more like a helpless human than the powerful Sidhe Lady I was supposed to be. And he was here —unreliable as all hell, openly telling me I couldn't trust him, and yet—

"Yes," he said quietly. "I am now. I'll try to warn you if she —if the vow takes hold."

My hand reached out towards him of its own accord, whether in reassurance or whatever, I didn't know.

A scream came from ahead.

"Viola." I ran towards the sound, my heart sinking. If she'd got caught, I was the one who'd dragged her into this.

A laugh followed, deep and menacing. I ran faster, clearing ground fast, and skidded to a halt beside a dip in the ground.

Viola was trapped in a net. A tall spindly fae creature stood over her, one I'd never seen before. Its long arms were the colour and texture of tree bark, reaching out towards Viola. Hunger gleamed in its pitch dark eyes.

"I caught a little fish," said the creature.

I held the sceptre up in warning. "Let her go!"

"Another half-blood?" The spindly fae's forked tongue flickered over its teeth. "I'm lucky today."

"You asked for it," I said, and raised the weapon.

Before my attack hit, Cedar moved first in a blur of green light, and the fae creature fell with a scream of pain. I fired magic at the earth and the nearest tree root smacked the creature in the face. Cedar glanced at me, his face tense. "I was trying to act before you used magic. If anyone had seen…"

"Then they'd have mistaken it for Summer magic. You're not the only one who can mess around with trees." I tore at the net around Viola with my hands, but it wouldn't give. I used my sceptre-free hand to take out my knife instead. The blade easily sliced through the mesh-like substance, and Viola climbed out, grimacing.

"Forgot about those sneaky buggers," she said.

"You don't get them in Winter," Cedar remarked. "Do you? Either way—the forest shouldn't be this quiet."

"Then we'd better get a move on." I glared pointedly at him. "Viola, did you see anything at the… jail?"

"Never got that far. I thought there was a shortcut here, but it's changed since our last territory visit."

"No, it's that way." Cedar pointed through the trees. "Not five minutes from here."

"Lead the way, then," I said.

He didn't move. "They heard the screaming. I can't go any further. As for your friend, I wouldn't go anywhere with her, either."

I glanced at Viola, frowning. "What? Am I missing something?"

"I—" she broke off, cursing. "Can't say."

Cedar eyed her. "So your vow binds you, too. Even though the one who cast it is dead."

"Stop that," I said sharply to him. "What in the world are you two talking about? Did you know one another?"

"No," he said softly, "but I'm not the one who's failed to tell you something important that might affect your mission here."

I looked at her despite myself. "Viola?" Why he'd lie to me at this stage, I had no idea, but I trusted Viola a damn sight more than anyone else I'd met in Faerie.

"He's the one deceiving you," she said. "He's Lady Hornbeam's pet thief. I always thought he was pure-blood."

He shook his head. "No pure-blood would consent to be a slave."

"I always thought he was a child, at any rate," she said.

A grim smile flashed across his face. "What do you think? Children grow older, even here."

"So you're Sidhe?" I asked.

"Half," he said. "But you knew that already. I never hid it."

"You're related to—*them?* Which?"

"Lady's Hornbeam's bastard offspring." He grinned at me. "Don't worry, I've never felt a particular attachment to her, nor her to me. That's why she never sent anyone to check up on me. I'm one of a dozen thieves sent to steal from you. But I happen to be the best."

"You need an ego check," said Viola. "Not that it's surprising, considering who she is."

"Save it for later." I marched ahead. If they wanted to bicker, they could do so in their own time. My priority was finding my father. I followed the direction Cedar had pointed out, even though a small voice of resistance inside me whispered that leaving Cedar behind was a bad idea—and that he wouldn't have called Viola's trustworthiness into question without good reason. But she'd saved my life, helped me more times than I could count, and was vow-sworn to my family so she *couldn't* betray or hurt me. I needed to save all my misgivings for the Hornbeam family.

The path abruptly stopped. A huge building lay nestled between leafy branches. Unlike the ice palace, it appeared to be made entirely of living trees, overlapping branches forming a tough exterior without a single gap. But I wouldn't say it resembled a palace as much as a long blocky building, grim and uncompromising. *Cheerful.* I was kind of surprised, considering the pomp and ceremony of their arrival at the Gathering. They hadn't struck me as militant, but that was how I'd describe the building.

Viola stepped up beside me. A hiss of alarm escaped her, and several people walked past the building in front of us. Soldiers. I raised the talisman, aiming it at the trees between us and them. Blue light ignited and the trees I'd hit moved in, forming a barrier between us and the area in front of the building.

"Good thinking," Viola whispered. "That's the jail. I know a secret entrance."

But are you on my side? I didn't want to believe she was working against me. She'd sworn a vow to serve my family, one that couldn't be broken. I took in a breath. "Okay."

We crept through the trees, around the outskirts of the building. Viola pushed one of the branches carefully aside, revealing a worn wooden door set into the back. I didn't dare break the silence for long enough to ask how she knew it was there.

My heart drummed against my ribs as she used her magic to push the branches apart, allowing her to ease the door open. She looked at my coat, then pointed at her own. *Oh. A disguise.* I glanced at her carefully nondescript uniform and imagined a similar one, directing the talisman's magic to my clothes. Blue light flowed briefly over me, and then it was done.

I looked like a Summer soldier… carrying a Winter Sidhe's sceptre. Maybe it'd buy us a few seconds, but I didn't have all the information I'd need to pull off the act convincingly. Well, if they saw me smuggling my dad out of the cell, it'd give the game away pretty quickly. Too bad for them. I had enough magic in this talisman to make things seriously difficult for anyone who wasn't a Sidhe. Any thoughts of getting away without confronting the Hornbeams had perished when they'd kidnapped my father.

Viola closed the door behind us, and we walked into the dark.

16

My talisman's light shone, igniting the way ahead, but I tucked it inside my jacket to hide the blue glow. Good job, too, because two guards ahead walked between rows of barred cages. I held my breath, walking alongside Viola. Her military-style march ensured neither looked twice at us. They continued to walk, passing us by on their way back. When they'd passed beyond hearing, she whispered, "I'll divert their attention. Find your father and bring him outside. They keep all the humans in here."

My response died on my lips as I moved close enough to see into the cages. A dozen humans sat in each cage. Staring eyes peered at me from the dark, drunk on the haze of faerie magic distinct even beneath the iron bars on the cages. The smell was unbearable. The chains were worse. And… none of the humans was my father.

I walked from one cage to the next, checking every face. Had they put him somewhere else? Or was this a setup from the start? I needed to leave, but I wouldn't abandon these humans to rot and die in the dark. But if I set them free, they'd perish out there in Faerie. For the Sidhe's sakes, was my magic good for nothing?

"I'll come back," I whispered to them, re-tracing my steps. Viola would be creating a diversion somewhere, but maybe—

One of the humans stood behind the bars of the cage, reaching a hand out to me. I hesitated. He was in a cage on his own for some reason, standing in the dark.

"Sorry," I whispered to him. "If I let you out, you'll run into the guards."

His hand snagged my sleeve. "Come to stay in the dark where you belong, have you, half-blood?"

I gasped as he yanked me forwards, into the bars. The iron's effect was instantaneous, smothering me as my magic's spark died out. All the strength drained from my limbs as I fought to break his grip. He bared his teeth at me in a grin, his teeth startlingly white, his eyes too bright...

He's... half-blood.

His foot connected with the cage door, knocking it open, our hands locked against the iron door. My body sagged against it, my grip loosening on the talisman—

No!

I flailed, aiming my magic at the floor. The stone barely cracked. Iron... there was so much iron down here, it dampened even my talisman.

I pulled back, my shoulder wrenching, and I was free. The air thickened like soup, my skin blistering where the iron had touched it. My shoulder burned. I had to get outside.

Shouts rang through the corridor. The guards were between me and the back entrance. *Hell.*

I ran forwards, the only other direction unguarded, towards the sunlight shining through an open door—

And dozen guards waiting outside, all carrying iron weapons. A hand locked around my wrist and dragged me forward, and the pain from my blistered hands nearly made me pass out. A knife stabbed in the direction of my ribs. I dodged, my free hand scrambling for my own knife, but my fingers hurt too much to move quickly. Dizzy with pain, I didn't even feel the sceptre in my other hand until someone tore it from my grip.

"Give that back," I croaked.

It was the guy from jail—who suddenly looked nothing like an underpowered human. He wore the same uniform as the other soldiers but less put together, his dark hair dishevelled rather than combed, and dirt splattered across his tanned face. A mask—he'd been pretending to be weak. His green eyes were bright as evergreen trees. Like a Summer Sidhe's. He smiled at me, the light of the sceptre glinting in his eyes.

Anger snapped inside me like the taut string of a crossbow and I launched myself past the other guards, tackling him. Apparently he hadn't expected such a direct assault. We crashed into a heap, my hand locking around his wrist and tearing the sceptre free. I dodged his wild stabs and leaped to my feet, kicking him in the face in the process. My hands trembled on my sceptre, my skin burning from the iron, but my weapon hand was functioning fine. The other half-bloods froze when I pointed the sceptre at them.

"Go on," I growled. "Do you think you can stab me before I take at least one of you out? Are you willing to risk it?"

The half-Sidhe who'd assaulted me let out a coughing laugh and scrambled to his feet. Blood dripped from his nose where I'd kicked him. He didn't look afraid, just mildly curious. *Who is he, then?* Not a soldier—his clothes were too finely made, but his muscular build was similar to the other soldiers. Surely not a pure-blooded Sidhe, though his confident stance suggested he thought he could take me.

I was through being a joke to these people.

I fumbled in my pocket for the iron knife, pointing that at

the group, too. They remained frozen as though awaiting orders—from whom, I didn't know.

"I wouldn't," said the half-Sidhe, his eyes glittering with malice. "We're on orders not to kill you."

"You sure did a good job trying," I said, and punched him in the throat with the hand that held the sceptre.

I hadn't even used magic, but the force sent him stumbling back, gasping for breath. The sceptre's sharp end had caught him in the nose, which dripped blood onto the forest floor.

The half-Sidhe hissed in anger. His green eyes burned like flames, now furious. "You'll pay for that, mortal."

"Kill her!" shouted a guard.

"Don't move," said another sharply. "We're supposed to bring her in alive."

"Then why did this fucker try to choke me with iron?" I demanded.

Nobody answered.

"I'll leave your territory if you tell me where my father is," I said. "Tell me. Now."

"What's she talking about?" asked one of the soldiers.

"Your Lady Hornbeam has him prisoner," I said, my heart already sinking. "Where?"

"That's the only place we keep mortals." One of the guards jerked his head at the building behind me. "It looks to me like you're trespassing."

"Yes," said the green-eyed half-Sidhe, with a flicker of a smile. "It does. I'd like to see Lady Hornbeam carve pieces out of her."

Iron surrounded me. Too much iron, caging me in as they surrounded me, driving me into the jail again. Left, down a corridor, and into a cage. Iron bars formed two walls and the door, while the back wall was cold stone. And in the cell beside mine...

Viola. They caught her, too.

A sharp jab to the spine sent me stumbling into the cage. The door shut before I could whirl around and fight my way out. Viola sat on the floor of her own cage, her eyes urging me not to fight back. My hands throbbed from the iron wounds, the chill creeping into my bones. *My talisman's gone again.* Of all the tricks to fall for...

"I'm sorry," said Viola. "I didn't see them—I didn't know they'd bring a prince with them."

"Prince?"

"The man with the green eyes. Half-Sidhe."

"The guy I punched?" Shit. Like things weren't dire enough.

"You did what?" Viola stared at me in horror.

"He tried to kill me." I sat down on the cold floor. "The prick was waiting in here to ambush me, pretending to be human. And—and I think he might have been the one who set me up. Dad—he's not here. He was never here."

"The prince did it?" She cursed under her breath. "Aspen. I should have known—he's her son. He has access to magic none of the other soldiers do. It'd have been easy for him to send that message."

"And kill Frances, too." I swore. "And they took my talisman away. They can't steal it from under my nose just because I'm not Sidhe. Isn't that illegal?"

"Yes," she said, "but there's never been a half-blood in charge of a family before. You'd never win in a case against a Sidhe. They know *you're* a thief, and will use it against you. Assuming we get out."

"The Sidhe don't get the concept of fairness, do they?"

"No, they don't." She paused. "This is all my fault. I never should have come back."

Cedar's words came back to me—*I'm not the one who's*

failed to tell you something important. "You say that," I said slowly, "as though you've been here before."

Viola took a shuddering breath. "I thought you'd worked it out. My former family…" She moved into the light, showing her fake uniform. Summer, but not marked as such. It might have belonged to any Court.

And the Hornbeam family was the one who'd brought the most soldiers to the Gathering.

I stared at her. "You… you once belonged to the Hornbeams—to Summer."

She nodded. "I did. Until your mother's magic erased my —vows—" She broke off, cursing. "Blasted vow."

"You can talk about it if I guess, right?" My mind whirled. I'd never heard of someone taking on the magic of a different Court before. Not without— "The talisman," I said. "The sceptre. She used that on you. *That's* what it does."

"Yeah." She cleared her throat. "I think I can talk about it now you've figured it out. It… it's her magic. Somehow, her magic is so powerful, it can *replace* someone else's. My own magic was never strong, but she obliterated it. And once I was hers—the connection of our magic gave her a hold over me that went deeper than a vow."

"You did give me a clue," I said. "You told me she gave you some of her magic…"

"I didn't expect you to guess it was the Hornbeams I belonged to," she said. "I wasn't able to give you any more clues, not even at the Gathering. I was worried someone would recognise me, but I was known by another name when I lived here, and I changed my appearance when I left." She shrugged in an attempt at nonchalance. "Your friend Cedar, though—he worked it out. I don't remember him, but he's her thief, it's his job to observe and know everyone. I suppose he's reporting us as we speak."

"He won't, unless they caught him," I said, though more to

make myself believe it than anything. *Her* thief. Like a possession. "But—do the Courts know that Lady Whitefall could use the sceptre to turn anyone's magic into hers? Because… damn. That could start a war. I mean, I assume it works on Unseelie faeries the same, right?"

"It wouldn't surprise me," Viola said. "She had an unusually strong influence over her court, and—and I think that's why they broke away after she died. It wouldn't surprise me if she'd recruited them in person, from both Summer and Winter, and blasted away their original magic until they could do nothing but obey her."

"Sidhe's blood," I said. "Now I know why everyone wants it." No other talisman, or magic, could put someone under that level of influence. Never mind that I'd met a few half-bloods who wouldn't have actually minded switching their magic from Summer to Winter, or vice versa—the talisman's magic gave nobody any choice in the matter, and if other talismans were anything to go by, the spell couldn't be undone. Instead, anyone hit by the talisman's magic would be eternally bound to the wielder, until someone else stole it… or destroyed it.

And now I know why Cedar wanted to be rid of it.

"Wait," I said. "Just *how* do the Courts not know about it? They must do, right?"

"I wouldn't count on it." Viola grimaced. "I'm not even sure where the talisman came from, and I was forbidden to speak of it with anyone. Your mother owned it before my time, but I had the impression she had little contact with the Winter Court in recent years. Only the borderland families have had direct experience with her magic over the years. Lady Hornbeam's had years to figure it out, and if Cedar's her son—that must be how he knew."

Her son. Like that prince who'd tried to kill me. The Hornbeams were twisted, evil, and yet from what I'd seen of

Cedar—he'd told me under a vow that he'd intended to defy them and destroy the talisman himself. He wasn't on their side. If he'd really betrayed me… then we had no allies remaining.

"Why did she pick you?" I asked. "I mean, she used the talisman's magic on you openly, right? Why risk everyone finding out?"

"She did it deliberately," said Viola. "She knew I wanted to escape. I was an easy target. I couldn't make a vow to obey her as a Summer faerie. But mostly she did it to prove a point to Lord and Lady Hornbeam, who were the biggest threat to her power. They were the only witnesses, and I thought they never told anyone else. Think of what harm it would do to their reputations if everyone found out one of their soldiers defected to the Unseelie."

"You didn't exactly defect, though, did you? You wanted to leave the army, not switch Courts."

"Technicalities," said Viola. "I made a vow to serve Lady Whitefall."

"She just didn't explain the small print." I nodded. "I don't blame you, at all." Considering those brutal guards. They'd all carried iron weapons—and that meant her stories about her family using iron as punishment referred to the Hornbeams. "Is that the only time she's used the spell?"

She shivered. "To my knowledge—but don't forget how old she was. All I know is that using that spell shook the borderlands up. I swear the forests weren't right for weeks afterwards, on either territory."

My breath caught. "So if the talisman passes onto someone else… they could do that. To anyone." Create an army of faeries with the same magic, vow-bound to serve only them—and mow down or convert anyone in their way.

All it took was the talisman deciding someone else was more worthy to wield it than I was.

"They could try." She frowned. "If most people tried to use the spell, it'd probably kill them. We're talking a total upsurge of power across the realm. Most magic can't hold a candle to it, even here. But Lord and Lady Hornbeam? They have easily as much power as she did."

"Dammit." It wasn't at all hard to imagine how anyone in the Courts might misuse the power to win literally any faerie over to their side—let alone the owners of this horrific prison. "How could something like that even be allowed to exist?"

"Because it's disguised as a simple transformation talisman," said Viola. "What it can do isn't that unique, not here. Turning water to ice, even freezing people into statues—there are a thousand lesser faeries with the same ability. The palace itself is similar to others. She flaunted her power, but never gave away the depth of it. Everyone knew she had a secret, but nobody guessed."

"But—if she had enough power to build an army, why did she die alone?"

Viola shook her head. "I don't know. Using her power on me seemed a waste, but I never truly understood her motives. I was a fool to trust her. She never wanted to help me. She only wanted a servant. I will serve this family until I die."

"Not if I have anything to do with it." My fists clenched, though dread trickled down my spine. If one of the leading Sidhe decided to claim the talisman, that was it. Their superior Sidhe blood would win over mine, and I'd be at their mercy forever.

Viola gave me a grateful look. "You're too kind."

"Apparently Faerie thinks so, too," I said. "I think I'm pretty selfish, actually. If I hadn't tried to sell the bloody thing—"

"This would have happened no matter what. The pieces

were already on the board before you arrived. Even before she called me over from the palace. I always thought she had a plan, but it's Lady Hornbeam who did."

"And not her husband? Is he not involved in this at all?"

"No. She won't want him to have the chance to get hold of the talisman before she does."

"Shit." I rested my head on my knees. "Would they go to war with one another over it?"

"War? No. But things could get nasty. Nastier than they already are, I mean. Both of them will want to keep you out of the picture."

"Surprised they haven't killed me yet."

"They're planning something," she said in a low voice. "I've no idea what. If I were a better spy… this used to be my job. Your mother liked to send me back to spy on my former family, but I got out of the habit after the past year."

"Considering all the attacks on the palace, it's probably for the best. Why did she have to die and leave the rest of us to clear up the mess left behind?"

"She wasn't *supposed* to die," said Viola. "The Sidhe—aren't immortal anymore. That's why they want to kill one another. Because now death isn't an impossibility, they can steal talismans from one another without repercussions."

I looked up sharply. "What? The Sidhe aren't immortal? None of them?"

"They can still live forever, but they can be killed." Her gaze dropped. "Think about it. Have you ever heard of a Sidhe dying who wasn't an exile?"

"No. But I've been out of touch with Court gossip for a while."

"Something went wrong," said Viola. "I never knew a Sidhe who died before her, but common knowledge is that when a Sidhe dies, their body is consumed by their own magic. Then, a few days later, they come back, as though they never died at all. But when she died, that didn't happen. I waited. Days. Weeks. She didn't come back. And then I started hearing rumours from the Courts—that when any Sidhe dies, they're no longer reborn."

"Seriously?" I hadn't known *how* the Sidhe lived forever. They just did. It was a fact, an inevitable one. Even after hearing about my mother's death, it hadn't truly hit me until now that something in Faerie had gone horribly, horribly wrong.

"So," Viola went on. "When they die, it's the same as when a mortal dies. They're as vulnerable as we are now." Her voice grew louder. "They think they're superior, but we're on an even playing field. A Sidhe's life is worth the same as a half-blood's. And that's why you *must* be strong enough to beat them. Even the Hornbeams."

"Little late," I said, but my mind whirled at her words. The Sidhe were, according to all reports, eternal. That my mother had died in the first place was so rare as to be impossible, but if something had gone wrong to stop the Sidhe from living forever, then... then everything in Faerie would change. "That doesn't change the fact that murder is, well, murder. Right?"

"Of course not," said Viola. "Murder of a Sidhe is punishable by exile, same as always. But they didn't used to *stay* dead. Now they do."

"That doesn't have anything to do with my sceptre, right?"

"No, but it makes the Sidhe even more likely to kill anyone who gets in their way. The talisman is powerful enough to stand up to the Courts. If one Court went to war with the other, with the talisman at their head..."

And killed or converted all the enemies? The whole of Faerie might be destroyed.

"That," said a voice in the dark, "is why you can't let anyone else get their hands on it."

Cedar leaned as close to the bars on my right as possible without touching them.

I sat upright. "You."

"I didn't mean for this to happen," he said in a low whisper. "I'm engineering a way to get you out. Your dad's not here. It was—"

"A trick. Like everything you've ever said to me."

"I told you, I didn't lie. I was forced to hide from their armies in the forest, but I'm working on a plan." He leaned forward, further, his hand slipping through the bars—and he held the sceptre.

"*Cedar.*"

He carefully manoeuvred his hand so that it didn't touch the bars as the sceptre's awkward shape became stuck between the narrow iron bars. I reached for it, too, so careful to avoid the iron that my hand brushed over his instead. Magic trailed up my arm, along with the smell of woodsmoke and scented candles. I wanted to hug him, despite all the trouble he'd caused me.

He had other ideas.

Carefully, he pressed the sceptre into my hand, using the other to guide mine back through the bars without contact with the iron. The sores on my palm began to disappear and the sharp pain of the iron's touch vanished as his fingers brushed my palm. Instead of withdrawing his hand, he trailed it up the side of my face. "I can't tell you how sorry I am, Raine," he murmured, and for a brief, unhinged moment, I wished the bars of the cage would fall away. *He gave me back the sceptre. I can use it to get out...*

He leaned forward until our faces almost touched, but the iron bars blocked the distance between us. "Hang onto it."

His feathery whisper trailed past my ear. "Keep it hidden from them. You can get out."

"Thanks," I whispered, gripping the talisman hard. "Cedar—"

But he'd gone, slipping away into the shadows like a thief in the night.

17

I stared after him numbly. The talisman was a solid weight in my hand containing the power to get us out. I hoped the iron wouldn't interfere too much. I tapped the talisman against the stone floor. Maybe it could break through.

"He gave you the sceptre?" whispered Viola. "How'd he get it?"

"He's a thief." A grin broke out across my face, though it didn't last. "Lady Hornbeam will be pissed when she finds out. We need to go. Can I transform the floor?" Into what, though? I tapped it with my talisman—and the gemstone split open. A note fell out.

My heart sank and I dropped to pick it up. "That's not right…" I trailed off, the words of the note sinking in.

Sorry, Raine. This talisman is fake, but I needed a way to get words to you that I'm unable to speak aloud. The magic in the talisman never left you. As long as you can access the magic, you can use it. Iron dulls it, so be careful. I truly am sorry, but I cannot tell you what I did with the real talisman. If they know the truth, they will kill me.

"Cedar, you…"

"Let me see that," whispered Viola.

I passed her the note, my hands shaking with anger. I wanted to scream in incoherent rage. He'd deceived me, acted like he was genuinely sorry, and I'd fallen for the act *again*. "What now?"

"What he said." Viola studied the note. "You have magic, and it's not in the talisman. That means we can get out."

"We're locked in an iron cage." I crouched down. The ground beneath was stone, which was hardly better than iron. At least it didn't hurt my hands. Cedar could transfer his healing magic to another person, apparently. Just one more thing he hadn't told me.

"Transform into sand, damn you," I muttered to the floor.

I didn't expect it to work. But the magic had chosen me, and the sceptre was just the vessel for its power. Most Sidhe and their talismans were inseparable, but that didn't mean it was impossible to use magic without it. Unless someone else had already claimed it… but Cedar had clearly taken the talisman elsewhere. If I trusted his word. *Hmm.*

Magic was still here, but I'd never used it under these conditions, with cold iron sapping my strength. I concentrated on my anger at Cedar, picking up the false talisman. Without my palms throbbing, I could better feel my way through to the magic lurking under my skin. *The sceptre is the key to your magic,* he'd said. It'd unlocked my power, but didn't control it.

I also didn't need to destroy the whole floor. Just part of it.

Blue light pooled in my right palm, and I tilted it, spilling the magic onto the floor like water. I aimed the trickle of magic at the part of the ground where our cells joined. Careful not to touch the iron, I kept pouring magic at the ground. Stone became earth, easy to shift aside with my free hand. I dug through a layer of it. Viola leaned forwards and added her magic to mine.

My feet skidded and I jumped. "Whoa."

We'd turned half the stone beneath our feet into earth. I scooped a handful from between the cages, and a noise from outside made me freeze. I stopped moving, waiting for someone to rush in. Instead, more noise came, wild howling and screaming like a pack of dogs set loose.

Had Cedar done something? Maybe. I wasn't about to stick around and find out. Scraping layers of earth away, I cleared a gap deep enough for Viola to wriggle through into my cage, and then for both of us to crawl out. Earth scraped against my elbows, and the iron's metallic touch inches from my head made me shudder—but we'd made it out.

Now all we had to do was get out of the prison.

We weren't in the same section I'd found the humans in. Most cages were empty, though all of them had iron bands on the walls and floor. Iron shackles, manacles, torture instruments…

"This is where they keep half-blood transgressors," she whispered. "They aren't common, not in this family. We're lucky they wanted you alive. For now."

"So what's keeping them?"

A tremendous roar came from outside.

Viola turned to face me. "I think I know what he did."

"Cedar?"

She began walking quickly down the corridor. "There's an underground section to the prison where they keep their war-beasts. Ogres, trolls, things like that. For fighting Winter's monsters."

"Oh hell. He didn't."

"I think we're going to have to make a run for it into the woods."

"Okay. I hope you know the way."

Of course she did—she knew the whole territory, maybe better than she knew Winter's. The fake talisman didn't hold a candle to the real thing, but I couldn't help eyeing it with suspicion. The power to turn your enemies into allies, the power to dominate a whole Court. If the Unseelie Queen or the Seelie King found out, who knew what they'd do? That's if Lady Hornbeam didn't usurp them. Who knew... maybe my mother had wanted to do the same. No wonder Cedar wanted to destroy the talisman.

Up a staircase, along a corridor, down another. I lost track of the way, but soon enough, Viola stopped beside a back door. The way we'd come in the first time.

"We used to meet here," she explained. "It's not the most heavily guarded part of the jail. Most escapees—on the rare occasion that anyone gets out—aren't able to find it. They're never in any condition to run, anyway." She bit her lip and looked down. "I did help one of them get away once, but he was killed before he'd made it into the woods."

"Damned Sidhe. I wish I could help those humans in the other part of the jail." Self-preservation kept me going through the back door and into the trees beyond. I kept walking, Viola at my side, until another roar brought me to a halt.

All hell had broken loose—or slipped its chains. A troll rampaged past the jail, fists swinging, chains hanging from its arms. Trolls were notoriously difficult to subdue, and in wild form like this, even iron chains weren't enough to do much more than piss them off. Several armoured soldiers circled it warily, but couldn't get close enough to strike without being hit by its rapidly swinging fists. More roaring noises came from an open shaft next to the prison. I didn't know where Cedar had disappeared to, but I'd bet he was behind the noise.

I have to get that talisman back.

We turned our backs and ran into the woods behind the jail, avoiding the soldiers—not that they noticed us, with the troll making such a racket. Trees closed around us instantly, somewhat muffling the noise. Viola walked swiftly, forcing me to jump over undergrowth to keep up with her. When Cedar appeared, I nearly ran into him.

He gave me a light smile. "I'm glad you got out. I knew you could do it."

"You're a fool.," Viola broke in before I could speak. "If you wanted to get the Lady's attention, you just did."

His smile faded. "Do you think I don't know that? I had to improvise with what I had, and it happens all I had was a key to the dungeons."

"Which you stole, I guess," I added. "I'm still pissed off at you." Not least because of his antics in the jail. What the hell had been going through his head?

"You have every right to be."

"C'mon." Viola beckoned, leading the way into the woods.

I walked after her, not taking my eyes off Cedar. "What are you doing here, then?"

"Repaying my debts. You saved my life."

"I already called in my favour."

"You picked the wrong moment." He paused. "I never wanted to deceive you. I'm sorry."

"Then give me the real talisman and we'll call it even."

"I can't."

"Stop screwing with me." I whirled on him, so our bodies were inches apart. Underneath his coat... *I knew it.* "You still have it."

He raised his hands and stepped back, and the tree roots by my feet wrapped around my ankles, holding me in place. His expression, though, was tortured. "You can't. It's too late. The final part of my vow came into effect, and—" He choked off.

Viola turned back, eyes widening. "Raine… he means he can't give it back. The vow will make him kill you. If you take the talisman from him… one of you will die."

I stopped struggling against the roots, momentarily stunned. "You—"

He coughed, then said quietly, "Destroying it is the only way."

Lady Hornbeam… she trapped us both.

Shock gave way to fury, and magic tingled over my palms as my hands itched to snatch the talisman back. *No. It's what* she *wants.* The Sidhe had played us all against one another, and would have us destroy each other for sport. There was no other use for a half-blood in their eyes.

Destroying the sceptre would be the perfect revenge. On Lady Hornbeam… and on my mother.

"All right." I nodded. "Let me out of this trap, and I'll come and destroy it with you."

I didn't imagine the momentary flicker of relief on his face before he raised his hands and the tree roots let me go. "Okay. Be careful. Her people are everywhere, and if she knows I'm here, my life is forfeit."

"But you're her son." I walked quickly to keep pace with him, Viola marching ahead.

"That doesn't matter here," he said. "Lady Hornbeam needed a thief, and I was the best candidate. It has to be a half-blood, because our magic isn't as strong and easily detected on enemy territory. We're also less susceptible to iron, though there are exceptions."

"Then why the hell do their soldiers carry iron weapons?"

"They trained us to build up a tolerance to it," said Cedar. "It does work, as long as our skin isn't touching it. And if it breaks the skin—it all but destroys our magic."

"That sounds like torture to me," I told him. "The Sidhe are so fucked up—"

Cedar started to speak, then tensed, instantly alert. "Someone's here."

A rustling came from the bushes, and then several figures appeared. Arrows fired at us from all corners, surrounding us in a circle. We were trapped.

18

A ssassins surrounded us, wearing dark clothes that didn't betray their Court. But the silver-haired man with them was too familiar to me. My brother approached, icy blue eyes boring into mine.

"Give me the talisman," he said.

"I don't have it," I told him. "The Hornbeams took it from me. Good luck stealing it back. Would they like that you're trespassing?"

His gaze slid to Cedar. I held my breath. If he sensed Cedar might have it, I was in trouble, but I doubted it'd cross his mind. To him, we looked like allies.

My bother—Valour's—teeth flashed white. "If I'd claimed the talisman, I would have united all our territories, not divided us."

"I'm not the one sending assassins after people," I spat at him. "Besides, the talisman chose me."

"Then our mother's magic made a terrible error I must correct."

"Guys," I said out of the corner of my mouth. "Run. I can take him."

"Oh, can you?"

He charged, swinging a blade at my ribs. I reached for my iron knife and found nothing. They'd taken my weapon away, of course. But I had the fake talisman. Whipping it out, I deflected the blow. He didn't fight with iron, but with some faerie-made substance. *Oh, you're in trouble now.*

Magic flared from my fingertips, colliding with his blade. The shape warped and clung to his hands, the material melting as my magic took hold of it. He cursed, lunging forwards. I swept aside and hit him over the head with the fake talisman. Then I brought my knee up into his ribs. He yelled in pain, twisting onto his back, unable to let go of the sword… which I'd turned into a useless lump.

I kicked him in the ribs again, and he bellowed in rage, trying to drop the melted weapon. Apparently he hadn't thought to use it to attack me. The thing about living in the mortal realm is that you learn pretty quickly to improvise with what you can get. And the fake talisman was all I had. It might be made of cheap glass, but still hurt when you got hit with it. He moaned in pain and rage, and the other assassins moved in.

Two arrows criss-crossed over my head, inches from my hair. Another snagged my arm. The ground trembled under my feet, and a collective yell went up from the assassins as the nearest trees' branches curved, blocking them from moving. Cedar's magic. I turned back to my brother, and a starburst of green light shone overhead, dazzling my eyes. Then all faded to black.

———

Familiar music woke me from my stupor. I blinked, confused that I was standing—and not in a cell. Instead, I walked down a path cloaked in leaves. Not Winter. There was no snow, only tall, thick trees. Was I dreaming? I hadn't been hit, so why had I blacked out?

Magic. Threads of Summer magic pulled underneath my skin. Somehow, I'd ended up back on their territory, and someone had used a spell to block out my senses. But why I was I still on my feet? And walking, as though I had no control over my own limbs?

Music drifted, carried by the magic. A rush of déjà-vu halted my steps. This definitely wasn't the theatre—but I'd know that music anywhere. And now I recognised the path. It led to the Gathering place, but on Summer's side of it. The shape of the stage became clearer beyond the trees. As for the music, it drew louder. Dizziness made my head swim. I was under the influence of some sort of compulsion—a mild one, because I'd know if it wasn't. And underneath the flood of Summer energy, my own magic pulsed, like a second heartbeat. Thank the Sidhe for that. For a second, I'd worried that I'd somehow been switched over to the Summer Court without knowing it.

But... where was Viola? And Cedar? Soldiers caged me on either side. The prince I'd hit before caught my eye and gave me an ugly look. A chill raced down my back. *Compulsion magic... someone wanted me to march with the army. But why?*

"Did you know," Aspen said, "that you're lucky to be alive right now?"

"Why am I here?"

"For a Gathering, naturally. The Darkwaters trespassed on our territory, so we come to claim compensation."

Okay... But none of that explained how in hell I'd ended up walking with them like an ally.

"You didn't answer my question," I said. "If this is a Gathering, I shouldn't be with your family. I should be on my own stage."

"Since you were found wandering in the woods on your own, we took you under our wing."

"That's not what happened." I scanned his face, looking for clues. "I'm not joking. Tell me what the hell is going on. I wasn't alone in the woods. My servant was with me." I didn't dare mention Cedar.

"There was a strange incident near the jail," he said. "Someone set free some rather dangerous animals. Oddly, this occurred around the same time you were found to have escaped."

So they blamed *me* for it, not Cedar? Wherever he'd gone, he wasn't with the other soldiers. I didn't particularly want to get him into trouble with the Hornbeams, knowing what depravity they were capable of, but what if they punished Viola, too?

"I saw," I told him. "They escaped before I got out of jail. They probably did it themselves. It's not easy to keep a troll chained up in iron. Besides, what did you do with my servant? She had nothing to do with it, either."

"Relax, she's fine. However... she won't be if neither of you can tell the Lady what you did with the sceptre."

So that's what this is about. Of course. Cedar still has it.

"I don't have the talisman." Implicating Cedar would make sure they caught him instead, but I saw no signs of him anywhere. Maybe he'd taken off with the talisman to destroy it like he'd promised. But why leave me alone with them?

"Then who does?"

"I don't know." The lie slipped easily past my teeth. "I was on my way to look for it when you put me under a spell. What was it, compulsion?"

"Yes." He tilted his head. "You're more resistant to it than I realised. I'll have to use a stronger spell next time."

"Try it and I'll do worse than break your face. I won't forget you lured me onto your territory and tried to kill me."

His mouth curved in a cruel smile. "That was something of an experiment, too. I was curious about your magic, and what made it so special. There were rumours you were immune to iron poisoning. Nonsense, clearly."

"That was worth murdering Frances and trying to kill me?" I growled. "You're despicable."

"I'm a prince of Faerie." His eyes laughed at me. "I'm also your watcher, and it's my job to punish you if you try to run. I assume Frances was that half-blood kid who tried to claw out my eyes when I went to ask around for details of your life. That you care so much for strangers is such a very human trait, Raine… you won't survive long in this realm if you don't embrace who you really are."

Like you have a clue, you murdering prick.

I didn't say anything. I might be unarmed, but traces of blood remained on his face from where I'd hit him earlier. A reminder that I'd bested him. On the other hand, a whole army surrounded us, penning me in. If the other families saw me with them—what would they think? Assuming they didn't start a war there and then, because of the Darkwaters trespassing on enemy territory. What was my brother thinking? And how had he known I'd be there?

Our group halted beside the stage. Opposite was another small cluster of people—the assassins, and my brother, in front of the Hornbeams' stage. Rather than making a move to ascend the stage, the soldiers continued to walk to the clear earth between the stages, where the dancers had performed last night.

The sound of rushing water filled the air accompanied by a shiver of intense Winter magic. Lady Darkwater walked towards us, her dress blue and flowing, like a mountain stream. She looked at my brother with distaste on her face. "What are you doing with my assistant?"

Lady Hornbeam stepped forward. Even from the back,

she was a force to be reckoned with. Power radiated off her, masking everything else, feeding on the flood of energy from the music playing somewhere in the background.

"He was found on our territory," she told Lady Darkwater. "Someone also freed our war-beasts from their cages, and they're baying for blood. Have you an explanation?"

"Don't be ridiculous," she said. "This child wasn't sent into your territory."

"I wouldn't lie to me," Lady Hornbeam said softly. She didn't wear her usual green attire—in fact, her uniform was close to the other soldiers', patterned with overlapping black scales covering her body. Only her forbidding stance gave her away as a powerful Sidhe. That, and her staff. Power crackled from it like a barely contained entity of nature. It took everything I had to keep still, to keep my teeth from chattering. Faced with that power, I understood why some Sidhe thought themselves gods. And I had the impression I was about to witness a clash between two of the most powerful Sidhe in the borderlands.

"Well?" said Lady Hornbeam.

Lady Darkwater didn't back down. "I don't know what game you're playing, but I want no part in it. My people have done nothing wrong."

"Not to me, perhaps," said Lady Hornbeam. "But they're about to do a great deal wrong to you."

She waved a hand, and the assassins turned on Lady Darkwater, caging her in. Every last one of them.

What...?

Oh, I thought, far too late—they were double agents. The assassins belonged to the Hornbeams' army, not Winter at all. Their nondescript uniforms hid their allegiance—and for all the times they'd tried to kill me, I'd never seen any of them use magic.

As for my brother, he'd already proved he didn't care who held his allegiance. Even to the enemy Court.

Slowly, everyone moved onto the side of the Hornbeams. And that's when I realised… nobody else was on Lady Darkwater's side. She was alone, surrounded by the enemy.

I tried to catch her gaze, desperately, knowing what was coming. *The Sidhe didn't used to be able to die, but they can now. Like my mother.* Damn the Sidhe, had one of *them* killed her?

I blinked frantically at Lady Darkwater, trying to communicate—*run!* But I might as well have yelled at the wind. The soldiers—her own soldiers—surrounded her in a blur of iron and steel, and she raised her own talisman. A current of air stirred, then struck with the force of a storm, sending the army reeling sideways. And us, too. Even the prince stumbled, the crowd breaking apart. I took my chance to run, but the storm knocked me onto my knees, my whole body shaking. I wasn't the only one. I managed a crawl, but before I'd moved more than a metre, a surge of Summer magic split the air like a lightning bolt.

The storm died abruptly, and a scream came from the Winter Lady, cut off in an instant.

Her body crumpled forwards.

She was dead.

19

I swallowed bile, reeling, horror rooting me to the spot. *The soldiers just killed a Sidhe.* On Lady Hornbeam's orders. She herself dropped elegantly to one knee and picked up... *Lady Darkwater's talisman. That's what she wanted.*

The air hummed as magic whirled around her—thick blue strands of it, wrapping around Lady Hornbeam, and particularly the hand that held the talisman. My breath stopped. Had she just claimed it, in less than a second? *I'd say yes.*

Shit. Like she wasn't overpowered enough.

Lady Hornbeam turned to face us, smiling a terrible smile, and caught my gaze with her impossibly bright eyes. I got her meaning as clearly as though she'd spoken aloud. I wasn't getting out of here alive.

But no soldiers turned on me. Instead, they reversed their steps, heading back down the Gathering path.

Leaving the body of the dead Lady behind.

Numb shock dogged my steps. Somehow, I kept in line with the soldiers, searching in vain for a way out. If I hit one of them, a dozen more would take their place. With the Sidhe that close, having just killed another of their kind, I didn't dare. And they had Viola somewhere. Maybe in the jail again. They must know it was my magic that'd helped us escape. Sure enough, we halted outside the jail first, the soldiers moving in groups in different directions. A circle of them surrounded me, but not the prince. Lady Hornbeam herself stood apart from the others, as though waiting for something. As the crowd thinned, the others dispersing, she moved towards the soldiers surrounding me. Then our gazes locked.

Now Lady Hornbeam carried the power of Lady Darkwater in her right hand and her own in her left, the sheer staggering presence of her knocked me sideways. Her magic was stark and terrifying, a force of nature all on its own. My vision swam, my mortal mind trying in vain to keep eye contact with her, but I was forced to break my gaze first.

"The new Lady Whitefall," she said quietly.

"What?" I responded.

Several audible gasps escaped the lingering crowd.

"I see," she said. "Now I know who you are."

"I know who you are, too," I countered. "A murderess. How many more have you killed?"

"A fair few," she said dismissively. "There were once twice as many families. None were as easy to capture as you, however."

"Is there any reason you're taunting me? Because if you don't mind, I'd like to pick up my property and my assistant and return to my own territory."

"I think we both know you'll never return to your own territory again."

I searched in vain for a gap in the soldiers, but they'd kill me instantly if I ran. My magic couldn't take all of them out. The iron of their weapons was the ultimate defence—deadly to any faerie who touched it. And she stood in front of them, burning bright with a magic strong enough to block out the sun.

"Let me out of here," I said. "You're imprisoning a fellow family leader—an equal."

"You'll never be equal to any of us, you thin-blooded mortal." She gave me a pitying look. "It's almost not worth killing you. You don't even count as a challenge. But the other families will expect proof that I took care of the problem in a suitable way. I shall have to decide how to give it to them."

"You're breaking the laws of the Courts," I said. "The law states that murder is forbidden."

Surely someone knew that what she was doing was way off the rails even for Faerie. But everyone here was half-blood, without half the power she had, and killing us had never mattered to them. Even a mortal heir.

"The murder of pure-blooded faeries, particularly the Sidhe, is forbidden," she corrected. "The murder of an interloper who doesn't belong here… will anyone miss you when you're gone?"

"I will," said Viola.

I spun around. I thought they'd jailed her. Instead, she stood apart from the others, holding a knife she must have taken from one of the soldiers. Her hands visibly shook—*the weapon's iron. She shouldn't be holding it.*

"You," Lady Hornbeam said. "You're the traitor."

"You hate that you lost me to another family," said Viola. "Don't you?"

"Viola," I whispered—even I knew that arguing with a Sidhe was a bad move, and Viola of all people should, too. But there was steel in her gaze, and her weapon-free hand glowed with magic. *Viola. You can't beat her. Neither of us can.* Then it hit me—she was trying to draw Lady Hornbeam's attention away from me.

The other soldiers didn't react to her words. Even if they had magic—and they probably did—the iron weapons they carried dulled it, and they couldn't hold a candle to a pure Sidhe carrying two talismans. Maybe more. She'd picked up Lady Darkwater's like it wasn't a big deal. How many other times had she done the same?

"Go on." Lady Hornbeam looked sideways at her. "If you try, you're breaking the laws of the Courts yourself. As though a half-blood could ever outmatch me."

We're losing. Despair settled in my chest like a dead weight. The Courts couldn't even accuse her of killing Lady Darkwater either, because she'd deliberately given the job to her assassins. If accusations of murder came into play, they'd take the fall. Gladly, no doubt, because they obeyed her without question.

"I'm not interested in fighting you," I said. "Your delightful son tricked me into coming into your territory by claiming you kidnapped someone I care about."

"My son. Aspen. You nearly killed him, he claims."

"He tried to kill *me* with iron," I retaliated. "I had to teach him a lesson."

"You're an interesting mortal."

"I'm the heir of a powerful Sidhe," I told her. "What do you want with me? You got me to come to the Gathering already."

"I had insufficient chances to take your measure. Now I have. You're more than a match for most half-bloods—except my thief, perhaps... but I still know so little about you, mortal."

"The name's Raine, and you haven't earned the right to that information."

She gave a soft laugh. "So you do know how to play our games."

"Is there a part where you let me go because I've done nothing that wasn't provoked?"

"A valiant attempt, but no, there isn't." She gestured to the soldiers. "Bring her in. I'll find a cell that can hold her."

Another soldier moved to her side, and my blood turned to ice colder even than the palace. Cedar. He moved close to Lady Hornbeam… and he was holding the talisman. Not the fake one.

The last threads of my hope slipped away.

He's with her. That's where he went.

"Wait," croaked a voice from amongst the assassins. "Let me take care of her myself."

My brother. The traitorous worm stood a little apart from the others, his face bloody, one eye swollen shut. Two soldiers caged him on either side.

Lady Hornbeam tilted her head. "Hmm? Aren't you the one who failed to kill her before?"

"She has nothing left now. Don't bother with her. She's not worth the effort."

So much for sibling love. Though he didn't look too happy. Plainly, working for her hadn't worked out in the way he'd hoped. More's the pity.

The green-eyed prince sidled over, smirked at me, then leaned over to whisper in Lady Hornbeam's ear.

"What?" she snapped. "The Court—fine. Give them any excuse. Make sure nobody steps out of line. And you—lock these two up. You're lucky not to be jailed yourself."

My brother looked from me to her. "What? These two? You mean that one as well, right?" He jerked his head at Viola.

"No, I mean you and your sister."

"But I worked for you!"

"You're too stubborn, mortal, and your blood is tainted with the 'Whitefalls'."

The soldiers holding him stepped forward, dragging him along with them. The soldiers surrounding me, meanwhile, moved into a similar position.

"I thought I was going to the palace," I said.

"A filthy thief like you doesn't deserve to lay their eyes upon it, mortal," said Lady Hornbeam. "Don't let her escape this time. As for my traitorous soldier, I'll let you decide the punishment, Aspen." She addressed the prince, who smirked again, his attention sliding over to Viola.

No.

I couldn't break past the soldiers. They surrounded my brother and me, pushing us on towards the jail. Lady Hornbeam followed closely behind like she expected me to make a run for it. Pausing at the jail doors, she peered inside.

"It's grim, isn't it? My husband doesn't like me keeping the mortals here, but they have to be kept contained. He usually leaves his pets outside to die. I think my way is kinder."

My stomach turned over. *She's sick. They're both sick.*

"I'm *not* a mortal," my brother said desperately. "I'm not—"

"You can die, can't you?"

So can you. I clamped the thought down. If I'd read the situation right, the Court had already learned of Lady Darkwater's murder. Lady Hornbeam was clearly trying to come up with a reasonable explanation. Maybe they'd try her for treason. But only her assassins would take the hit, because they'd been the ones to deal the killing blow. And... they could lie. Even to the Sidhe. I could see the scene as clearly as though it took place right in front of me. The assassins would tell any lie, gladly lay down their lives for her. Because they knew their place, as half-blood slaves to an immortal wannabe-goddess.

And now she planned to lock me in a cell with my lunatic

brother, who was apparently working for three families at once.

The soldiers dragged my brother and me into the first available cage. Three sides of the cage were iron, and a grating sounded as it lifted from the ground.

"Hey!" I yelled, but too late. We were off the ground, on a cage tilted at a slight angle, and if either of us hit the iron, we'd be dead in seconds.

Lady Hornbeam had gone. The soldiers checked the doors were locked, then walked away. The iron's presence had sent all magic fleeing, and I didn't even have a fake talisman this time. Or my knife.

My bother pushed to his feet, glaring at me.

20

I held still, meeting his gaze. "Don't bother fighting me again," I told him. "You'll die if you hit the iron."

"We'll both die in here anyway." He ran a hand over his bruised face.

"Giving up already?"

He shrugged. "It was worth a try."

Valour's ice cold Winter Sidhe demeanour had vanished entirely. Had it all been an act?

"Which part?" I asked. "The attempted murders, or being a sycophant to Lady Darkwater—or Hornbeam? Who do you even work for? Are your powers from Winter at all?"

"That doesn't matter to her. And now it doesn't matter to me, either," he muttered. "I'm not working for Lady Hornbeam. I never was. I let her *think* I was, because the alternative was death. I knew she planned to kill Lady Darkwater, and I'd be killed as collateral damage if I didn't turn traitor. She wants *all* the family leaders dead, and this isn't the first time she's done it."

"Our mother?"

"It wouldn't surprise me."

Now he'd dropped the creepy threatening act, I couldn't summon up any fear of him, not compared to the terror that gripped my very soul at the idea of Lady Hornbeam using my talisman. Now Cedar had betrayed me for real, had handed it over to her, we were all screwed.

"She needs to die," I said.

"Good luck with that."

"Thought you wanted me dead. You've tried to kill me twice now."

"The second time was on orders. The first, I lost control. I wanted that talisman, so I could get it away from her."

"Sure you did. Are all you half-Sidhe deceitful bastards, or did I just get lucky?"

"I'm telling the truth," said Valour. "You don't know what she could do with that talisman. Or maybe you do."

"Yeah. I do." Maybe it was better off elsewhere, but it'd been placed in my hands, and it was *mine*. Not hers. Nor anyone else's.

"Our mother was the same," said my brother. "She wanted to unite the families, Summer and Winter both, and make her own Court to rule over both."

"Then why didn't she use the talisman? Nobody's even left in the Court."

"Something went wrong," he said. "I don't know what. I wasn't actually raised in Faerie, but in a half-blood community in the mortal realm. But I knew there's been unrest everywhere for a while now. Especially amongst these families, far from the main Courts. They're old, their power is waning, and they need more talismans."

"So that's why Lady Hornbeam's stealing them, huh."

"Yes. But I can't say I know what she wants to do with—" He broke off. "Someone's coming."

At once he rose to his feet, delivering a kick that sent me sprawling onto the cage floor. Winded, gasping, I clambered upright in time to see green and blue light slide over his skin in a way I'd never seen before. The blue light was his own magic, which I recognised even now. And the green—was hers. I felt the taste of it, sharp and cold in the back of my throat, an echo of the formidable power she possessed.

And she'd used it to bind him under a vow.

"I have to kill you," Valour said, and reached into his pocket for a knife. So he hadn't been disarmed, unlike me. The cage had no way out, save for a quick death by iron. If the vow told him to kill me… one of us would die.

I dodged the first blow, kicking at his knees to knock his legs out from underneath him. He fell, heavily, and gasped in pain. His knife hand jerked forwards as though pulled by an invisible force, but missed me by inches. He stabbed, and I backed away, the cage's iron bars brushing against me through my clothes. The cage was too small to dodge him for long without touching the iron.

He stabbed again, but the knife came nowhere near me. *Wait...* he was fighting it, somehow, each stab veering away at the last second as I fended him off. Blood streamed from his mouth, though I hadn't hit him there, and his eyes glowed white. The vow was literally killing him for sparing me.

Come on, magic! I tried to summon up a trickle like I had in the other cage, but the iron's proximity dulled it to nothing, and there was nothing to hit inside or outside of the cage.

Except us. I could still transform my clothes. And that armour the soldiers wore looked pretty resilient.

I channelled the magic into myself, creating armour that covered my vulnerable mortal body. Then I stepped in front of the knife, which simply glanced off. I'd won us a few more seconds. My brother dropped to his knees, strangled sounds escaping him. His knife hand jerked towards me, uncontrollably. A sick taste rose on my tongue.

Then his hands moved to the iron bars.

"No!"

His body sagged, the hand that had touched the bars turning grey. I screamed, but too late. The iron effect was too fast—even as I reached him, he fell, mouth dripping blood, skin turning greyish-white.

As his body convulsed, the knife slipped from his free hand, and he grabbed mine, pulling me closer to him. I tugged back, suddenly positive he planned to take me down with him—but his hand brushed the mark on my jaw, and a surge of energy jolted through my whole body.

"I—that's my gift," he choked. "Magic... transfer..." His voice faded to nothing.

He was dead. And he'd given me what magic he'd had left.

I fell to my knees, dizzy, numb. Cedar had betrayed me. My brother was dead. And I was alone, aside from Viola, who was probably next on their execution list.

Not if I can help it.

Someone must have heard the commotion. Escaping the vow in death hadn't been his only motive. Sure enough, after a couple of minutes, two guards approached the cage. I remained very still, eyes on the gap where the door opened. Just far enough away that they'd assume I couldn't reach it.

As they reached in to remove the body, I lunged at them.

The world blurred as I shot through the gap, colliding with the guard in a clash of iron and steel. My body was still covered in the armour I'd conjured, and the cage bars didn't hurt me as I tackled the guard to the ground, holding my brother's knife in one hand. One quick stab, and I leaped to my feet. As I pelted outside, into the shadow of a huge tree, I fired magic at the trunk.

The tree bent beneath the power, bowing over the prison's exit, blocking the path. I didn't stop to see if the others had got through, but kept going, clearing ground.

I had to stop eventually, but breathing in the taste of freedom, the absence of iron, removed the fog from my head. My brother had died to save me, and now for both of us, I needed to get the talisman back. The problem was, of course, the damn thing was in her hands now. Thanks to Cedar.

Nothing about the way he'd played me made sense. Okay, so a vow was pretty much impossible to fight, but I'd thought he'd found a way around it. I'd thought he was at least *trying* to fight it, even the unbreakable words of the Sidhe themselves. Just look how my brother had had to kill himself to escape.

The breath stuck in my chest, choking me. This was the game we were all playing, in which one mistake meant certain death. Because there was no undoing a vow, only replacing it, and even I couldn't think of a way to subvert the command to kill. What my mother had done to Viola had only switched her allegiance, and she hadn't been under any vow but a command to be loyal.

But… what if Lady Hornbeam had stolen her back? And the talisman? If Lady Hornbeam used it the way it was intended, she could even challenge the Courts themselves.

A figure appeared at my side, leaping down from the nearest tree. Cedar watched me, his face unreadable. My heart drummed. After watching my brother die, I wasn't sure I had the heart to let someone else die in front of me. But those were the thoughts of a mortal, one with no chance of surviving here. To spare everyone the talisman's wrath, I had to be every inch the Sidhe my mother had been, even if it ate away what remained of my mortal heart.

"So you're hers." I conjured magic to my fingertips, readying an attack. "Give me the talisman back, or you're dead."

Cedar took a step back, and I ran at him, tackling him to the ground. My knees pinned him, and my hand locked around his wrist, the other reaching for the talisman inside his coat.

"I—can't." He wrenched his hand away. "Unless you want to leave another body behind you—"

"Maybe I do," I snarled. "Your family killed my brother."

His eyes widened. "I thought—I thought he tried to kill you. He's dead?"

"Yeah, because he killed himself rather than take my life. What the hell are you doing? Did you see what they did with Viola?"

"They're taking her to the palace. I barely got away. I intended to help you escape."

"You're too late. Didn't she make you leave the sceptre with her?"

"I left the fake one."

I stared for a moment in disbelief. "You didn't."

"I did. She conveniently left a loophole when she told me to hand it over to her."

I laughed, half shocked. "You had it there. Right in front of her. And she didn't know?"

"She'll know when she tries to use it, but she's a little preoccupied at the moment. The unfortunate escape of the Hornbeams' war beasts caused more damage than she expected."

"But she still has Viola." I released him, and waited a second before getting to my feet. "All right. I'm going to set her free. Then I'm going to undo that vow, so I can see if you're really a man of your word."

He rose to his feet, too. "You're not going to kill me."

"No. I'm not. We're all pawns in their games."

"I know." His forehead pinched. "Oh—and you might need this." He reached into his pocket and handed me my iron knife. "I think that'd be more useful than magic against the guards."

"Thanks." I looked down at my armoured clothes, which still looked like the soldiers'.

"That will work as long as *she* doesn't see you," he said, eying my uniform. "She's the most dangerous—though she's arrogant with it. I can come with you up to the side entrance to the palace, but I can't be seen. When she finds out what I did..."

Not *if*, but *when*. For one wild moment I wondered what'd happen if I just let all the magic inside my talisman loose with abandon, and tore up everything in my path. But I didn't dare risk Viola's safety, not when she'd put herself in danger to protect me. I needed to do only what was necessary to get out of this mess alive. Besides, most of the magic remained inside the sceptre, in Cedar's hands. I sensed it as we walked swiftly through the trees—my own magic, the power begging to be used. Except I couldn't take it, because it'd trigger Cedar's vow, we'd be forced to fight to the death, and Viola might never escape her former family. We were bound to one another—Viola to me, me to Cedar, Cedar to Lady Hornbeam. And the person controlling us all had killed a Sidhe today already.

Between the trees, I spotted brambles grown into the shape of a fence, barbed with spikes along every inch.

"The gate's around that way," Cedar whispered, pointing. "I'll have to stay back here. I can't go inside, they'd know I was there. Wait for the next group of guards and join them."

Because I looked like one of them. I exhaled, wishing the tight sensation in my chest would go away. "All right."

His breath was inches from my ear. "Please stay safe, Raine."

I remained still, hoping my disguise held up. Cedar's presence wouldn't help either of us, but I'd never felt quite as alone as I did now, waiting beside that deadly wall for more soldiers to show up. And they did—small groups of them, all dressed in the same uniform. Some carried crossbows, some had swords strapped to their backs, and every one of them was half-blood.

I veered away from the trees, positioning myself behind the group, and concentrated on walking at a steady enough pace to catch up to them without alerting their attention. My light feet didn't give me away, and I reached the gates without incident. The two spear-wielding guards at the gate didn't even check who passed them by—their attention was fixed on the space in front of the palace, where a crowd had gathered.

In any other circumstances, the palace would have rendered me speechless. White and gold and imposing, it towered above us, radiating vitality and power. Magic hummed from every facet of its walls, but my eyes paused only for a second before focusing on the crowd.

Lady Hornbeam appeared to stand in the crowd's centre —but someone else stood beside her. Viola. I couldn't hear what Lady Hornbeam was saying, but the crowd remained deadly still. Transfixed, or waiting for orders.

Nobody could fight so many at once, especially not the vicious predator in the group's centre. *Don't intervene. Not yet.*

I walked quietly amongst the guards until we reached the group. As we did, the Lady fell silent, her gaze sweeping the crowd. My breath stuck in my chest, but most guards wore the same awed, terrified expressions. She looked back at Viola. "I've had about enough of your insolence. If you are truly unable to swear to serve me again, then let's see what happens when I use this."

Lady Hornbeam held out the false sceptre so it nearly touched Viola's forehead.

There was a sound like beating wings, and my heart hammered so frantically I was sure her sharp ears would pick up on it.

Lady Hornbeam laughed. "What better way to test this than to undo the spell Lady Whitefall used to take my servant from me?"

Viola stood still. *The spell can't be undone.* She knew it as well as I did. Her vow bound her to me, and the only way to undo it was death. And everyone would know I was still alive the second Lady Hornbeam used the fake talisman.

She'll also know Cedar betrayed her.

Lady Hornbeam held the fake sceptre out, and blue threads spun up her arm. So it did contain some power. Maybe enough to convince her.

The light brightened. I edged closer, concealing myself behind the other soldiers. The dazzling light blinded one side of the crowd, offering me a chance to get behind Viola, then to the side of her. As the light brightened, she looked away, and our eyes met.

I gave a slight nod, telling her not to give me away, and then deliberately knocked into a soldier, hand over my eyes so as to pretend the light was the cause of my clumsiness. The soldiers hissed in annoyance as I elbowed two of them in the ribs, then tripped sideways into another, moving forwards at the same time. Another soldier tripped, and their formation broke. I lunged for Viola, grabbing her arm and pulling her back through the crowd—

"Nice try, Raine," said Lady Hornbeam. "Did you think I wouldn't sense your magic?"

22

I stood frozen as the light faded, and in a flash, Lady Hornbeam struck Viola with the fake talisman. Viola fell, gasping, bleeding from her head.

"Stop!" I shouted, my voice hoarse. "Don't hurt her. None of this is her fault."

Her deadly gaze landed on me, arresting, paralysing. "Nobody betrays me."

"Killing us won't change the fact that my mother got the best of you."

"Soldiers!" she barked. "Pull back."

The ground cleared as the soldiers moved away. Music struck up in the background, a steady beat that pulsed through the ground. My heart drummed faster. What had she concocted this time?

"Let her go," I said. "Both of us. You've proved your point." The talisman was gone. And all I had left was… "I want to make a bargain with you."

Alarm rippled through the soldiers. Lady Hornbeam tossed back her head and laughed. "I thought so, mortal. As it happens, I devised a test just for this. Win, and you walk away free."

A test. It's too easy. Easy… yet tempting. What choice did I have? Her magic went beyond me, beyond anyone. She was power incarnate and the only thing keeping her from finishing me off was the lure of playing a fun game with the mortal who'd strode willingly into her territory.

"If I win this test of yours," I told her, "you'll let us leave without being harmed."

"Agreed," she said, waving her hand. The air warped, the palace scene changing to the jail. Viola pushed to her knees, wiping blood from her forehead. Lady Hornbeam had rearranged the entire territory *around* us, and now we stood beside the prison, in the empty space where I'd seen beasts rampaging around after Cedar had set them free…

Thud. Thud. Thud.

Wait. That wasn't a drumbeat, but footsteps. In front of the jail, walls sprang into existence, turning transparent to reveal the crowd on the other side. All the soldiers waited, watching, as it dawned on me that the walls caged Viola and I into a small space. An arena-like space.

Lady Hornbeam herself stood behind the glass, too. I pressed my hand to it, then tapped it with my fingers. "I wouldn't," she said softly. "The walls come down only when I choose. Save your energy, mortal. You'll need it."

Thud. Thud. Thud.

Viola made a strangled noise. I spun around, my heart sinking somewhere below the earth. The troll I'd seen before lumbered into view, the walls of the arena moving and snapping into place behind it. Sealing it in here… with us.

Chains still hung from its huge, battered body, and the iron had cut into its muscled arms and shoulders deep enough to draw blood. Trolls had so little magic that the iron hadn't killed it yet—another creature would be long dead after such abuse. But this monster just looked really, really pissed off. Its pitch-black, pupil-less eyes narrowed, white clouds crossing its dark irises. Had someone blinded it, or damaged its eyes? Maybe, but its other senses would work just fine, and the arena—sustained by Lady Hornbeam's magic—had no exit at all.

Lucky for both of us that she hadn't taken my weapon away.

I pulled out the iron knife and ran towards the beast, ignoring Viola's warning shout. She was unarmed, so I needed to draw its attention away from her—and deal as much damage as possible before it started one of its deadly rampages. It carried no weapon of its own, but its giant hands were strong enough to crack a skull, while one stomp of its feet could shatter bones. As for those chains, they could do enough damage on their own. A mere brush of iron against my skin and it was game over.

The chains swung overhead. I dropped into a forward roll and cut at the troll's thick legs, my knife biting into the flesh. Even a beast this size would fall if you cut deep enough, but its leathery skin was tough as hell, and I'd tire before it did.

We can't die here.

The music continued, a pulsing drumbeat under our feet nearly drowned out by the troll's roaring and yelling. I sank my blade to the hilt in its foot, and it jerked away, knocking me onto my back.

Viola screamed my name. The troll's foot stamped in the direction of my head, and I rolled over, barely dodging in time. She hit out, but the troll's chain caught her, sending her flying into the wall.

"Viola!" I shouted.

She didn't get up.

Viola.

I climbed to my feet and renewed my attack, but I was

weakening. The presence of the troll's iron cuffs sapped my energy, too. I rolled out of the way of another swing of the chain, hearing the crowd's excited screeches. She'd turned our deaths into a performance.

Rage filled me, steadying my hand. My knife sliced into its ankle, and the edge of its foot caught me in the face, sending me tumbling onto the ground. I managed to land on my feet through sheer instinct—but the knife stayed where it was, stuck in the troll's thick ankle. The crowd howled with laughter as I was forced to drop to my front and roll between the beast's feet to avoid its retaliatory strike, but fear and fury masked all humiliation.

Without my knife, my palm tingled with the presence of my magic, even underneath the sharp spears of Summer energy holding the arena's walls upright. Lady Hornbeam's.

I splayed my hands against the nearest section of wall and pushed, trying to transform it. Lady Hornbeam's magic pushed back, hard. The buzz of energy lifted me off my feet and slammed me onto my back. Gasping, winded, I rolled over. My knife had lodged deep in the troll's ankle, and it flailed, trying to pull it free.

Blue light lit up my hands again, and this time, I aimed my attack at the floor beneath the troll's feet. But the earth was packed tight and didn't budge an inch. *Think, Raine. Think...*

Rain. Water. I'd conjured ice from the moisture in the air the first time I'd used my magic. The earth here wasn't dry, otherwise plants wouldn't thrive.

I aimed magic at the earth again, and this time, water bubbled to the surface, flowing over the ground, and the troll slipped, steadying itself against the arena's side. Water flowed over the surface, swirling higher, and the earth swallowed the troll's feet. I might not be able to affect the iron, but it didn't matter. The ground itself would eat the enemy alive. I moved to stand beside Viola and directed my magic away from us, leaving the small area where we stood clear, but flooding the rest of the arena.

The troll sank to its knees, swallowed up in the earth. I kept pouring energy into the earth, willing it to break underneath the arena's walls. The crowd's cries became shouts of anger. The troll flailed, the ground giving way and pulling it further underneath. As it fell onto its back, its huge feet came up, the knife still sticking from its ankle.

I leaped, and the crowd held its breath as I soared, slamming down onto the troll's knee and yanking the dagger free. As it surfaced, arms flailing, I lunged again, slicing open its throat. Then I jumped clear, flipping in the air then landing beside Viola. I almost thought I heard applause.

But the arena was still standing. The swirling water had stopped, even as the troll's lifeless body floated to the surface.

The crowd was deadly silent. I took in a breath, scanning for Lady Hornbeam. "The game's over," I called loudly. "I won. Let us go."

"You should have thought more carefully before cheating me," she said. "Your friend goes free. But you, deceiver—you will pay for the treason you committed against me."

Viola disappeared in a rush of green light, as did the troll. Even the water disappeared, leaving packed earth behind.

In their place stood a single person.

Cedar.

And he held the talisman. The real one. She knew, and she hadn't taken it away from him for this reason… to punish both of us for daring to conspire to destroy it. Horror trickled down my spine. I couldn't move, could hardly breathe.

Lady Hornbeam's voice reached me. "I'm told you're an excellent thief, Raine. Let's see how you last against mine."

Cedar's eyes were panicked, desperate. In his hands was

the true talisman, at the whim of a bloodthirsty immortal. She was going to force me to kill him, like she'd done to my brother. Nobody, no matter how powerful, could fight a faerie vow.

Unless his desire to live outweighed the impulse to spare my life, and he tried to kill me anyway.

I opened my mouth to tell Lady Hornbeam to get stuffed, and he shook his head imperceptibly. Wait…was it possible she didn't know we were allies? To outsiders, we stood face to face, each waiting for the other to attack. If we stayed like this, Lady might guess he was on my side, and exploit the hell out of it. I had no choice—if he wouldn't attack me, then I'd fake it for both of us.

I raised my knife and swiped at him, but apparently he'd been waiting for me to. He dodged and caught my arm, preventing me from grabbing for the talisman—I'd hoped he'd do exactly that, because I'd had no intention of actually taking it. I pulled my arm free and circled him. He did likewise, and only the clearness of his gaze indicated he wasn't under the vow's thrall.

As long as I made sure not to touch the talisman.

Impatient shouts came from the crowd while we circled one another. The Hornbeam soldiers saw this as a disappointing follow-up to the troll fight. They wanted blood.

The air flickered, and where there'd once been empty space, a cluster of trees shot up from the earth, nearly impaling both of us. I danced to the right, forced to climb onto a root to avoid being hit, and Cedar did likewise as the trees grew higher and wider, filling the whole arena and blocking out even the sky.

If they keep climbing, maybe I can get out. I doubted she'd built in such an obvious weakness, but you never knew. Cedar's vow had a loophole—as long as I didn't try to take the talisman back, he'd remain in control of his own mind. I *had* to think of a way to stop him, so we could finish her off before one of us died.

The ground was completely covered in sprawling roots. We'd have to be careful to keep our balance—but this was hardly the first time I'd experienced this particular dilemma. In no time, the drop was sheer, and worse than broken bones awaited below. He had a healing ability. I didn't. But I doubted she'd spare either of our lives in the end.

"KILL. KILL." Words rang over the trees, and the branches continued to move, boxing us in, blocking the sky. Cedar looked at me, still gripping the talisman.

Mine.

The talisman gleamed, enticing, its power luring me in.

Magic swarmed over my hands, tugging me towards it. *No...*

I aimed the magic at the branches, intending to transform them, but collided with a solid barrier. Lady Hornbeam's magic must be *inside* the trees—which meant I couldn't use magic on them. Of course she wouldn't let me escape that easily. I climbed higher, firing magic at the branches over my head, but to no effect. There was no escape.

"That's enough," snapped Lady Hornbeam. "Thief, she has already tried to take the talisman from you. I command you to kill her."

I held my breath.

She'd twisted the vow's meaning. I didn't need to know the original words to work out she'd found a loophole. Cedar only had to kill me after I tried to take the talisman—but I'd done so before. Several times. She knew, or she'd guessed. It didn't matter.

I grabbed a branch, pulling myself higher as green light ignited around Cedar, flashed in his eyes... which then went blank, as though her magic had wiped them clean.

He jumped onto the same level as me, knife in hand, face calm.

Her puppet. Not Cedar, who'd I'd allowed to help me against my better judgement.

Not the thief. Her toy. Like any other mortal.

A roaring sounded in my ears. I climbed higher, countering his attacks, knocking his sword hand aside. The unsteady footing barely slowed him, and every stab was certain, aiming to kill. I danced higher, dodging, blocking, hitting back with the side of my blade—stalling for time. *Think, Raine.* There was no escaping this arena, even if I killed him. She'd find a loophole in our bargain, same as with him, and keep me here for the remainder of my existence.

However short that time may be.

The branches shifted, pushing me towards him again, and my hand locked around his wrist, pushing the knife away from my face. "How'd you get that scar?" I asked desperately, searching his eyes for any trace of the person he'd once been. "Did she do it? With iron?"

Iron.

Iron dampened magic, and Cedar himself had said that iron in the bloodstream destroyed our magic…

One way to test my theory.

I yanked his weapon hand down, hard, wrenching his arm sideways. *Sorry, Cedar.* He made no sound as his wrist twisted, his grip on the knife giving a little—just a little.

I steadied myself on the branch, pushing my own knife towards his exposed wrist, and the branches underneath my feet moved without warning.

I fell, arms flailing, hands grabbing at the nearest branch. My own knife slipped through my fingers, slicing into the branch—

The branch gave way, crumbling beneath the iron blade.

Of course.

I grabbed another branch with my free hand, pulling myself upright. Cedar had jumped to a lower level, ready to meet me. His expression remained eerily calm.

I lunged forwards, and sliced through the branch underneath his feet. This time, my blade caught the bare skin of his palm as he fell, grabbing the tree branch opposite me for balance—

And clear hazel eyes stared into mine.

It worked. Faerie vows might not be like ordinary magic, but somehow—I'd got through.

Cedar pulled himself upright, breathing heavily, holding his injured hand. I'd cut deeper than I'd intended, and the iron poisoning effect was already out in force.

"Cut the branches," I whispered.

Cedar shook his head. "I gave you the clue, Raine," he whispered. "In the note."

The note. What had it said?

He stepped closer to me, inching along the branch, and grabbed my free hand. Before I could pull myself free, he'd pressed the talisman into it.

I froze in shock, opening my palm rather than taking it. "Your vow... I can't take it."

"Then don't." He smiled.

"But I'm not...." *Wait.*

A shock jolted up my arm, followed by a flood of magic. I wasn't trying to take the talisman, but its power was transferring to me anyway. I could take the *magic,* without the talisman. Both were mine. But magic was bound to my very soul, not an object. *That's what he meant. Of course...*

Then Cedar's eyes glazed over again, and he kicked the knife from my hand. It sliced through branches as it fell through the trees, out of sight.

No.

Wait. What else had the note said? *Iron dulls it.* Of course…

Magic waited for me. All I needed to do was grab the reins—and pull. The talisman's light died as the power surged into me, and Lady Hornbeam's voice screamed, "Kill her, you fool!"

Sorry, Cedar.

I grabbed his wrist again, still holding the magic in my other hand, and let go.

This time, the trees trembled with the force of the power I'd wrenched from the talisman. Branches exploded outwards, shattering into pieces. The magical barrier crumpled as my magic collided with hers, raw and untamed and *mine.*

Her scream of fury reverberated in my ears as the ground rushed up to meet us.

23

Magic shot from my palms, hitting the earth and softening the fall. I landed in a roll and came to my feet to find the audience had gone. And so had Cedar.

Lady Hornbeam and I were outside the palace, the arena and audience gone. Green tendrils of light spun around her, making her whole body glow with radiance. A mortal who beheld her might think they looked upon an angel, until she proved them horribly wrong.

Cedar. Viola. I hope they're okay.

"Do you know how many talismans I possess, Raine?" she queried.

"You mean how many you stole?"

"Won," she said. "Conquered. You acquired yours by a trick and a technicality. It should be mine."

"Keep telling yourself that," I said. "We're not so different."

"We are nothing alike, mortal."

"No, we aren't," I told her. "Unlike you, I keep my word. You promised I'd walk away free."

"You invalidated that agreement by poisoning my thief against me. I'll deal with you—then I'll take great pains to ensure nobody else ever tries to defy me again."

Magic hummed in the air, surrounding her in green light. She had multiple talismans, Summer and Winter both, but I'd never asked if someone with more than one talisman could use all of them at the same time. Surely not. Everyone's magic had a particular focus, even if they had multiple abilities like a lot of the Sidhe. Some could heal… it was pretty safe to say she probably had that ability, because it was more common in Summer Sidhe. And of course, she had control over her entire territory.

A blade appeared in her hand, bone-white, honed like a sharpened branch. *A talisman.*

"I think I know what I'm going to do to you," she whispered.

Abruptly, the sensation of her magic changed, sharpening, becoming colder. Like… *Winter.* It must be one of the talismans she'd stolen.

The air rushed from my lungs as the world froze, trapping me in a block of solid ice. I gasped, struggling for breath, but the magic choked me, freezing the air in my lungs, my whole body rigid, trapped.

Both kinds of magic did her bidding, and she'd chosen to use magic belonging to my own Court against me.

"You…" I croaked. "You don't deserve this magic. You didn't win it with your own hands." I barely got half the words out, but the movement of my lips against the ice dulled the numb sensation momentarily, and I sensed my own magic beneath the suffocation. Unfortunately, the ability to transform things didn't help when I couldn't breathe.

But I could still transform the ice into something else.

Magic flowed from my palms. Water surged around me, drenching me as all the ice melted at once.

And rose to attack her, shards of ice aimed to spear her all over.

Lady Hornbeam raised her hand and the ice bounced off an invisible shield. I fell to my knees, coughing, trying desperately to regain control over my own limbs.

The air whipped around us and suddenly we stood in the forest between trees. Blue light swirled around her, merging with her own green aura into a turquoise torrent of deadly magic.

"Both Courts will bow to me, mortal," she hissed. "Winter and Summer waste their time with stubbornly pursuing peace by having nothing to do with one another, not realising that their goals are the same, and if they united, they could conquer all."

"And you plan to unite them?" I wheezed. "Or kill them all for daring to challenge you? Why does my talisman matter, if you plan to conquer them both?"

"It doesn't," she said, "but I never allow anyone to get the best of me."

Oh. My mouth parted in surprise—she didn't want the talisman at all. She was still, after years, hung up on the fact that my mother had stolen away one of her soldiers. She just wanted the talisman because of this petty, ridiculous feud.

I struggled to my feet. "Does your husband know you're trying to kill me? What does he think of your habit of collecting talismans? I thought you were meant to rule this territory as equals."

She laughed. "Equals? Never. His allegiance is to me alone, but he'll never dare intervene. Not as long as I have the family's magic in my own hands."

"You stole *his* magic?"

"He handed it over willingly." A vicious smile curled her lip. "I've long wanted to punish him for consorting with so many mortals. An eternity is a long time to enact punishment. Pity *you* don't have that long."

Shears of ice fanned from her palms. I danced out of the way of her attack, alarmed that Winter magic had so much effect used against me. She must have mastered its power. As for mine, it was no use transforming anything when she had absolute control over her territory.

A new wave of ice spread across the ground, locking me into place, freezing my legs up to the knees. As she stalked towards me, I spat at her feet.

She looked at me with pure disgust. "You filthy little mortal. You have no respect."

"Your son tricked me into coming here. *You* tricked me into making a bargain then changed the terms. I owe you no respect, Lady Hornbeam, because you've shown me none at all."

I wrenched my foot free, turning the ice to water, but it froze again almost immediately, crawling up my leg. Our magic collided, and my teeth rattled against one another as my power fetched up against hers. Her perfect face swam in and out of focus, and even this close, all I could see were her eyes—green, bright with power, laced with malice and cunning. Inhuman. I was nothing more than a toy to be cast aside, yet she hadn't killed me outright. I was entertainment, likely the first mortal to ever directly challenge her.

Her next attack sent me sprawling, spots dancing before my eyes as my mouth sealed shut, frozen over with ice. Eyes watering, I countered her magic with mine—blue light shone from my hands, but it bounced off her as though she had a shield around herself. Instead, I melted the ice. Water flowed over my mouth, and I gasped for air, spitting it out. If I could just *think*—

She pointed the sword at me with feigned boredom, then took out the sceptre in her other hand. "Pity. Handing this over would have been the simplest way for you to escape. I'm going to enjoy making you scream."

Shards of ice pierced my hands, materialising from the air. A cry of agony built in my chest, but I clamped it down. I hadn't thought such tiny wounds could cause so much pain. The ice crept up my sleeves, and I tore at each of my hands as though to rip it free. Yet for every shard I pulled free, they kept appearing, a thousand tiny instruments of torture gouging my skin. Worse than iron, worse than anything. A whimper escaped as the ice stabbed underneath my sleeves. She could reach my entire body, inch by painful inch, and torture me until I broke.

But tormenting me took all of her attention, and she'd left a gap in her defences.

I wrenched my screaming hands apart and found the little magic I had left, aiming it at the ground under her feet. The earth shook but didn't break. The pain abated for a second and magic pulsed from my skin, melting the ice, sending droplets of water spiralling to the ground. She let out a yell of rage and her hands came around my throat, squeezing, icy cold. Her grip was tight, unyielding, impossible to break.

Shattering pain shook my body as blue light ignited again. My magic *moved,* as though pulled away from me and towards her. Never mind the talisman—she was trying to pull my magic out of me by sheer force.

I didn't want to find out the hard way who the magic was truly loyal to. She'd killed a Sidhe, without even dirtying her own hands. And she was power incarnate, a figure mortals would tremble to look upon. I stood locked into place, helpless, her hands reaching deep inside my soul for the magic.

"You're nothing more than a worthless human," she whispered, a smile playing on her lips. "And I'd like nothing more than to break you."

Break me. Like all the humans the Sidhe captured. Like my own mother did to my father. I should be more afraid than I was, maybe, but I'd never wanted to be one of them. The idea of wielding the talisman so long that any semblance of humanity melted away—I'd rather die.

Instead, I let her take it, pushing *more* of the power over to her side. The energy rushed out of me towards her, not acting, just swirling around her in a blue haze. I'd run out of oxygen. I might pass out at any second, yet her grip had slipped a little in surprise at me giving her what I wanted.

Her smile turned into a snarl as I kept pushing, my magic lapping against hers. It was entirely possible that my last-ditch plan would end in my death, but she didn't know the heart of my family's magic, not like I did. It wasn't the power to change a person's allegiance—it was the power to replace anyone's magic with mine. She was already holding the talisman, and had some of its power already, even if it wouldn't fully obey her. Her core magic was lost beneath mine, and all I had to do was push, until I found the heart of her—the magic that bound her to this Court. To this territory.

Pain racked my body. The ground continued to warp as it was hit by flecks of power from both of us. Plants sprang up and spun into strange patterns and disappeared, rain whipped around us in an icy tornado, magic of all kinds formed a vortex as we struggled for control.

I'm dying. I felt it—felt the world slipping, felt my mortal body on the verge of collapse, my soul splintering, and I knew I'd lost. She was still alive. I'd tried everything, and it wasn't enough...

Then we stopped, without warning, crashing into the mud. We'd landed in front of the jail, her hands still locked around my throat. The prison's iron sapped both of our magic, and it must have been enough to momentarily stop my progress. The tornado raged on, engulfing the forest around us, but we'd landed in the one spot of land where iron kept magic from functioning as effectively.

A howling wind engulfed the territory, ripping limbs off branches, tearing even the prison apart as the ground trembled underneath our feet. Roars sounded as the other beasts kept under the earth tore their chains off and came out, rampaging, thirsty for blood, only to be caught in the relentless vortex. My skin stung with the aftermath of her attacks, my limbs shook from the brush with death—but for a moment, she hadn't been in control.

I used the last of my strength to wrench her hands from my neck and push her into the vortex.

Her laugh of delight ended in a scream.

I lost sight of her in the torrent of debris—the iron chains, torn up earth, tree branches, and the freed beasts running for the forest right through the vortex. I crawled towards the jail, seeking the iron like a lifeline, clinging onto consciousness through sheer willpower.

And then it stopped. The wind died instantly, as though someone had flicked a switch. Branches, chains, beasts—all fell to the ground.

I hardly heard the impact. Because the only way a talisman's magic could stop like that was...

If its owner had died.

Her limp body lay amongst the now dazed looking trolls and other beasts. Behind, slowly, several humans had begun to emerge from the jail, pushing the broken doors aside with their frail arms. The vortex had knocked down part of the exterior, revealing the cages within.

The sight of the humans snapped me out of my shock.

"Raine!"

And Viola was behind me, pulling me away. "Get the

humans out!" I shouted, but my voice was hoarse, and the words unrecognisable.

"Get the humans out," I mumbled, already slipping into unconsciousness.

All went dark.

24

I woke up in the palace, on a soft bed, amazed to feel… alive. And tired as though I'd run several marathons back to back and scaled a fifty storey building. I fought to open my eyes properly, and a familiar face looked at me with concerned eyes.

"Viola?" I croaked. "You're okay? I thought she—"

"I'm fine." She smiled. "Glad you are, too. You had me worried there. You've been unconscious for three days."

Three days. Something told me I should be worried. But the bed was soft, and I was so, so tired. "I feel like total crap, but considering…"

Considering what I did. Used magic so powerful it sent the whole world sideways. Pushed Lady Hornbeam into a tornado.

"She died," I whispered. "For real. Right?"

A nod. "Yeah."

"Shit. It really happened." And I'd been responsible. Directly or indirectly, I suspected it'd make little difference in the eyes of the Seelie Court. I shoved the thought firmly away, lacking the energy to deal with it. My vision was still fuzzy around the edges. "And—after? How'd you get away? Did Cedar?"

"The soldiers fled into the forest when her magic started tearing the territory apart," Viola said. "Cedar and I tried to catch up with you, but her magic held us back. We were behind the jail. Cedar had to stay—it'd have looked suspicious for him to follow us back here."

"So he still belongs to the Hornbeams?"

"Yes. His vow will probably have transferred to Lord Hornbeam by now."

"Damn. Is he as bad?"

"Not by reputation. And he hasn't won over her talismans yet, as far as I know."

"At least neither of them have mine." Because the magic was in me, not the talisman. Even here, exhausted as it was, I could still feel it. I'd survived. The magic was mine. Two of the families who wanted to find it had been eliminated... but at a heavy cost.

I drifted in and out of sleep, borne through dreams which seemed part of another existence. Cedar appeared sometimes, speaking words I couldn't hear. He might have survived, but his family would never allow him to come here, so I ignored those dreams and let them fade away to worlds where none of these problems existed.

Once, I managed to stay awake long enough to ask Viola, "What happened to the humans?"

"I took them through the rift. Don't ask me what I had to promise the Little People in return."

"You didn't have to do that."

"Apparently you're rubbing off on me."

I blinked. "Even if my dad wasn't with them, I couldn't let them die like that."

Her throat bobbed. "Most of us hated that she kept human prisoners, but obviously—complaining about any of her methods would get you a lashing, at least. I hope—I hope Lord Hornbeam will stop capturing them."

"Yeah."

Her mouth quirked. "I can't believe Lady Hornbeam nearly went to war over me. I didn't know I meant that much to her."

She offered the humour as a lifeline. I took it. "Me neither. I can't believe the immortal Sidhe are capable of bearing such absurd grudges. Against dead people, even."

"The Sidhe are all spoiled brats, really." She smiled.

"Yeah," I said. "They really are."

———

The next time I woke, it was Cedar who stood on the other side of the room. He wore his uniform, but looked pale and tired. "Raine?"

I squinted at him. "Am I awake?"

"Looks that way to me." He moved over to the bed. "I was worried."

"What?" I closed my mouth and tried to remember how to string a sentence together. "I'm not in your Court. What are you here for?"

"To see you. Viola told me you were in a bad way, but recovering. You weren't awake the first couple of times."

He'd been to see me more than once? "Turns out screwing up a huge section of Faerie is really tiring. Who knew?"

"You nearly died."

"Yeah. That wasn't deliberate." I woke up a little more with each word, managing to focus on his face this time. He didn't look like he'd suffered any lasting damage from our duel to the death. But when he reached to brush his hair from his eyes, I spotted the faint mark on his palm where I'd cut him with my knife. "Unlike someone."

His eyes followed my gaze. "You'd have preferred me to carry out the command?"

"No, but…" My brother had appeared in my dreams, more times than I'd have liked to admit. I hoped my sister was far away from here, where at least one of us could avoid being caught up in faerie games. "But you must have known there was no way out, unless one of us died."

"I think we all knew that, Raine," he said quietly. "I can't stay long—but now she's dead, I can tell you what my vow said. It's not affecting me any longer."

I blinked. "You can? But—you belong to the Hornbeams."

"Technically. But her specific commands are mine to speak aloud as I wish now."

"Oh. Okay." It didn't seem to matter. I knew enough.

Enough to know that whether what I'd felt in the jail was real or not, we were from enemy families, and I'd killed his mother. I wondered why he hadn't mentioned that little detail yet.

Cedar spoke. "Her command that I take the talisman from you came into effect right away, but I knew you wouldn't have the talisman when I came to your house in the mortal realm. Once I realised the hellhound had targeted you, I stayed to watch you, but I couldn't stop you from going into Faerie to claim your inheritance. If you'd declined the offer and stayed behind, then I wouldn't have been obliged to steal the talisman. The moment you took it is when my vow came into effect. I felt it even in the mortal realm. *You will take the sceptre from its next owner, and if they steal it back, you will kill them.*" His words came quicker. "When I realised someone else had taken the sceptre, I could have left. But I didn't want you to run into trouble with the new holder, and I—I almost hoped it'd pass over to them. You know, if someone else took the sceptre and claimed the magic, it wouldn't kill you."

"Even if they ripped it out of me, like she tried to do?"

He winced. "No. It'd hurt like hell—and will only get worse the longer you spend here in Faerie. So will the effect iron has on you."

"So iron's worse here. What's the deal with the jail, then? And the weapons the soldiers carry?"

"Like I told you—she wanted all half-faeries to be able to wield iron as a human would. She wanted to take care of our weaknesses."

"Because she was afraid of dying," I said. "She was terrified, because the Sidhe can die now. Her grudge... that was why she picked me, but the real reason she collected talismans is because she and the other Sidhe are all set on gathering as much power as possible. Right?"

He nodded. "You're an important piece in the game, not just because of your magic, but because you're the first half-blood who *can* face the Sidhe as an equal."

"But I won't live forever. And they don't see me as an equal, no matter what I do. I don't *care* about being like the Sidhe. I want to go home and see Dad."

"Your father's safe," he said. "I did check up on him. Someone had already installed guards."

"Oh." I paused, my mind fuzzy. "Good. Thank you."

"You're welcome." He cleared his throat as though he wanted to say something else, but didn't speak.

I cast around for another question. "My mother... is there anything you know about her death?"

"No. If Lady Hornbeam knew, she never told me. I don't think she was the killer. She *did* tell me the talisman was left behind in the palace, and that Lady Whitefall was found in the woods unarmed and dead."

"Unarmed," I echoed. "She went out without the sceptre. She left most of her magic in it. I don't understand why."

He shook his head. "I don't know. Lady Hornbeam might have been involved, but I doubt it. Even without her magic,

Lady Whitefall would likely have won a confrontation, as you did."

I still didn't know my mother, but she'd left me one clue. Maybe there were others. Someday, I'd find out how and why she died. Why she'd left the talisman behind. Why the Sidhe could die now. So many questions.

"Sometimes it isn't about winning," I said quietly.

"I suppose not." His hand unconsciously moved up his sleeve again, to the iron marks, testimony to some horrible torture at the hands of his Court. Iron, like the bars of the cage when he'd leaned through and…

"Cedar?"

"What is it, Raine?"

"At the jail. Why did you let me believe you'd handed over the real talisman?"

"I think you know the answer to that."

I raised my head. "Because you thought I'd kill you."

"Anyone else would have."

"Doesn't say much for your Court, really."

To my surprise, he smiled. "I suppose it doesn't. I don't know if I should be alarmed that you risked so much for someone who deceived you. It doesn't say much for your survival chances here." He spoke in a light, teasing tone, one he hadn't used since we'd set foot on his family's territory.

I rolled my eyes. "Don't flatter yourself. I spared you because I didn't want to give her the satisfaction of goading me into killing you."

He tilted his head, a smile playing on his mouth.

"As for my survival chances, I'm pretty sure besting a Sidhe in battle puts me above any other half-blood here."

Cedar's expression turned serious. "I know. What you did —it was incredible."

"What, tearing up your territory and murdering your

leader? Should I be worried about what you usually consider a high standard for entertainment?"

A glint appeared in his eyes. "Perhaps not, but you're the star attraction here, Raine."

I groaned. Was it too much to ask to have a peaceful existence? Apparently so.

"You never said whether Lord Hornbeam sent you here to steal anything from me." Like the talisman, which sat on my bedside table, a pretty ornament now it had no power left inside it.

"No, I didn't. I'm under no such orders. He does not share his wife's ambitions, and has no interest in your talisman."

I breathed a sigh of relief. "You have no idea how glad I am to hear that."

"Is it hard to believe I came here on my own account?"

I raised an eyebrow at him. He looked away, and I regretted my careless words. "Sorry."

"I can't fault you for asking. I came here because I wanted to see you. To apologise, and to explain myself."

I nodded. It was hardly his fault Lady Hornbeam had forced him to act against me. And my mind kept going back to the jail—to the way his hands had lingered on the side of my face, as though it was the first time in a while he'd been free to move of his own accord. He'd known the risk. He wouldn't have had reason to fake it.

But did I really want to broach the subject? After Robin, and our brush with death? I was too tired to think about either of those things right now.

"If you steal from me again, I'll make you sorry," I said instead.

He grinned, giving me another hint of the charm that had lured me in from the moment we'd met. Just then, I wanted to pretend we were two people who'd met under other circumstances, where there were no bars between us. "I suppose that's only fair."

My eyes drifted. He took one step closer, brushing his fingers across my hand, my cheek, lightly enough for his magic to awaken mine again.

You can transfer your healing magic, I wanted to say. *How?*

But dreams took me, carrying me back to the one place I wanted to go. Home.

———

Two days after I managed to get out of bed for the first time, there came a knock on the door.

Robin stood on the doorstep. "Hi. Raine. I'm glad you're okay."

"Me too." Silence spread between us. Nothing would be the same, and if he thought we could ever turn back, he was mistaken. "I thought you'd have left."

Robin cleared his throat. "I did go into the mortal world, briefly. I checked up on your father. He's safe. And... and I left enough money for the two of you, for a while. It's the least I could do."

"That wasn't necessary, but thank you," I responded.

He dipped his head in acknowledgement, awkwardly fiddling with his sleeve. His own iron mark remained where the cuff had been, a reminder of the enslavement he'd so narrowly escaped. "Also—I'm moving back to the mortal realm. I never swore a true vow to the Hornbeams, so I can walk away free. I wondered if you wanted to join me. Not as us—just, you know. This realm. It's... not what I want."

"Nor me, but there's too much I have to take care of here." I paused. "But yeah. I need to see Dad. Clear up things at home."

"I'm actually on my way now. If you can walk okay. I mean…"

"No sense in delaying," I said. "Dad will think I've been taken away by the faeries." It wasn't much of a joke, but he attempted a polite smile. I turned to see Viola watching me.

"Is that all right?" I asked her. "Do you want to come along, too, or…"

"I have a few things I need to take care of." She smiled. "Besides, you'll be back, right?"

"Sure." Faerie and I had unfinished business. My mother's death. The other talismans, and Lady Hornbeam's legacy. Cedar, and whatever we owed one another for the way this realm had screwed up our lives. But all of that could wait. The mortal realm beckoned, and I was more than ready to go back home.

I used the talisman's magic to transform my clothes back into normal human ones, and walked out into the snow, leaving the palace behind.

ABOUT THE AUTHOR

Emma is the New York Times and USA Today Bestselling author of the Changeling Chronicles urban fantasy series.

Emma spent her childhood creating imaginary worlds to compensate for a disappointingly average reality, so it was probably inevitable that she ended up writing fantasy novels. When she's not immersed in her own fictional universes, Emma can be found with her head in a book or wandering around the world in search of adventure.

Find out more about Emma's books at www.emmaladams.com.